"Because I am never going to marry," Carin assured Adrian. "And as far as I can tell a lady needs a reputation merely for that purpose."

"Not merely for that," Adrian said stiffly. "But we will not delve into that at this moment. Why are you never going to marry?"

"I promised my mother on her deathbed I would never marry," Carin said simply.

"Just why the devil did you do such a—a totty-headed thing like that?"

"It was not totty headed," Carin said, prickling herself up.

"It was damn stupid and ridiculous," Adrian said. "Every woman of good breeding must marry."

"Meg did not," Carin retorted. "And she is quite happy."

"Is she?" Adrian said, eyes narrowed. "Or does she just say she is happy?"

Carin floundered. He appeared so very positive of himself. "I—I believe she is happy."

"There you have it," Adrian said. "You *believe.*"

"I do," Carin said, her temper finally surfacing. "And you are quite wrong. Mother assured me men can only break your heart, and if you marry one, you will be doomed to misery for life."

"That's rot," Adrian retorted. "Marriage is a fine institution."

"Then why are you not married?"

He appeared offended. "You did not permit me to finish. Marriage is a fine institution for women."

BOOK YOUR PLACE ON OUR WEBSITE AND MAKE THE READING CONNECTION!

We've created a customized website just for our very special readers, where you can get the inside scoop on everything that's going on with Zebra, Pinnacle and Kensington books.

When you come online, you'll have the exciting opportunity to:

- View covers of upcoming books
- Read sample chapters
- Learn about our future publishing schedule (listed by publication month *and author*)
- Find out when your favorite authors will be visiting a city near you
- Search for and order backlist books from our online catalog
- Check out author bios and background information
- Send e-mail to your favorite authors
- Meet the Kensington staff online
- Join us in weekly chats with authors, readers and other guests
- Get writing guidelines
- AND MUCH MORE!

**Visit our website at
http://www.zebrabooks.com**

ON THE FIRST DAY OF CHRISTMAS

Cindy Holbrook

Zebra Books
Kensington Publishing Corp.
http://www.zebrabooks.com

ZEBRA BOOKS are published by

Kensington Publishing Corp.
850 Third Avenue
New York, NY 10022

First Printing: November, 1999
10 9 8 7 6 5 4 3 2 1

Printed in the United States of America

In Memory of Hero

Praise the Lord for all creatures small and great.
Especially those four-legged canine wonders of love.

I shall miss you, dog.
Try not to nip at too many angels' wings.

Chapter One

One Baby Partridge

"She's a good little puss, my Carinna," Lord Worthington said, leaning back in his seat. "Hasn't caused a day of trouble in her sweet little life."

"Indeed? How fortunate for you," Adrian Hazard, the marquise de Chambert, murmured as he adjusted his cravat in the large gilt mirror that hung above the parlor fireplace. He restrained a grimace of impatience. He never minded comrades from the war dropping by to reminisce about the old days, even if they appeared out of the clear blue and detained a man from meeting his mistress. However, when they began to ramble off onto their children and family, it was the outside of enough. In truth, Adrian felt doubly betrayed. Before this, he had always assumed from the earl's behavior that he too was an inveterate bachelor.

"True. True. You wouldn't even notice she was here if you took her in," Worthington said, nodding.

Adrian froze. He turned slowly to stare at the large, bluff man. "I beg your pardon?"

"Her governess, Miss . . . er . . . always forget her name. 'Mum' something or other. Mummington?" Worthington asked, his face scrunching. He shrugged.

"Well, whatever her name is, she takes good care of little Carinna. Quiet and unassuming, too. Won't be a spot of trouble, I assure you."

Adrian shook his head in bafflement. "I should hope not. But why would I wish to take in your little Carinna or this Miss Mummington-or-other?"

"Well, I . . . ah . . . must go out of town for a while. Er . . . certain affairs demand it," Worthington said. Adrian narrowed his eyes. He hoped the man at least had the grace to be blushing, but with the earl's naturally florid complexion it was difficult to tell. "And the trouble is, my wife has just recently passed on to her rewards. So it stands to reason she can't take care of Carinna anymore."

"Indeed," Adrian said.

"She was a good woman," Worthington said. He sighed and shook his head. "We didn't deal well together, but she was a good woman."

"Yes," Adrian said impatiently. "But what does this have to do with me?"

"With my wife gone," Worthington said, "er . . . all the properties revert back to her family. Won't tax you with all the legalities—know that would be a bore. At least, I have always found them to be a bore. But the one thing I can tell you is that they are coldhearted bastards, all of them. They don't like me. Never have. They don't want to take care of Carinna either. Not that I'd want them to. A more grim and proper lot I've never seen. Wouldn't wish them on my worst enemy. Wouldn't wish them on my little girl. That is when I thought of you."

"You thought of me?" Adrian asked, stunned. The man must have a tile loose.

"Yes, I did. Long and hard." The earl nodded. "God's honest truth. I thought to myself, 'Who? Who can I entrust with my little girl?' And then like a miracle it came to me. The marquise de Chambert. The marquise de Chambert is the man!"

"Like a miracle you say?" Adrian asked, his tone dry.

"Yes, a blinding light it was," Worthington said. His blue eyes became piercing. "Mean, we have a bond from the war."

"Ah, of course," Adrian said. His heart sank. They indeed had a bond: Worthington had saved his life. He had taken a ball in the shoulder to do so.

"I've always respected you," Worthington said, grinning now in apparent innocence. "You are a man of honor. You never shirk your duty. Never turn from doing what a man ought. I know that you'll take care of my daughter, far better care than my wife's relatives. Not that they are willing, mind you. And I can't be carting her off with me when I don't know where or what I'll be doing. Just wouldn't be right for her."

"Yes," Adrian said, biting back a curse. There was no miracle here, only sheer blackmail. Worthington apparently had no one else to unload his child upon.

"Wouldn't ask it of you," Worthington said, rubbing his shoulder—no doubt the one in which he had taken the fatal ball—"but as I said, I feel close to you, feel a bond. And I respect you. And . . ."

"You saw a blinding light," Adrian supplied.

"Yes." Worthington nodded. He smiled quite blithely. "I assure you, my little puss will be no trouble. If I thought she would be, I wouldn't ask it of you. I am not the type to burden another man . . . even if I have saved that man's life."

"Thank you," Adrian murmured.

"But she's not been a jot of trouble to me, I vow. So I don't see she'll be a problem to you," the earl said. He stood, beaming. "It looks like you have a well-run establishment here. Just let your servants and Miss Mummington take care of my little Carinna. She won't get in your way. You probably won't even notice she's here. I'll return for her as soon as I can."

Adrian's nerves uncoiled. Worthington's confidence was reassuring. "Very well."

"Good, good! Knew I could count on you," Worthington said, rubbing his hands together. "Now, those leeches said Carinna could stay one more week at the country house. So don't expect to see her here until the next week." He blinked. "Gadzooks. That will be December. The Christmas season and all. You'll like that, I am sure."

"I will?" Adrian asked, lifting his brow. "Why?"

"You'll have family for Christmas," Worthington said, smiling what appeared to be a fatherly smile.

Adrian narrowed his eyes. "I have never particularly cared for Christmas. It is a much overrated and mawkish season in my opinion. As for family, the few relations I have left know better than to try and draw me into such drivel."

"Er, yes," Worthington said. He shifted upon his feet. "Well, I must be going Shouldn't tarry. Have much to do. And I thank you."

"Think nothing of it," Adrian said through a tight smile.

"Knew I could count on you," Worthington said, grinning. He departed from the room, actually whistling.

Adrian stood a moment in deep contemplation. He went and yanked the bellpull. Within a few short minutes Nelson, his butler, appeared. "Yes, my lord?"

Adrian returned to the mirror to inspect his appearance once again. He smoothed back a lock of auburn hair from his forehead. It was already shot with gray. He grimaced. Since he was a mere twenty-eight years, it was not a pleasant sight. "We shall be receiving a Miss Mummington and her charge, Carinna Worthington, within the next week. Do what you can to make the left wing into a schoolroom with the proper respective chambers for a governess and child."

"Yes, my lord," Nelson said without flinching. "May I ask the age of the child in order that I may command the proper supplies?"

Adrian frowned as he added the last flick to the folds of his cravat. "Lord Worthington never said. It is of no significance. He assures me she is a good little puss and will present no difficulties, so do what you deem necessary." He smiled, casting off the past aggravation. Worthington was correct. He had an excellent staff. They could manage the child. "I really must leave. I have a pressing engagement requiring my attention. Do not expect me back for the evening."

"Yes, my lord," Nelson said, bowing.

Adrian strolled from the room, his mind at ease. Worthington's request was rather offsetting, but it could not be considered overly presumptive. After all, Worthington *had* saved his life. Adrian did not believe in much, but he did believe in being a man of honor. Personal respect for oneself was the only thing a man truly needed.

He would look upon the bright side of the matter. To meet his debt of honor he need but withstand a child within his house. Or rather, his staff would. Adrian's lips twisted. It could have been much worse. After all, it was not as if Worthington had asked him to give him his life in return or some such thing.

"Do not expect me back for the evening, Nelson," Adrian said, throwing his cape about his shoulders and drawing on his gloves. He must hurry or Almack's would not permit him entrance. He had promised Delilah Randels he would attend. The bountifully endowed widow had started casting out lures for him and he looked forward to discovering what the delightfully experienced Delilah desired to offer. Of late, Nanette, his paramour of the moment, had become more and more demanding. Indeed, much too possessive. Without a doubt it was time to seek out different waters while the sailing was still smooth. A mistress turning greedy was one thing; a mistress growing jealous was quite another. After all, it was much better to set sail before the storm. He did dislike a scene. Such could only be considered unrestful at best.

"Yes, my lord," Nelson said, opening the door for Adrian.

Adrian, prepared to step out, halted. Two women stood upon the stoop, effectively blocking his path. The one—a brown-haired woman of middle age, her nose brilliant red from the cold—had her fist raised toward the knocker. The other was cloaked and hooded, which made her age indeterminate. She held in her arms an infant whose gurgles and coos determined its own age readily.

"Do forgive me," the brown-haired lady said, jerking her fist down. "Is this the residence of the marquise de Chambert?"

"Yes. Yes, it is," Adrian said, frowning as a sudden squall rose from the baby.

"Thank heavens," the lady sighed. "It is only the third establishment we have tried. Lord Worthington has never been one to be clear upon addresses."

"Lord Worthington?" Adrian asked. It took a moment of recollection, but with recollection came consternation. "Good God, no!"

Nelson, behind him, cleared his throat and stepped forward. "You are Miss Mummington, I presume?"

"Miss Mumford," the lady said, nodding her head with a pleasant smile. "Yes, I am."

"We have been expecting you," Nelson said.

Outrage shot through Adrian. "No, we have not!"

"Oh, dear," Miss Mumford said, her eyes stricken.

"I mean," Adrian said, attempting to recover, "Lord Worthington did not inform me his daughter was but a baby. We are not prepared for a baby. He led me to believe she was . . . er . . . older."

"Faith, what a tangle," the cloaked one said with a trill of laughter. With a strong jerk of her head, she shook her hood back. Adrian sucked in his breath. The most beautiful girl with silver hair and deep blue eyes smiled at him. "I am Carin Worthington."

"No," Adrian breathed. "You cannot be Carinna Worthington."

"Carin," she said, smiling. "Only Father still calls me Carinna."

Adrian flushed. That infernal Worthington had misinformed him about everything. "By either name, you cannot be his daughter."

"Indeed, I am not a baby," Carin Worthington said. "Doesn't that please you?"

"*You* are too old," Adrian said.

"First you do not want me to be a baby, and now you say I am too old," Carin said, a perplexed expression crossing her face. "Which do you want?"

"I do not want a baby and I most definitely do not want a young woman," Adrian retorted before he could stop himself. A sudden chilling thought numbed him. "Good Lord, is the baby yours?"

"Of course not. It could not be mine. I am not married," Carin said. Her tone showed she thought that to be irrefutable proof it was not her child.

Adrian sighed. "Whose baby is it then?"

"A Miss Partridge's if I am not mistaken." Carin frowned. "At least that is what the coachman told me. I never met her personally, of course. She deserted the baby, you see. Right there in the inn. Can you imagine that?"

"Certainly," Adrian said. The girl's eyes widened in disbelief. He frowned, attempting to ignore her look. "What I cannot imagine is why *you* took the baby."

"It seemed the only thing to do," Carin said. The bundle let out a squall. "Shh, I know. Please do not take it to heart about your mama. Aunt Carin will take care of you now."

"Well, Uncle Adrian does not intend to do so," Adrian growled. "Nor can you, young lady, remain here. It would be most improper."

"Why would it be improper?" Carin asked.

"I am her chaperone," Miss Mumford interjected quickly.

Adrian bit back a stinging retort. He did not know Miss Mumford's credentials, but with Carin's beautiful looks, it would require one of the highest title and standing for the ton to accept her as a proper chaperone. Adrian cast a glance at Carin. His blood heated immediately. No, he corrected himself, he feared it would require a mother superior. "I am sorry, but her reputation would still be endangered."

"Is that all?" Carin asked. She smiled quite blithely. "Do not let that concern you. I have no need of a reputation. Not anymore."

Adrian stared at her. Her eyes were so very innocent. Who was this duplicitous child before him? His voice came out in a roar. "What?"

The baby set up a shriek.

Miss Mumford jumped. "Good heavens!"

Nelson stepped forward. "If you will excuse me, my lord. I do believe the ladies and infant should step in out of the cold. Their chambers are prepared . . . or will be, with some alterations. You have an appointment you wished to keep. Perhaps this may be settled in the morning."

"No. She can't sleep under this roof," Adrian persisted.

"Very well," Carin said. Her chin jutted out. "Meg and I will return home."

"Do cut line," Adrian said, exasperated. "You know you cannot."

"Why ever not?" Carin said. Her eyes showed hesitancy with a fine dash of bravado. "It was Father's wish we come for a visit. I personally would have preferred to remain home, thank you very much."

Adrian leveled a cynical stare upon her. She neither flinched nor wavered in her attitude. Damn and blast Worthington. Just what kind of devilish imbroglio had he created? He gritted his teeth as the thought of seeing the delightful Delilah died. "You'll not go home, but you will bloody . . . er . . . very well explain yourself."

"Explain myself?" Carin asked, cocking her head to the side. "What should I explain?"

Adrian choked, unable to decide which question should come first. "You . . . you . . ."

"Perhaps the ladies should settle into their rooms first," Nelson offered in a helpful tone.

"Yes." Adrian grabbed onto the tossed lifeline. "Then we can talk."

Carin smoothed down her skirts before entering the library, where Nelson had informed her the marquise awaited her. Her heart jumped erratically. No doubt it was due to exhaustion and a growing trepidation. Meg had impressed upon her how fractious men became when confronted with surprises, especially when the surprises were infants.

Carin bit her lip. She had never meant to present herself as a taxing houseguest. Her father had bade her, "Be a good girl and give the marquise no trouble." After one week with her mother's relations, she had sworn to herself to be in every way amiable to his lordship.

She could never have imagined how her childhood home would suddenly turn into a place of depression and constant condemnation with the simple advent of her mother's relations. Yet it had. They had made it clear they did not wish her there. Her father was a great sinner. Her mother had reaped only what she had sown. Carin, as the spawn from that unblessed union, could not be anything but tainted blood—and a case of unwanted charity to boot.

In truth, when Carin and Meg had left, she felt as if she had escaped a dark prison. Her spirit had been failing her, she knew. Yet she had drawn up her hope. With Christmastide arriving, one could not but do anything else. To lose hope during this time—this special time that happened once a year for that very reason—would be wretched. After all, if the good Lord had not given up hope for mankind, who was she to do so?

She drew in her breath. Yes, it took but a little faith. She would do all she could to assure she didn't cause any problems here. The marquise had been surprised by baby Partridge. However, once she explained the situation she was positive he would understand. Who would not?

She entered the library. The bracing breath she had drawn in before entering swiftly deserted her. The marquise stood before the fireplace, tall and stern, a bumper of brandy in his one hand. He was dressed in formal attire, the sort of which Carin had not seen before. She had seen many of the young men in the village dressed queerly and had been informed their attire was all the crack in Londontown, but when presented with the true image of what elegance should be, a girl could not help it if her knees weakened.

The marquise looked at her, his water-gray eyes dark. "Now explain yourself, madam."

Carin blinked. She attempted to unobtrusively drift to a chair, seeking its support rather quickly. "You mean about baby Partridge? Meg has explained it to me now.

I understand that baby Partridge might have come as a surprise. And that grown men do not care for babies until they are grown themselves—the babies, I mean—but I simply could not leave the child at the posting house like her mother had done before me. They told me she was a drunkard and . . . well . . . they called her many other things, which are unrepeatable. Yet you should have seen the pitifully cruel note attached to baby Partridge. Mrs. Partridge said she was tired of the—" Carin flushed.

"Yes?" Adrian asked.

"Of the little bugger and she'd have no more to do with it. She was leaving with her man Jacko." Carin frowned in consideration. "It was fortunate I was there to take baby Partridge, now that I know how grown men dislike infants."

"I did not say I disliked infants," Adrian said, an indignant look in his eyes. "But we certainly cannot have a baby here. We are not prepared for one. Nor do I see why you did not leave the baby with those at the posting house. They would have applied to the proper authorities."

"I . . ." Carin looked down. "I did not like the appearance of any of those men either, to tell you the truth. None of them looked . . . er . . . reliable or able to care for a child."

"And I do?" Adrian retorted, his brow raised.

"You do not look as mean as they did," Carin said with a hopeful smile.

"Well, I am just as mean, I assure you," Adrian said with a menacing growl.

Carin leaned back in her seat. "Yes, my lord."

"And just what the devil were you doing traveling by post anyway?" Adrian continued growling.

"Father arranged it," Carin said, wide-eyed.

"Another thing I must thank your dear father for,"

Adrian said, rolling his eyes heavenward. He trained narrowed eyes upon her. "Just how old are you?"

"I am seventeen," Carin said.

"I thought so," Adrian said, his tone grim. "What was your father thinking about? You are seventeen. You cannot stay here. He must have been insane."

"No, I do not think he is," Carin said sincerely. "I do not see father often, so I fear I cannot vouch for such, but I think it is simply that he still considers me his little girl. Most likely he truly did forget that I have grown somewhat over the years."

"Somewhat?" Adrian asked, his tone dry.

"Yes." Carin flushed. She drew in a breath. "However, if you are worried about my reputation, you need not concern yourself. As I said before, I do not need a reputation."

She saw the marquise suck in his breath. "Why, pray tell, do you not need a reputation?"

"Because I am never going to marry," Carin assured him. "And as far as I can tell a lady needs a reputation merely for that purpose."

"Not merely for that," Adrian said stiffly. "But we will not delve into that at this moment. Why are you never going to marry?"

"I promised my mother on her deathbed I would never marry," Carin said simply.

"You what?" Adrian cried. He stared at her as if not only befuddled, but incredulous.

"I promised my mother I would not marry," Carin repeated.

"Just why the devil did you do such a—a totty-headed thing like that?" Adrian said.

"It was not totty headed," Carin said, prickling herself up.

"It was damn stupid and ridiculous," Adrian said. "Every woman of good breeding must marry."

"Meg did not," Carin retorted. "And she is quite happy."

"Is she?" Adrian said, eyes narrowed. "Or does she just say she is happy?"

Carin floundered. He appeared so very positive of himself. "I—I believe she is happy."

"There you have it," Adrian said. "You *believe.*"

"I do," Carin said, her temper finally surfacing. "And you are quite wrong. Mother assured me men can only break your heart, and if you marry one, you will be doomed to misery for life."

"That's rot," Adrian retorted. "Marriage is a fine institution."

"Then why are you not married?"

He appeared offended. "You did not permit me to finish. Marriage is a fine institution for women."

"I do not see that," Carin said. "Mother never seemed happy. Yet the few times Father came to visit, he was always jovial. It appears to me Mother was correct."

"It is not always that way." He frowned. "Or so I have heard."

"Then you intend to marry?" Carin asked.

"No. No, I do not," Adrian said, sharply. He glared at her suspiciously.

"Neither do I," Carin said, smiling. "I do not see what the difficulty is then."

"I know you don't," Adrian said. He seemed to grit his teeth and he ran his hand through his hair. "Blast it, this is impossible. You were supposed to be a child. Maybe six, seven, even eight, but not seventeen. Your *governess,* not your chaperone, was to take care of you."

"And Meg will," Carin said quickly. "She and I are accustomed to living quietly. And . . . and living self-sufficiently. We will not require much attention."

"You will not?" Adrian asked with narrowed eyes.

"Most certainly not," Carin vowed. "We are accus-

tomed to entertaining ourselves. Father has explained—
well, he wrote it actually—that you are being kind enough
to take me in until he is settled. He respects you highly.
He says you are an honorable—"

"I know, I know," Adrian said. "Please do not belabor
the issue."

"No, I won't," Carin murmured. "I was only attempting to let you know that Meg and I appreciate your kindness and that we do not expect much. I mean, we do
intend to live quietly. We certainly do not expect to meet
any of society."

"Thank God for small mercies," Adrian said bitterly.
"If you were to enter society now, the gossip mill would
churn out the worst kind of fodder."

"The worst?" Carin asked, frowning.

"Yes," Adrian said sharply. "They would think that
surely we are having an affair."

"But why?" Carin asked, astonished. "I am but seventeen and you are old."

"Old!" Adrian shouted. "I am only twenty-eight. That
is not too old to have an affair with you."

Carin gaped at him, knowing she had made a severe
faux pas. Twenty-eight was old to her, but with his graying
hair, she had thought him much older. "Oh, I—I see."
She spoke quickly, attempting to retrieve her ground.
"Even if—if you are not that old, and even if I am not
a child, it should not matter. Society need not know.
And—and from what I've seen, your mansion could
house Meg and me three times over without you ever
seeing us. We will try very hard to stay out of the way.
We shall be no trouble, I promise."

Adrian stared at her. "That is what your father said."

Carin smiled. "See?"

"Very well," Adrian said, sighing. He looked at her
sternly. "However, you must take that baby to an orphanage tomorrow."

Carin's eyes widened. "Must I?"

"It is the best thing for the child," Adrian said firmly. "They will know how to tend and care for it, and they will find a family who may wish to adopt it."

Carin flushed. "Yes. Yes, indeed. That is important."

"Very well. Now if you will excuse me, I am already late," Adrian said. He glanced at the mantel clock. "Blast. Almack's will never permit me entrance now."

"I am sorry," Carin said contritely. "Is there anything I can do?"

Adrian looked at her in an odd way. He turned his gaze away. "No. I believe I shall go to my club. Only make sure to take that baby to the orphanage tomorrow."

"I will," Carin said, standing. "Thank you."

"You are welcome," Adrian said. He bowed and left.

Carin stared after him. Her heart fluttered madly. She should be relieved. She need not return to her relatives. She had a safe haven. Why then did she suddenly feel so much more insecure and nervous at this moment than she ever had before in her life? And why did she keep thinking about the fact that the marquise did not consider himself too old for her?

Chapter Two

Two Turtledoves Cooing

Adrian sat poker stiff in a plush club chair at White's. He deliberately lifted a bumper of brandy to his lips with only the slightest waver and swallowed from it with equal definitude.

"Adrian, my man," a voice called out.

Adrian slowly turned his head and narrowed his eyes to gain focus. "Ah, Gerald! H-how are you, old friend?"

"Not as happy as you apparently." Gerald Nathan Vincent, viscount of Severs, lowered his short, stocky frame into a chair arranged across from Adrian. His blue eyes twinkled in a broad, fair face. An arrant lock of blond hair fell over his brow, which was customary to his breezy, comfortable personality. "Been celebrating, what?"

"No," Adrian said. "Far from it."

"What is the matter?" Gerald asked, frowning.

Adrian considered a moment. Gerald was one of his best friends. They'd seen their share of action together in the war. "Can you keep a secret?"

"You know I can," Gerald said. He grinned. "I have never got you in Dutch with any of your various lady loves yet, have I?"

Adrian frowned severely. "This one isn't a lady love of mine."

"Ah, but it is a woman," Gerald said, leaning forward. "It is the only thing which can make a man drink like you are doing. Haven't seen you this taphacket since you sold out."

"Yes," Adrian nodded. "Life has been good since then. B-been very good. And I deserve to have it that way."

"Well, who is saying you ought not?" Gerald said, his tone amused.

"You know old Worthington?" Adrian asked, sighing glumly.

"Of course I do." Gerald nodded. "Wouldn't forget the fellow. He saved your life. The man's an old reprobate, but he came through for you that day."

"He's left town," Adrian said, taking another precise swallow of brandy. "Had to from what I can g-gather. He's all to pieces."

"Is he?" Gerald asked. He shook his head. "Never pleasant, that."

"He left his l-little girl with me," Adrian said, his voice finally slurring. "He asked me to take care of her until he can settle his affairsh."

"Gads!" Gerald exclaimed. He looked quickly about and lowered his voice. "I didn't know he had children."

"He doesn't," Adrian said. He hiccuped. "He has a seventeen-year-old girl. Not children."

Gerald stared. "He left a seventeen-year-old girl with you? B'damn, if that isn't asking the wolf to tend the sheep."

"I am repaying a debt of honor, man," Adrian growled. "Worthington asked me and I said I would. I thought she w-was a child. Not a baby, but a child."

"Old Worthington must be dicked in the nob," Gerald said, shaking his head.

"Or desperate," Adrian said. "H-he bamboozled me."

"Never thought I'd see the day," Gerald said. "He gulled you. Best send the girl to him."

"Don't know where he is," Adrian said. "He left town a week ago."

"Well, send the girl somewhere else then," Gerald said, shrugging.

"No," Adrian said, shaking his head and then blinking from the blur of it. "I am paying a debt of honor. I said I would. I will do it. A man must have his honor."

"Sounds more like pride than honor," Gerald murmured. Adrian glared at him. "All right, have it your way. But I think you're as touched as old Worthington."

"I'm not touched," Adrian growled. "Not touched one bit. And I won't be."

"I meant in the head, old man," Gerald interjected.

"She promised she'll b-be no problem," Adrian said. "And that is how it's going to b-be."

Gerald's expression turned innocent. "Er . . . tell me about this girl? What does she look like?"

Adrian lifted the bottle of brandy and poured himself another bumper. He remained silent as he drank.

"Gads," Gerald said. "She can't be *that* beautiful!"

"She's p-passing. Silver hair, blue eyes," Adrian muttered. "And what does it matter?"

"What does it matter?" Gerald asked. He shook his head and whistled. "Damn, if you're saying that, you *are* in the suds."

"No," Adrian hiccuped. "I'm not. I will fulfill my duty. That's all."

Gerald stared at him. He chuckled. "Guess you got a present early this year. Merry Christmas."

"You know I don't believe in that tw-twaddle," Adrian said, frowning. "And that won't change. Sh-she promised. I shouldn't even notice she's there."

"Sorry," Gerald said, his face falling.

Adrian burped and frowned suspiciously at him. "Sorry for what?"

"Er . . . nothing," Gerald said.

"Sorry for what?" Adrian persisted with a glare.

Gerald sighed. "Well, if you must know the truth, I'm sorry that that won't change. Your attitude about Christmas is . . . well . . . cold, old man. I know you haven't had a family since you were sixteen and lost your parents."

"Didn't lose them," Adrian said stolidly. "Never knew them in the first place."

"I know," Gerald nodded. "They weren't very . . . er . . . paternal from what I've heard. But having a family is a good thing."

"Good?" Adrian barked. "Gads, if I had as many sisters and nephews and all as you, I'd kill myself."

"I do have rather a lot," Gerald said, grinning sheepishly. "But I wouldn't give any of them up."

"I am not asking you to," Adrian said more calmly. He twirled his glass. "Just don't ask me to be the same as you."

Gerald sighed. "Very well. But it's got to be lonely sometimes."

"Lonely?" Adrian stared. "No, it's not lonely. I-I come and g-go as I please. I do what I please. I c-can enjoy every pleasure there is to be offered." He stared off into space. "I promised myself when I sold out I'd not w-waste life. It is all too fleeting."

"That is what I think," Gerald said, nodding. "Makes a man want to settle down. Find the lasting ties."

"Ties?" Adrian shook his head. "That's what a man doesn't want. Didn't you see that in the war? You care too much and it will only hurt the more."

Gerald remained silent a moment. "Guess I wasn't in the same war."

"No," Adrian said, grinning. He wagged a finger. "You were. But you are an idealist. That's what you are!"

Gerald grinned. "Guess I am. But you don't have to make it sound like a sin."

"No, it's not a sin. Just foolish," Adrian said magnanimously. He lifted his glass. "But you have m-me. I'll be there when you change your mind and see the truth."

"Or I'll be there when you change your mind," Gerald retorted.

"I won't," Adrian said. He suddenly sat up, blinking. "Gads, why have I been drinking like this?"

"I don't know," Gerald said, shaking his head in apparent innocence.

"Nothing's going to change," Adrian said, drawing in a strengthening breath.

"True," Gerald nodded. "Not if you stick to your guns. You've been to war. You've commanded regiments."

"Blast it, yes!" Adrian said loudly. "I've survived the bloody war. This is nothing!"

" 'Course not," Gerald said. "It's your duty—nothing more. So what if the girl is beautiful?"

Adrian swiftly reached for his brandy and took a swig. "That's right."

Gerald coughed and yawned widely. "Er . . . best be going. Care to walk out with me?"

"No," Adrian said, looking away. "I intend to sleep here tonight."

"I see," Gerald said, nodding. "Good plan of action."

Adrian growled. "What do you mean by that?"

"Nothing," Gerald said. He appeared worried. "Truth is, I've got to go out of town for the next week. Sorry to do it, old man, but it's business, you understand."

Adrian frowned and burped. "Business is always important. No need to apologize to me."

Gerald flushed. "Only thought you might need me . . . for support."

Adrian stared. He laughed and clapped his hand to Gerald's shoulder. "D-don't be ridiculous. What could go wrong?"

"Are you certain, Miss Worthington, you do not wish for me to accompany you?" Nelson asked, standing straight and tall as he held the door open the next morning.

"No, thank you," Carin murmured as she held baby Partridge close to her.

"You have already been so very kind, Nelson," Meg said to the butler, "in commanding a carriage for us and discovering an orphanage."

A flush actually rose to Nelson's face. "It was nothing, Miss Mumford. I wish I could have had more time in researching the choices."

"No," Carin sighed. "I am sure the marquise is correct. Baby Partridge needs to be taken where she will have a chance of finding a mother and father. She is such a sweet, dear little thing."

"Indeed," Meg said, a broad smile crossing her face as she peered down at the baby. "You were a much more difficult child, Carin."

"Was I?" Carin asked, wide-eyed. She caught Meg's teasing look. "I was not. Do let us go before you tell Nelson other taradiddles."

"Thank you, Nelson," Meg said, smiling at him.

The two ladies walked down the steps and entered the carriage. Both were silent as the carriage started up.

Carin, feeling the oddest of emotions as she held the foundling baby close, looked hesitantly at her longtime governess and truest friend. "Meg, are you . . . are you happy?"

Meg's brow rose. "What do you mean, am I happy?"

Carin looked down. "The marquise said last night that

a woman who wasn't married couldn't be happy. I told him you were. He told me you couldn't be." She studied Meg with concern. "You are happy, aren't you?"

"Yes. Yes, I am," Meg said, laughing.

Carin's fears lessened. "Then I was right."

Meg grew more solemn. "I have been happy because I have had you to raise, Carin. I cannot say if I would have been happy in another household. But in yours, I have been. I feel more as if I am family than anything else."

"You are," Carin said, nodding eagerly. Never would she confess it, for she was, or at least tried to be, a dutiful daughter, but Meg had been a far more important figure in her life than her mother. She had loved her mother of course, but it was Meg who had guided and comforted her. Meg had always been there for her. Her mother had taught what was good and right, but Meg had shown her the heart behind that which was good and right.

Meg smiled gently. "Do you remember when you were young and felt sad that you never saw your father like the other children did?"

"I remember."

"And I told you that we may not always have what everyone else has, but if we choose to care and love what we do have, it will not matter."

"Yes." Carin nodded. Her confidence rose.

"I have never married or had a husband," Meg said softly. "That is one thing I was not given. But I have been given the opportunity of raising you. Indeed, the years have flown by and I have no regrets."

"And I can be like you," Carin said. "I can be happy without marrying. Indeed, Mother was right. I-I would not like to suffer what she did."

"Each life is different and each person is different," Meg said, her eyes becoming guarded. "My choices need not be yours." She paused. "Nor should your mother's choices be yours either."

"No," Carin said firmly. "I promised Mother I would never marry, because that is what *I* wished."

"Very well," Meg said. She peered out the carriage window as they felt it slow. "I believe we are here."

The coachman opened the door. A cutting wind whipped into the carriage. Carin shivered and held baby Partridge closer. She alighted and shivered for a different reason as she looked at the orphanage before her. It was a large red brick structure darkened to a gloomy cast by the soot of the city—an aspect that was not alleviated by the apparent lack of windows across its facade. Only a large, scarred door broke the forbidding exterior.

"Oh, dear," Meg murmured as she climbed down from the carriage. "It—it is not very inviting, is it?"

"Perhaps it will be much nicer inside," Carin said in a hopeful tone.

"Pardon, miss," a crackling voice said. "Could you spare a ha'penny for an old lady?"

Carin tore her gaze from the dark edifice. An equally frightening visage was close by her. The old lady's white hair was blown by the icy-cold wind into a wild, knotted upheaval. She appeared more an ambling mound of tattered shawls and skirts than a human. A strong, pungent smell of some sort wafted to Carin.

Only when the old lady stepped closer and Carin saw into her eyes did she calm herself. The old lady's eyes were an alert dark brown. They sharpened as she peered down at baby Partridge. "Here now. Looks like you've got your own bundle of troubles, what?" She jerked a chafed blue thumb toward the orphanage. "Ye're thinking about going there, ain't ye?"

"I beg your pardon?" Carin asked.

"We all make mistakes, dear," the old lady said. "But I'd think twice afore you give your baby up to the likes of them."

"Oh, she's not my baby," Carin said. "I found her in a posting house."

"A posting house, did ye say?" The old lady cackled. "Now that's a new one. Well, it ain't no bread and butter of mine." The old lady turned her gaze to Meg. "Could *you* spare a ha'penny for an old lady?"

"I believe so," Meg said, delving into her reticule.

Of a sudden, the door to the orphanage burst open. A reedy voice shrilled a string of curses, and a small, scrawny body tumbled into the snow. A hulking brute then lumbered out, followed by a tall, bony woman dressed from chin to toe in dull black.

"You bleeding lout!" The body sprung up to define itself as a boy. "Treat me rough, will ye!"

He charged at the hulking brute, who stopped the boy with one large paw to his shirt. He began to shake the boy mercilessly.

"Stop that!" Carin exclaimed, aghast. The child appeared a rag doll in the man's clutches.

The man, rather than stopping "that," cuffed the boy resoundingly with his other great fist.

"Stop that!" Carin cried again. Rage and fear rose in her. She spun to Meg, shoving the bundled baby Partridge into her arms. Then she ran up to the man, who was lifting his hand for another swing. "You shall not hit the boy!"

He did not. Carin had advanced too swiftly and received his fist to her cheek instead.

"No!" Meg cried. She spun to the old lady. "Here!"

"Get in there, lass," the old lady cheered, her arms outstretched to gather baby Partridge to her, tucking the infant within the protection of a layer or two of shawls.

Meg, "the lass," legged it into the fray at a sprightly pace. The boy let out a howl and charged. They hit the man at the same time, toppling him to the ground. Carin dove into the roiling mass as well. With grunts and shouts and flailing fists, they finally succeeded in pinning the large man down. Meg, Carin, and the boy sat on top of him, all of them panting.

"Let Brutus up," the tall woman ordered. She had retreated a good distance away. "Let him up, I say."

"Like bloody hell we will," the boy said, grinning. He winked at Carin. "Don't listen to old Friday-faced Fenton. She's a nasty one, she is."

Carin flushed. She peered down and caught the fierce but bulging gaze of the man who was presently their cushion. "If we release you, you must promise you will not strike this child again."

"The thieving little blighter had it coming," Brutus rumbled.

"I did not!" the boy cried. "I told ye I didn't steal nothing!"

The man grunted and cursed. Carin interrupted. "Promise!"

"It does not matter, Brutus," the dark-clad woman said, her voice vicious. "He's out on his ear this very day."

"I don't care," the boy cried. He pushed himself off Brutus with one bony elbow to the breadbasket. Brutus *oofed* loudly, glaring at the pint-size miscreant. The boy stood with clenched fists. "I don't like living here anyways."

"Then go back to the streets where you belong," the woman retorted, her steely eyes cold.

"What?" Carin objected. She scrambled off of Brutus. Another pained *oof* arose. "You cannot turn the child out into the streets. It is so very cold."

"He should have thought of that before he stole again," the woman said. She crossed her arms, lifted a pointed chin, and glared at Carin. "What I choose to do is my decision. I run this orphanage. You do not."

"You run it?" Meg exclaimed. She bolted up. A sole wheeze came from Brutus this time.

"She *says* she runs it," the boy said, snorting. "But she's only taking the money in, she is. And she says *I'm* thieving."

"Told ye to think afore ye give yer baby up to the likes of them," the old lady said, nodding to Carin.

"You have a baby for us?" Friday-faced Fenton exclaimed. Her entire demeanor changed. "Well now, do come in."

"Please don't, miss," the boy said, his eyes pleading. "She gets them charity funds double for taking care of babies, but she don't feed them nothing."

"Shut up, you bratling," Friday-faced Fenton hissed. Then she creaked out a scary smile. "You have misunderstood. This child is naught but a troublemaker and a thief." She shook her head and sighed. "We tried to reform him. We strived to correct the errors of his ways and find him a good and loving home. But to the end, he is a thief."

"That's her charity talk," the boy whispered aside. "Hoity-toity, ain't it?"

"Indeed it is," Carin said, staring at the woman in awe. Ignoring the strange feeling running along her spine, she stiffened and looked the woman in the eye. "I am sorry, Miss Friday-faced Fenton, but if you wish to throw one child out into the streets in weather like this, I see no reason why you would wish to take in another instead."

"Huzzah," the old woman cried. "Tell her whot for!"

"Very well. Keep the child," Friday-faced Fenton snapped. She twitched in clear anger. "And may you suffer for your sins. As for you," she added, glaring at the boy, "may you—"

"Oh, don't worry about me," the boy drawled with a grin. "I'll get on fine, I will. Much better without you, 'fact!"

"Come, Brutus," Friday-faced Fenton said. Like a

swooping crow she darted back into her dark fortress. Brutus crawled to a stand and hobbled behind.

It grew quiet a moment as they stared at each other. Baby Partridge suddenly wailed.

"Oh, dear," Carin said. She flushed as the consequences of her actions struck her. "What shall we do now? The marquise will be quite displeased with me."

"Is he the one making ye give up yer baby?" the old woman asked, rocking baby Partridge.

"No, indeed not," Carin said. "I—I am only residing with him for the present. I truly did find the child abandoned. The marquise told me I must bring her to an orphanage, where they could take care of her and find her a home." She worried her lip. She gazed at the boy. "Nor can we permit you to remain out here in this cold."

"I'll be all right," the boy said. He lifted his chin defiantly. "I don't want no charity no more."

"I'll take a ha'penny," the old woman said with far less pride. "Fer my good advice, and takin' care of the sweet baby while ye settled the disagreement."

Carin studied the boy and the old lady. She could not bring herself to leave these two waifs to the street, both on opposite ends of the scales in age. What a cold and bleak Christmas they would face. Then she was struck with a notion. Her eyes widened. "I know! The marquise objected to baby Partridge because we were not prepared for her. But if I have a nurse for her and—"

"And . . . ?" The boy looked hopeful.

"Ah . . ." Carin thought swiftly. "A page. Yes, a page for the baby. To run all the errands that are necessary."

"I could be a page," the boy said. "I'll run me legs orf if I have to."

"And I can be a nurse to this dear little one," the old woman said. "Just you wait and see. I'm experienced at nursing, I am."

"Then do let us go to the coach," Carin said, nodding

in excitement. It always amazed her how things left to their own accord had a tidy way of working their way out. One only needed to believe and the good Lord provided.

"Yes," Meg murmured. "Do let us go."

The old lady was swift to crawl into the coach with baby Partridge. And the boy, *oohing* and *aahing* at the sleek design of the wheel caps and the enameled doors of the carriage, followed in her wake. Meg, casting a wry smile, then entered and so did Carin.

The coach started up as Carin watched the two sitting across from her in growing wonder. Their attention was fully upon the baby.

"Coor," the boy pointed his finger at the baby's chest. "She's a fine little mite."

"Coo, ain't she just?" the old woman said.

The baby gurgled, and flailed a small hand, catching hold of the boy's finger. "Coor!"

"Coo," the old woman said. "She's strong and healthy she is."

Carin looked at Meg. Meg nodded in satisfaction. They both sat back and listened as the others billed and cooed over baby Partridge like two turtledoves.

Adrian entered his home just before the dinner hour. He had enjoyed a pleasant day. He had spent the morning at his club. Considering how his head had hurt him, he could do nothing else. However, with a few shots of the hair of the dog that bit him, he had revived. Then he had gone to his tailor and the bootmaker. He had attended an afternoon soiree where he had partaken in a delightful *tête-à-tête* with Delilah. She had pouted and performed an intriguing act of anger because he had not come to see her at Almack's. They had both known it was an act, the first steps in the game of romantic dalliance.

Indeed, the day had been good. Only the slightest cloud

hovered over his day. It felt suspiciously like a guilty conscience, but Adrian told himself it could not be. Even during his drunken bout the night before, he had not mentioned to Gerald the baby Carin had brought into the house, or his demand that she take it directly to an orphanage.

He had only done what any right-thinking person would. And it had been right thinking that dictated he remain away from the house this day in order to avoid any possible unsettling scene when Carin took the foundling to the orphanage. Certainly not cowardice. No, in truth, he was merely being diplomatic. In this manner, they could overlook the disagreeable issue and proceed in a much better fashion.

He nodded to the footman who dashed forward to take his coat. He was one of Adrian's newest employees. "Hello—Gaskins, is it not?"

"Yes, my lord," Gaskins nodded, his voice squeaking.

Adrian smiled. The lad was apparently quite nervous about performing his duties for the first time. "How are you today?"

"F-fine, my lord!" Gaskins choked out. He promptly dropped Adrian's hat. His voice was muffled as he bent to reach for it. "Everything is fine, my lord."

Adrian frowned. The hat was one of his finest beavers. "Good, good. Where is Nelson, by the way?"

"My lord?" Gaskins jerked up as if shot, leaving the hat abandoned upon the marble tiles.

"I asked where Nelson is."

"I—I could not say, my lord," Gaskins said, flushing.

"I see," Adrian said, his eyes narrowing. Gaskins was clearly lying. He could feel it. A strong premonition took hold of him. "Do you know where our two guests are? Miss Worthington and Miss Mumford."

"I could not say," Gaskins said, his face miserable.

"I suppose you could not say whether they still have a baby with them or not?" Adrian asked, his tone cool.

"Yes, my lord," Gaskins said. He started. "I mean, yes, I could not say."

"You need not then." Adrian gritted his teeth. "I am perfectly capable of discovering what is going on within my household even if my servants cannot say."

"When would be the best time to tell him, do you think?" Carin asked as she gingerly lifted a cut of steak to her eye, settling farther into the comfy chintz chair of the newly prepared schoolroom. The boy at her feet gaped in awe that anyone could use such an expensive piece of meat for such a purpose.

Carin had discovered his name was Hez. He had looked shamefaced when Meg had observed that it was an uncommon name. He confessed that it actually was short for the longer and much more queer Hezekiah. Meg and Carin had contained their amusement, but Mrs. Bertha Hammersham had broken into cackles, owning that he was supposed to be a righteous boy because that name came from the Bible. A strong altercation had almost occurred until baby Partridge had started crying and both had immediately stopped to bend over her crib and coo at her.

"How about never telling him?" Bertha suggested.

"No," Carin said, "that would be dishonest."

"Not to speak of impossible," Meg sighed.

"Indeed, it would be," Nelson said as he approached Meg with a cotton piece doused in iodine. Meg had, somewhere in the melee, acquired two scratches over the brow. He halted. "Excuse me. May I have your permission, Miss Mumford?"

"Certainly. There is no need to stand upon ceremony," Meg said. She laughed. "It would seem odd, since we are all sharing a secret as it were."

Carin frowned. "But we won't keep it for long. Well,

not for an extended amount of time. Only until we can decide what is the best circumstance in which to approach the marquise."

"I have warned the rest of the servants to remain quiet," Nelson said. "Though I fear I cannot promise their loyalty. I fear Mrs. Knightsbridge, the housekeeper, is fractious at the moment. However, I have ordered up his lordship's favorite dishes from the chef. Perhaps this evening, after the meal and his brandy, you might choose to approach him."

"Good thinking, that," Bertha approved. "A man is always ready ter listen when his belly's been filled with good food and drink. That or when—"

Nelson coughed loudly and Bertha's face froze. "Good food and drink—that's the ticket."

"So it is, madam. I believe I should go to oversee the chef now," Nelson said. He rose and bowed, then departed the room.

"Nice chap," Bertha muttered, her face red. She held baby Partridge upon her lap with one hand. With the other hand she burrowed beneath her many shawls and withdrew a pewter flask and uncapped it. Carin's eyes widened in curiosity. Meg gurgled in apparent alarm.

Carin didn't have a moment to question her reaction, for Nelson bolted into the room, his coattails flying. "My lord is coming!"

"Good gracious!" Carin breathed.

The words muttered by both Hez and Bertha were far stronger and quite unrecognizable to Carin. Bertha, dropping her flask, took off with baby Partridge through the connecting door leading to the quarters intended for the governess. Hez circled the room crazily, dodging first toward the table, then toward the cabinets. Squeaking, he finally straightened his path and followed Bertha.

"I'll try and detain him," Nelson whispered and spun. He reached the door, only to skitter to a halt, colliding with Adrian. "F-forgive me, my lord. I—I was . . . er . . . I was just leaving."

"Were you?" Adrian asked, his gray eyes narrowed.

"Y-yes. I was . . . just seeing to the ladies," Nelson said, straightening up and regaining a more dignified demeanor.

"Excellent, Nelson. I have always admired your conscientiousness," Adrian said, his smile tight. "In fact, I thought I might just do the same. I fear I was not as receptive as I should have been last night."

"It was quite understandable," Carin said quickly, hoping to be soothing and diplomatic. She swallowed hard when the marquise turned a piercing look upon her. She felt rather like the mouse that had squeaked to the cat, "Hello. Look at me."

The piercing look deepened and Adrian growled. Brushing poor Nelson aside, he stalked toward Carin. "What the devil happened to you?"

"Nothing!" Carin said, her breath quickening when he halted before her and he reached out a hand to her cheek. His touch was amazingly gentle.

"Nothing?" Adrian asked lowly.

Carin felt her blood rush to the cheek he tended. "Nothing . . . much is what I meant to say. I—I fear I wasn't watching and . . . and ran into a door."

"Ran into a door?" Adrian asked. His tone had turned to silk.

"She did, my lord," Meg said. She cast Carin a supportive and sympathetic look. "I have often worried over Carin's eyesight. Indeed, I recommended to her mother that it should be examined."

Carin nodded gratefully to Meg. "She has, my lord, and often."

Adrian was not attending. He had bent his gaze upon Meg. "Are those scratches above your eye?"

Meg's face grew alarmed. It was Carin's turn to offer

a supportive and sympathetic look. "Why, yes. Er . . . a . . . a cat scratched me."

"It appears you two have had a rather eventful day," Adrian murmured.

"N-Not one of our best," Carin said weakly.

"My lord," Nelson said quickly. "Chef has decided to prepare one of your favorite meals tonight."

"Has he?" Adrian asked. Once again his attention had swung. His demeanor was more of a tensed tiger in a jungle than a polished lord of the ton.

"Indeed," Nelson persevered. "Perhaps you would care for a brandy before dinner?"

"Yes," Carin said, jumping up. She could not understand the marquise's stillness, but it made her nerves tingle. "Meg and I would be pleased to join you."

"You drink brandy then?" Adrian asked. The man was drawing in deep breaths and sniffing, actually sniffing.

Frightened at his actions but determined, Carin forced a smile. "Yes. Yes, we do. Let us go now and have one."

Adrian appeared not to listen. He eyes narrowed and slowly focused upon the spilled flask lying on the floor. He walked over and picked it up. He did not even raise it to his nose, but held it out with a sardonic look. "Do you drink Blue Ruin as well, Miss Worthington?"

"Blue Ruin?" Carin asked.

"It must be alcohol," Meg murmured.

"Alcohol?" Carin gasped, her eyes flying to Meg in consternation. Meg shrugged helplessly. Her heart sinking, Carin returned her gaze to Adrian. She swallowed. "No, that was for Meg's scratches. Alcohol is very beneficial for wounds, you know."

"I know," Adrian said, peering about with narrowed eyes. "But gin is a rather singular choice."

Still sniffing, Adrian walked as if in a sensory trance toward the door to the adjoining room.

"My lord!" three voices said in unison.

Unfortunately, a baby's wail arose in response from the other room.

Adrian looked back at them for one moment. "I do hope the infant does not cry for its flask of Blue Ruin." With that, he turned and disappeared into the room.

"Oh, dear," Carin murmured, picking up her skirts and going to the rescue.

Hez's voice halted her. "Leave me alone, guv! I'll pop your daylights out, I will!"

Hez's brave threat held no effect since Adrian reappeared in the doorway, the boy dangling from his outstretched arm like a puppy held by the scruff. "Is this young cockerel an intruder?"

"No," Carin exclaimed, "he is not."

"I'll fight ye, I will," Hez cried, squirming and flailing. "Come on. Man ter man!'

"Later," Adrian said. He dropped Hez and dove back into the other room.

Everyone remained silent. They could hear baby Partridge's cries. Then Carin breathed more easily as she saw Bertha scurry past the doorway to the hall. She had evidently gone around and was escaping.

"Stop, woman," Adrian bellowed, and they then saw him go by. "Now!"

Carin held her breath as everyone did. Within the shortest of tense moments, Adrian entered the schoolroom, escorting Bertha, who hugged baby Partridge to her.

"She is not an intruder either, I presume," Adrian said to Carin.

"No," Carin admitted.

"Pity," Adrian drawled. "If she had come to steal the baby away, I would have applauded her."

Carin bit her lip. She could not help herself. "How did you know they were here?"

Adrian's eyes darkened. "I've been in every kind of pub. I've also been in war. Now I want an explanation."

Five voices dutifully rose in a babble of proclamation and declaration. Adrian's face grew thunderous as the pitch rose with everyone's attempt to be heard.

"Stop!" Adrian roared, lifting a commanding hand. The bedlam ceased abruptly, except for a sweet, low gurgle from baby Partridge. Adrian narrowed his eyes. "I am not going to ask anything right now. I am going to have my brandy." His gaze raked the occupants of the room. His lips twisted. "Then we will have my favorite meal . . . together. As I do not imagine that you were *uninvited* to that as well."

He turned to leave, but spun back. He looked at Bertha and Hez. "Both of you will, of course, indulge in baths first. You, madam, leave behind a scent of gin that is quite overpowering." He glared at Hez. "You merely smell."

He glanced at Nelson. "I do not appreciate subversive tactics from my butler. If a man cannot trust his butler, then who can he trust?" Nelson flushed red. Adrian looked at Carin, his gaze dark. "However, I know at whose door to lay the blame. You had better have a fine explanation, madam, a *very* fine explanation!"

Adrian studied the feast displayed before him. Indeed, all his favorite removes were prepared. Normally he would be enjoying them with fine wines and a few select friends.

He lifted his gaze from the food to the guests at his table. By no stretch of the imagination could he classify his present dinner mates as select. Mrs. Hammersham, whom he had refused to call Bertha, even though she had told him she'd not mind him being less formal, was indeed bathed. However, since she wore the same clothes—if that is what the rags could be called—the aroma of gin still snaked down the table to him. No doubt the scent would soon be mingled with a more elite bouquet. She was tucking away his fine Bordeaux in the same manner most drank water.

Beside her, Hez sat. Adrian, of course, was forced to call the boy simply Hez since the child possessed no surname. The boy's face was either scrubbed raw or else he was perpetually flushing. His clothes added to the aroma. Adrian remembered such acrid smells from his time around campfires in the war. He had sworn when he sold out he'd not suffer them again. Now he suffered them at his own table—and with his favorite meal before him.

These perambulations caused him to direct his gaze at Carin, the choreographer of this unappealing dinner party. Even with the dark blue bruise beneath her eye, she appeared fragile and angelic. He bit back a snort. She was clearly no such thing. She must be a demon come to curse him. Her demon companion sat next to her, her face equally serene though it was graced by two vivid red scratches. Neither appeared concerned with their battle scars. Indeed, neither had attempted to powder or paint them the way most proper ladies would.

"We did take baby Partridge to the orphanage as you had asked," Carin was saying, her blue eyes sincere.

"Ah, that must have been my mistake," Adrian said, nodding. No female should have ever been permitted such clear and beautiful eyes. It only proved his theory that she must be a demon. "I should have impressed upon you that I was not asking, but ordering."

"Y-yes," Carin said, flushing. "But we did follow your order. We truly did. Only when we arrived the most dreadful thing occurred."

"They refused to take the baby?" Adrian asked in dulcet tones.

"Not exactly," Carin said. "But once I explain, I am sure you will agree we could not have left baby Partridge with them."

"You'll come a cropper on that," Mrs. Hammersham said even as Adrian said, "Will I?" He stiffened and cast a quelling look at the old woman. She merely returned his glare with a bland one of her own.

"Yes," Carin said, nodding her head vehemently. "You see, just as we arrived they were striking poor Hez."

"Who was?" Adrian asked, frowning.

"The people of the orphanage," Carin said, her voice aghast.

"It was old Friday-faced Fenton and Brutus the Brute," Hez said, his tone pugnacious.

"And why were they doing such a thing?" Adrian asked.

"They said I stole something," Hez said. "I didn't."

"Of course not," Adrian said dryly.

"Brutus the Brute would not stop," Carin said, her eyes wide. "Meg and I were forced to stop him."

"Et tu, Brute? I feel for him," the marquise murmured under his breath.

"Guv," Hez said, his face brightening, "ye should have seen it. They trounced old Brutus, they did. Leveled him to the ground. We got to sit on him like he was a bench. Finest day I've ever had in me life."

"You what!" Adrian exclaimed, staring in astonishment at Carin and Meg.

"We could not permit him to continue beating poor Hez, now could we?" Carin said. "What else were we to do?"

Bertha guffawed, spraying Bordeaux across her plate. "He's thinkin' ye should have lifted yer dainty skirts and noses in the air and acted like nothing was happening. Now that's what proper ladies would have done, wouldn't they have, m'lord?"

Adrian stiffened. The look of knowledge and challenge was clear in the old beldame's eyes. He refrained from retorting since in truth she had hit upon his very thoughts. Only somehow she made them sound petty. "Just how did you become involved, Mrs. Hammersham?"

"Me? I was just passing by," Bertha said, her tone innocent.

"She was kind enough to hold baby Partridge for us when we . . ." Carin said quickly. "Bertha kept her out of harm's way for us."

"I see," Adrian said.

"And that is why she is with us." Carin nodded. She smiled at Adrian as if she not only made perfect sense, but had performed a brilliant feat.

"I am sorry. I believe I have missed something here," Adrian said. "She is here because she held the baby while you were trouncing this Brutus the Brute?"

"After we saw how they treated poor Hez," Carin said, her tone indignant, "there was certainly no way that we could leave poor baby Partridge in their care."

"He's thinkin' there was," Bertha chuckled.

"My good woman," Adrian said, his ire rising, "please do not continue to attempt to guess what I am thinking."

"Then you weren't thinkin' that?" Bertha asked.

"Of course he wasn't," Carin said, her tone staunch. "And that is why we have also brought Mrs. Hammersham and Hez with us. I know a great concern of yours was that we were not prepared for a baby." She smiled in pleasure. "Mrs. Hammersham can be baby Partridge's nurse. She has had experience at being a nurse."

"I have no doubt," Adrian said bitingly. "She's nursed the bottle, is what she's nursed."

"I nursed me three fine boys," Bertha said in a quiet tone. Her rheumy gaze was dignified, making Adrian feel like a peasant. "They're dead now. Killed in the war, they were, like their father afore them. But they were fine boys. They never died under my care—only under the Crown's."

Adrian flushed deep red. Knowing himself to have been cruel, albeit unwittingly, he also knew better than to say more. He refocused his attentions. "So Mrs. Hammersham is to be a nurse. I am afraid to ask, but just what is the purpose of the boy then?"

"I'm going ter be a page," Hez said, his small body stiffening. "I'll run the errands for the ladies, I will."

"A page?" Adrian asked. He winced. "I was right. I shouldn't have asked."

"He will make an excellent page," Carin said, her eyes pleading. "It wouldn't be charity whatsoever."

"I ain't ever takin' charity again," Hez said, " 'cause it only takes from you. I'll work hard, I will."

"Indeed, he will," Carin said. "You said baby Partridge would need care. We have enough care for her now."

Everyone nodded with beaming faces at Adrian. He blinked, a dawning fear rising within him as he began to wonder who was the craziest of the party. Apparently, their way of thinking made perfect sense to them. He refused, however, to go down so readily.

"We would not need their help if you had taken the baby to the orphanage as I had requested. That is still the point you are overlooking." He raised his hand quickly as a clamor arose. "I understand that this particular orphanage was not the proper one for the baby. Or at least I will strive to accept your decision. But there *are* other orphanages in London, I am sure. There are certainly enough contributors within the city to populate a countless number of them."

"Nelson said this one was the best," Carin said.

"Nelson is a butler," Adrian said in exasperation. "What would he know?"

"Nelson is right, guv. None of the others is any better," Hez said.

"And how would you know, pray tell?" Adrian asked.

"I've been to them, I have," Hez said, his tone quite proud. "All of them."

"I see," Adrian said, clenching his teeth. "You've certainly been around for one so young."

"That I have, guv." Hez nodded. He leaned forward. "Do you want me to tell you about them. I've got stories that will turn yer stomach inside out, guv."

"Then do refrain from them since we are attempting to eat," Adrian said.

"There's one place where the maggots were the biggest and fattest I've ever seen," Hez boasted. "The younger boys were squeamish about eating them. But not me. I figured they were just extra victuals."

"I said you could refrain," Adrian repeated sternly as Carin and Meg gasped. He leveled a narrow gaze upon Hez, who grinned unrepentantly. He then looked at Carin. "You cannot keep this baby indefinitely. At some time you must find it a proper home."

"True." Bertha nodded. "This here one ain't proper. Those reared in these kind of places are queer ducks. Forgive me, m'lord, but it is true."

"Surely we could keep baby Partridge for now," Carin pleaded. "It is Christmas, after all."

"Just what does Christmas have to do with this?" Adrian asked, frowning severely.

"Yeh?" Hez asked, scrunching up his face.

"Why, Christmas should be a special time of goodwill and kindness," Carin said.

"Rot," Adrian said briskly.

"I agree with that, guv," Hez said, nodding. "Christmas is just a bunch of do-gooders acting high and mighty for a month so's they can feel right proud for the rest orv the year when they *ain't* being good."

"Oh, no," Carin gasped, her eyes darkening in solemnity. "It is not that way. Indeed, it is not. It is the time when our dear Lord came to us as the dear baby Jesus."

"Oh, God!" Adrian said, rolling his eyes.

"We're in fer it now, guv," Hez said in disgust. "She's going ter preach."

"You do believe in God?" Carin asked Adrian, her voice concerned.

"I am reserving my judgment," Adrian said dryly.

"He might be up there somewhere. I won't say He ain't," Hez said in a magnanimous tone. "But if He is, He's turning his eye something fierce from what's going on down here."

"No, He isn't," Carin said. "He sent the baby Jesus to us. He didn't turn his eye. And that is why Christmas is so very important. It is a special time. It is a time for renewing one's faith."

"If you got some," Hez said, winking at Adrian in a chummy manner.

"And a time for family," Carin persisted.

"Families are highly overrated," Adrian said before he could stop himself.

"Had plenty of them," Hez said, waving his fork in an offhand manner. "Don't need one."

"It is a time for miracles," Carin finished with a determined voice.

"Miracles?" Adrian groaned. "You believe in those, too?"

"She's just a woman, guv," Hez said, shaking his head. "She can't help herself."

Adrian stared at Hez. Bertha laughed loudly. "Blimey, if you ain't two peas in a pod. One from the gutter and one with a silver spoon clenched in his jaw, but both thinking the same. He could be yer son, m'lord."

Adrian started, appalled—not at her rude suggestion, but at the clear truth of it. Then he glanced at Carin. Her eyes were dark and concerned. They were so blasted innocent and, yes, believing. He sighed. Hez had the right of it: She was just a woman.

Someday she would discover that Christmas was noth-

ing and that all her childish notions were just that, childish. Faith, she had just spouted the most mawkish senti-
ments, down to believing in miracles. Life could never
live up to her rosy vision. She would discover that all too
soon.

Yet somehow, he was loath to make her discover it tonight. Worse, he was loath to be the one to make her
face the truth. It was ridiculous beyond belief, but what
she must learn he did not want her to learn at his hand.

Attempting a cool manner, he turned his gaze to Bertha. Her look was all too knowing. "Madam, I have a
proposition. If—and I repeat, *if*—you and everyone at this
table will cease this discussion and merely eat, then everyone can stay for the nonce."

"Oh, thank you, my lord," Carin said, her face breaking out into a smile.

"Indeed, yes," Meg said, nodding. "You are so very
kind."

"But everyone will take a bath once a week," Adrian
said sternly. "You will also acquire new clothes. Burn the
ones you have. They reek."

"New clothes!" Hez exclaimed. "Blimey!"

"How very thoughtful," Carin said, her gaze approving.

"I am not being thoughtful," Adrian said, stiffly. "I
only wish to save my nose."

"You just proved the sweet lady right, m'lord," Bertha
said, chuckling low.

"I beg your pardon?" Adrian said.

"Miracles do happen after all." Bertha grinned and
hoisted her glass of Bordeaux to him in a toast.

Chapter Three

Three French Chickens?

"So this St. Nicholas bloke is going to come and stuff presents into me stocking?" Hez asked, his tone suspicious.

"Yes, if you are a good boy," Carin said as they walked down the busy London street.

They had just come from a shop, where Nelson had overseen the buying of wardrobes for both Bertha and Hez. She glanced gratefully at the butler. She doubted any of them would have known how to go on without his firm hand with the shopkeeper. The woman had been quite frightening and officious until Nelson had mentioned the marquise de Chambert's name; she then proceeded to act as if the butler were Adrian himself.

"But you must be very good," Carin said.

"If you are not," Meg warned as she strolled along cuddling baby Partridge close, "he will put coal in your stocking."

"Coal?" Hez asked, pulling in discomfort at the collar points of his new ready-made high-necked jacket. "Gore."

"Don't sound bad to me," Bertha said, grinning and all but sashaying in her new finery of deep grape bombazine, the bodice of which was paneled with black

crepe tucks. She appeared almost respectable, if one did
not know she had her trusty flask tucked into its skirts.
"At least it will let you build a fire and keep a body
warm."

"But presents will surely be better," Nelson said, his
tone luring.

"Just how good does one have to be to have this Nicholas fellow heave over?" Hez asked.

"Good enough to give up the pincushion and ribbon
you've hidden in your pocket in order that I may return
it to the proprietress of the shop," Nelson replied.

"What?" Carin exclaimed. She peered at Hez in astonishment. "Hez, you didn't steal them, did you?"

"I didn't steal them," Hez said, flushing. "I just borrowed them . . . in case I needed to sew something."

"That *is* stealing, Hez," Carin said. "And it is wrong."

"It ain't wrong," Hez said. "It's known as taking care
of yerself."

"You are taking what is not yours for your own benefit," Carin said. "That is not right."

"Come back, you thieving cur!" a voice bellowed from
behind.

"Oh, dear," Carin gasped even as Hez squeaked.

The entire group turned in unison. It was fortunate
they did. A monstrous black dog galloped down upon
them, a string of something flapping in its mouth. They
stumbled back as the mastiff charged past. Behind the
dog, a burly man followed, and behind him ran a shorter
man sporting a white chef's hat and brandishing a
butcher knife, while shouting out curses in French. The
dog disappeared around the corner into an alley. The
two men pounded behind.

"B'jesus," Hez cried. He sprinted after them.

"Hez, come back," Carin called and gave chase.

By the time she caught up with them, her heart was
pounding. It lurched into her throat. The massive canine

was hunkered down against a rotting crate. It growled and displayed impressive fangs. Hez stood fearlessly beside the dog, which was almost as large as he. The first man towered over them, his ham-size fists balled. The little chef was jumping up and down, flailing his knife in the air.

"Don't hurt it!" Hez said, his own small fists clenched.

"I'm not going to hurt it," the man growled as loudly as the dog. "Just kill it!"

"No," Hez cried. "It didn't do nothin' wrong."

Carin heard panting and Nelson arrived. Bertha, her new purple skirts hiked up to her garters, was directly behind him. Meg followed with baby Partridge, but at a more seemly pace.

"Excuse me, sir," Nelson said, stepping forward. "What seems to be the problem here?"

"What's the problem?" the big man roared, causing the little man beside him to slash the knife once more in a hacking manner. "That damn dog has stolen from me for the last time. It sneaks in the back of my kitchen and snatches the food before we know it. Then it is out the front, tearing through my eatery and upsetting the customers. This time it took my birds. Joseph had a very special recipe all planned for them."

Everyone peered at the nefarious felon. The dog growled, the string well lodged between its teeth, three plucked birds strung upon it.

"So what?" Hez said. "It's just some chickens."

"Ze capon! Ze capon!" the little man cried, spinning. He flourished his knife at them and his face twisted. Clearly he suffered severe anguish and he told them so in a blast of French, which lost much without translation.

"Humph," Bertha said, squinting. "If he wanted a cape on he shouldn't have run orf without one."

"Non, ze capon! Capon!" the chef cried, stomping his foot.

"He is talking about the birds," Nelson said. "Capon is French."

"Oh." Bertha nodded, attempting to look wise. "Them be French chickens."

"Yes," Nelson said.

"Told ye so," Hez said scornfully.

The little chef erupted in a frenzy. Nelson listened intently and nodded. "Very well. They are not just chickens. They are the male bird."

"Them ain't roosters!" Hez exclaimed.

"No, for they were castrated," Nelson explained.

"Coor. Is that wot those Frenchies do to their birds?" Bertha said, her eyes wide.

"What . . . ?" Hez began.

"Never you mind," Bertha said quickly.

"It makes for a better-tasting bird," Nelson said, flushing. He appeared grateful as the little chef shouted and proceeded upon a lengthy declamation. "Yes, yes. It sounds like a most excellent recipe. I am very sorry the dog stole your capons. However, we shall be glad to pay for them."

The little man became even more verbal, waxing eloquent and flailing his hands.

"Yes. Yes, it is unfortunate. I am sure the recipe is of greatest consequence and sure to place the name Joseph on every tongue in London. However, not only will we gladly pay for them if you will leave the dog be," Nelson said, "but I am the butler to the marquise de Chambert. His chef is also French and highly proclaimed. If you would care for his special recipe—the one the Prince Regent found most delightful when dining with my lord—I will give it to you as well, if you keep it secret."

The French chef, M. Joseph, lowered his knife, his eyes

lighting up. He sprang toward Nelson, kissing him upon first one cheek and then the other.

"Here now!" Bertha cried. "What's he doing?"

"It is just their way, madam," Nelson said calmly. "I believe we have come to an agreement."

"Humph," Bertha muttered. "Looks like they did to him the same as they did to those poor birds."

"Here now, we haven't come to an agreement," the large man objected. "I'm not having that dog loose about and thieving from me again."

"He won't," Hez said, " 'Cause he's coming home with us."

"Hez!" Carin exclaimed. "We cannot."

"But we gotta take him with us," Hez said. His eyes turned pleading. "Please."

"I don't think the marquise will permit—" Carin began.

"It is Christmas," Hez said quickly. "You said we are supposed to be good. We can't leave him out in this cold. You didn't leave me out in it."

"I suppose not," Carin said, sighing.

The man continued with a feral grin. "You're going to pay me for the birds, give Joseph the marquise's recipe, and take this here dog away?"

"Yes," Carin said, nodding. There truly was no other choice.

"Well, all I've got to say is good riddance to the bitch!"

"Watch yer mouth," Bertha said. "Who're you calling names?"

"That one," the man said, jerking his head toward the large mastiff.

Baby Partridge let out a cry of a sudden. The dog's ears perked up and rather than growling it barked. A series of smaller yaps echoed after.

"What in heaven's name?" Carin exclaimed. She walked closer. "Oh dear. Hezekiah! How could you?"

Three plump puppies were hidden within the crate amongst a mangle of rags and garbage.

Hez grinned. "Guess he's a she. Something like those roosters being chickens."

"Hez," Carin said, looking at him sternly.

"It is Christmas after all," Hez said.

Adrian entered his home. Within a moment he discovered a most unsalubrious fact: Once again Nelson was not at his post. Gaskins hurried forward, his face flustered.

"Where is Nelson this time?" Adrian asked curtly, offering Gaskins his hat.

"I—" Gaskins halted.

"You could not say?" Adrian asked, lifting a brow.

"Yes, my lord." Gaskins nodded, his face relieved. "I could not say."

"Gaskins," Adrian said, "I know about the baby now—and about the old lady and the boy."

"I am glad, my lord," Gaskins said, nodding.

"Then let me ask once more," Adrian said, "where Nelson is."

"My lord," a voice called out. Adrian looked up. Mrs. Knightsbridge, the housekeeper, was approaching him. Indeed, one could say she was steaming down upon him. Her face was stern with disapproval. "I have been waiting to talk to you. I must object."

"Object?" Adrian asked, his brow rising.

"I have worked for you for six years," Mrs. Knightsbridge said, drawing in a breath.

"Yes?" Adrian asked. He hadn't had any notion she had been in his employ that long.

"And always I have been pleased to work here," Mrs. Knightsbridge said.

"It is so good to hear that," Adrian said politely.

"But I will not—cannot work where there are animals," Mrs. Knightsbridge said.

"Animals? Is that not rather a strong view to take?" Adrian raised his brow in astonishment. "I myself own I am not quite pleased with the present company, but I would not call them animals."

"I do not know what else you would call them," Mrs. Knightsbridge cried. "Flea ridden and no doubt diseased. I will not have it."

Adrian frowned. "You will not have it?"

"I will not!" Mrs. Knightsbridge said, drawing herself up to her full height. "Either those creatures go or I go."

"Is that an ultimatum?" Adrian asked, his eyes narrowing.

"Yes," Mrs. Knightsbridge said though her gaze wavered. Gaskins could be heard to gurgle.

"Then you may go, Mrs. Knightsbridge," Adrian said, drawing himself up to his far grander height. "I shall not be ordered about by my servants. I believe I pay you an adequate wage. Who I choose to have in my house is my affair."

Mrs. Knightsbridge's face crumpled. "But, my lord, I am allergic to them. They make me sneeze and give me rashes."

Adrian stared. A strong presentiment came over him. Still, he held firm. "I said I will not be ordered about. You may stay or go, but if I choose to have animals in the house, I shall."

"Very well, my lord. I shall remain for as long as I can," Mrs. Knightsbridge said. She turned and fled.

Adrian watched until she had disappeared from sight. "Gaskins?"

"Yes, my lord?"

"She was not talking about the old lady and boy, was she?" Adrian asked.

"No, my lord," Gaskins said.

"If not them, then what animals was she referring to?" Gaskins remained silent. Adrian sighed and held up a hand. "No, do not tax yourself. I know where to find the answer."

Adrian strode through the town house, going directly to the wing now serving as the schoolroom, the nursery, and this day, God only knew what else. He slowed as the sound of laughter drifted out from behind the half-open door.

"Do not laugh," Carin said. "I do not know what we are going to tell my lord."

"Does his nibs ever smile, do yer think?" Hez's voice asked. Adrian stiffened immediately.

"I do not know," Carin returned. "I do not think he wants us here."

"Many men do not care for change," Meg said in a gentle voice.

"True," Nelson concurred. Adrian frowned severely. His butler should be supportive of him. "His lord has been a bachelor for quite some time. It is customary for those who live alone to become set in their ways."

Adrian stifled a curse. Nelson's tone made Adrian sound as if he were one of those cantankerous, eccentric old men who propped their gout-ridden feet on a stool and terrorized the rest of their establishment.

"Coor, set in his ways?" Hez said scornfully. "You mean he's a cool customer, he is."

"Hez," Carin's said reproachfully.

"I don't know," Bertha said, speculation in her voice. "I'd bet me new bonnet he'd be fine looking if he'd smile."

Blast it! Adrian thought, stiffening. He would show them exactly how fine looking and jolly he could be. Adrian pinned a smile upon his lips and stepped forward. He halted and adjusted the smile, realizing his first was too grim.

Deeming his smile correct this time, he stepped into the room. His fine, jolly smile slid from his face. There in a large copper-and-enamel bathing tub—*his* large bathing tub with the Chambert crest scrolled in gold along its side—sat a monstrous black canine, white suds dripping down its snout. Carin knelt beside the tub. Her sleeves were rolled up. Tendrils of damp silver hair plastered her cheek the same way her wet dress clung to her body. The others sat around in chairs and upon the desks. As Adrian's gaze scanned the room, he quickly noted three more smaller versions of the behemoth in the tub, all being cuddled and toweled dry.

"The devil!" he shouted.

Everyone turned to him in astonishment. Their astonishment immediately became horror. Their looks of fright were so great Adrian started. Surely he could not be as horrific as the dog in the tub. Then he remembered his intention to smile. He forced his lips to do so. "Hello."

"Er . . . hello," Carin said, her voice diffident.

"Hello, guv," Hez said. In his small arms he clutched a pup so tightly the poor mite yelped.

"Good day to ye, my lord," Bertha said. It was fortunate her response was not as tense as Hez's, for in her arms she held baby Partridge.

"My lord," Nelson exclaimed, rising with a wriggling pup in his arms. "You are home early."

"So I am," Adrian said, still valiantly attempting to smile.

The room fell silent. The large dog in the tub barked.

"I believe," Adrian said calmly, "that someone requires an introduction."

"This is Marie Antoinette," Carin stammered.

"And this here is Napoleon," Hez said.

"And this is King Louis," Meg said, smiling.

Adrian turned his gaze to Nelson. Nelson flushed. "This is Richelieu."

Adrian's smile quivered. "May I ask why we have such a stellar envoy visiting us?"

"It was because of some chickens," Hez piped up quickly.

"Capons, my lord," Nelson said.

"That's French," Bertha said. She shook her head. "Poor birds. What those foreigners won't do."

Everyone fell silent over that. Adrian frowned. "Please continue. You say it was because of some chickens . . ."

"Capons, sir," Nelson said.

"Yes, yes. You say because of some capons I now have a large dog in my bathing tub as well as three puppies?"

"Marie stole three capons from a restaurant," Carin said. Marie barked and bared her teeth in the semblance of a smile. Her large tail slapped the water, spraying Carin.

"Be quiet," Adrian said to the dog. "You should be ashamed of yourself."

"She only took them for Nap, Louis, and Rich," Hez said.

"The chef and the proprietor of the establishment were going to kill Marie because she stole the birds," Carin said, her face aghast.

"Imagine, guv," Hez said, shaking his head sadly, "killing a dog 'cause of some silly birds—French ones at that."

"We couldn't have permitted that," Carin said.

"No, of course not," Adrian said, sighing.

"We had to bring them here," Hez said. "We couldn't leave them on the street in the cold. It is Christmas, you know."

Adrian raised a brow. "I thought you didn't believe in Christmas."

"I do now," Hez said, a flush rising to his cheeks as he cuddled Nap.

"Amazing," Adrian said, shaking his head. "To turn into a believer so quickly just because of a dog."

"Never had one, guv," Hez confessed. "I've always wanted one."

"One? Strange. I count four myself," Adrian said.

"You couldn't take just one and leave the others, guv," Hez said. "They are a family."

"Ah, now you believe in family as well," Adrian said.

"We can keep them, can't we?" Hez asked, all his bravado disappearing. His eyes actually pleaded.

Adrian hesitated. Evidently Marie divined her fate hung in the balance. She barked and placed her two large paws on the tub, clearly intending to jump out.

"Marie, no!" Carin cried. She leaned over and wrapped her arms around the dog in an effort to stay her.

"Woof!" Marie replied and sprang. Carin, off balance, was dragged into the tub even as Marie escaped from it. The dog charged at Adrian, trailing water and suds.

"No," Adrian ordered as the dog prepared to jump up on him. "Down."

"Marie, how could you?" Carin's voice sputtered as she surfaced from the tub.

Marie hunkered down upon her haunches and barked. Her pups added their yaps in accord. Adrian did not notice. Carin's dripping, indignant face was all he could see. Despite himself, he laughed.

"Because she has no morals," he said, strolling over to Carin. He reached down. "Let me assist you."

"Thank you," Carin said, her face embarrassed. She put her hand in his. Instantly a jolt of electricity shot through Adrian. No doubt that was what caused him to draw Carin up so swiftly that she almost slipped. Adrian was forced to pull her close to him to keep her from falling—or at least he believed that was his purpose.

"Are you all right?" Adrian asked, his voice coming out hoarse as his body sent a clamor of messages to him. Her body was slender and supple and melded to his perfectly. She smelled of suds and a light jasmine perfume. Her eyes were the deepest blue and sweetly innocent. Her lips were full and glistening.

"I . . . ah . . . I . . ." Carin stopped. He could hear her breathe. He could feel it, he held her so tightly.

"I think that means she's fine, m'lord," Bertha said to Adrian. He heard her laugh.

He knew he should release Carin, but couldn't seem to do so. "Are you?"

"I—I . . ." Carin licked her lips. Adrian watched closely, heat flashing through him. "I think so."

"Very well," Adrian said. He slowly loosened his hold.

"You . . . you . . . ?" Carin asked quickly.

"What?" Adrian asked, stilling his movement.

"You aren't angry at Marie?"

"No," Adrian said. He couldn't be angry at anything at the particular moment.

"Can she and the puppies stay?" Hez's voice asked.

"Yes, can they stay?" Carin asked, flushing deeply.

"They can stay," Adrian said, unable to think clearly.

"They can?" Carin exclaimed, her eyes widening.

"They can." Adrian nodded slowly.

"Thank you," Carin said, smiling in sheer delight.

Adrian smiled back, totally mesmerized. What were a few dogs, if they could earn him such a smile and look. "It is my pleasure."

"That it is," Bertha was heard to laugh.

"Hooray!" Hez shouted. "They get to stay!"

Suddenly there were enough shouts and yaps that even Adrian was forced to turn his gaze from Carin. It was too late. Marie was bearing down on him. Reacting instinctively, Adrian released Carin and held his hands out to fend the large dog off. He failed. Her two massive paws hit his chest and he tumbled back, the dog on top of him.

"Confound it!" Adrian cried, shoving at more than a hundred pounds of fur and bone. "Get off of me, you beast."

He succeeded in shoving Marie from him. Biting back a curse, he sat up. Marie had gained her feet. She reached over and ran a long, slurping tongue across his cheek.

"Blast!"

"She's only thanking you," Hez said. "She likes you."

"Bet he wouldn't care if someone other than that dog were to kiss him in appreciation," Bertha cackled.

Adrian scrambled from the floor, irate and embarrassed. He attempted to dust himself off, only to discover he was damp and marked with two sodden paw prints. He glanced around. Everyone gazed at him with varying shades of amusement. Only Carin did not look at him, her eyes averted, a red flush painting her cheeks.

"I must go and change," Adrian said, quite unnecessarily. He set his focus upon Nelson. Fortunately, the butler's look was respectful. "I will be going out tonight." He glared at Bertha, feeling both goaded and driven by her amusement. "I intend to see a lady friend. Do not expect me home."

"What lady friend?" Hez asked, frowning.

"That is none of your business," Adrian said sternly. "Be certain to keep these dogs restrained. They may stay if—and only if—I need not suffer their overexuberance in the future."

"Yes, guv," Hez said, his tone frightened.

Not knowing what else to say, Adrian strode from the room. Only when he was well down the hall did he halt. He closed his eyes. Faith, what a total fool he had made out of himself. What a complete and total fool!

* * *

Carin stood starring after Adrian. How wonderful he had been. A warm and pleasant glow filled her and with it came the oddest tingle.

"He's got a mighty fine smile after all," Bertha said. "Don't ye think so, Carin?"

"What?" Carin asked, blinking.

"Who's his lady friend is what I want ter know?" Hez asked, frowning. He looked to Nelson. "Who is she?"

"My lord said it was none of your business," Nelson said, his tone dignified.

"Aha." Bertha nodded. "She must be his fancy piece."

"Fancy piece? You mean his mistress?" Carin exclaimed. The warm glow disappeared. She shivered. It was due to being wet no doubt.

"Heavens," Meg said.

"Well, why didn't he just say that?" Hez asked, frowning. "He was making it sound as if she was something or other special."

"Hez!" Carin exclaimed. "Do not speak so."

"Why not?" Hez asked, looking totally confused.

"Miss Carin is rather shocked my lord has a mistress," Bertha said, nodding.

"I am not," Carin said, flushing.

"Why should she be shocked?" Hez asked. "Of course his nibs would have a fancy piece. I said he was a cool customer, but I never meant ter say he wasn't a real man like."

"So he is." Bertha winked at Carin. "Don't you worry none, love. He was just letting us know he's a free man. You scared him."

"Scared him?" Carin frowned. "What do you mean?"

Bertha frowned in return. She glanced at Meg, whose face displayed extreme alarm. "Never you mind. I was only teasing a bit."

Carin, feeling completely lost and extremely uncomfortable, said, "I am not shocked that he has a mistress. Men always do."

"Not always," Meg said quietly.

"I agree with Miss Mumford," Nelson said, his tone solemn.

" 'Course not," Bertha said. "Marriage would be a sad thing if that were so."

"Marriage is a sad thing," Carin murmured.

"Here now!" Hez squawked.

Bertha frowned, her aged eyes piercing Carin. "Just what do you mean by that, missy?"

Carin swallowed. "What I mean is that marriage is that way—for women, that is."

"Coor, ducky. Wherever did ye get that bumfuddled notion?" Bertha asked.

"Men have their mistresses," Carin said from rote, "and women must accept and suffer quietly."

"God bless ye child," Bertha said, breaking into a roar of laughter. "Don't know where you come by that, but me man and I were together for twenty and more years. He didn't have no fancy piece 'cause he knew I'd slice him throughout the center if he did."

"Heavens," Meg murmured.

Carin could not speak. She could only stare.

Bertha grinned. "That and I made sure he was too bloomin' tired out to go lookin' elsewhere. 'Course, it was my pleasure to do so."

"Your pleasure?" Carin asked, wide-eyed. She frowned. "Marriage is nothing but heartache for a woman."

"Heartache?" Bertha asked. She shook her rheumy head. "No, dearie. I'd say heartache is when he is gone and ye don't have yer man there on those cold nights. And you don't have him to laugh with and fight with when yer in a brawling temper." Bertha shifted baby Partridge and delved into her pocket, drawing out her flask. "Heartache is when you've only got this here to warm ye and help ye make it through." Everyone fell silent as Bertha lifted the flask and, after tipping it to them, drank heavily. Only baby Partridge began to fret and Bertha immediately lowered the flask to shift her close and coo. "Don't ye fret, sweetings. Old Bertha is here. Never ye fear."

Marie Antoinette lumbered over to Carin and whined. Carin, blinking back what felt like tears, dragged herself from out of the tub and stooped to pet the large dog. "It is all right, Marie."

Hez, solemnly watching the ladies, held Nap up close to his cheek, rubbing his face against the pup. "It's all right, Nap. I'm here."

Bertha suddenly chuckled. "Well, yer don't need an old woman's blatherings. You'll find out what marriage is all about in yer own good time."

"No, I won't," Carin said, petting Marie all the more. "I am never going to marry."

"Don't ye talk that way," Bertha said sternly. "A fine, kind gel like ye. Of course ye will marry. And if I'm not mistaken, with all the love you have to pass out like sweets, you'll be keepin' him too close for him to look fer other fancies."

"You do not understand," Carin objected. "I do not wish to marry. I promised my mother on her deathbed I would not."

"Lawks," Bertha cried. "Why'd ye do a thing like that?"

"That can't really count, can it?" Hez asked, his tone nervous. "Promising someone who's dying? I mean, they ain't going to be around to see if you kept your promise."

"I am not worried," Carin said, her chin jutting out. She had not expected such a reaction from them. Indeed, they sounded just the way Adrian had. "I will not be sorry."

Bertha chuckled, but sadly. "Child, ye can't say it when

ye don't even know what yer passing up. And ye shouldn't have been makin' such a brash promise to yer ma when there ain't no saying what's going to happen in yer life. That ain't your decision nohow."

Adrian followed Nanette's maid up the stairs to her boudoir. He had made his decision.

He was going to forget about everything. He'd make rousing love to his mistress and forget about young innocents with supple bodies and all-too-knowing old beldames and dogs. His valet, Maritime, had all but wept when Adrian had appeared, damp and paw besmirched. He had moaned about how proud he had always been that Adrian was a neat and fastidious lord, never forgetting his station or appearance. He was the second servant in a day to cry to him because things were out of order.

Adrian entered Nanette's room. It was outfitted in soft pinks and mauves. No matter the cost, tapers were always lit. Hidden in corners and obscured behind festooned gauze, they offered a tantalizingly romantic glow. The air smelled of an indefinable exotic scent. Nanette's favorite.

"Nanette, my love," Adrian said.

"Adrian," Nanette breathed, spinning from her dressing table. Filmy, sheer muslin fluttered upon her movement. Her voice was low and husky, an odd and intriguing sound from such a diminutive brunette, though her bountiful chest, in that respect, could support such a contralto voice. That was her allure. A pocket Venus with a deep and hearty appetite for all things. "Dearest, I have missed you!"

She walked toward him provocatively, experienced and proud in that knowledge. Here was no innocent, either in body or soul. He winced and pulled Nanette close when she came within arm's length. He didn't need to think. He needed raw passion and the release of it.

"Adrian," Nanette laughed, wrapping her arms about his neck even as she rubbed her body against him. "I see you have missed me."

Adrian growled and lowered his head, ravaging her hot lips with his. He drew back in satisfaction. This was good, very good. Still, some perverse, nagging thought made him speak. "What do you think about Christmas?"

"Christmas? I adore it." Nanette's eyes glowed. She shimmied her body against him. "I love all the gifts. The more expensive the better."

Adrian laughed loudly and kissed her once more. Faith, her answer pleased him no end. She was an honest, greedy wench.

"Hmm," Nanette purred. "I think it is going to be an early Christmas." Her hand roved downward. "I was starting to fear you were forgetting me."

"Of course not," Adrian murmured, discarding for the moment his notion of finding a new mistress. He was not a cold customer, after all. He bent and kissed Nanette passionately—only he could hear Bertha's cackle in his head: *Bet he wouldn't mind kissin' someone else.* . . . He closed his eyes, shutting the words out, redoubling his efforts.

"Adrian," Nanette finally gasped, drawing back. Her face was confused. "What is wrong?"

"Nothing is wrong. Nothing," Adrian muttered. He remembered to smile. "Why?"

"Because—" Nanette halted. Her gaze flickered down to where her hand was intimately placed.

Adrian flushed. For all his passionate kisses, there was one part of his body still not convinced of his desire. The saving answer came to him quickly. "I am sorry, Nanette. I have drunk too much I fear."

Frustration and disappointment crossed Nanette's face. She sighed. "Damn."

Adrian smiled rather weakly. Not for all the world would he admit, even to himself, that he was not drunk. Generally respected as a three-bottle man, he decided that the two drinks of which he had partaken at White's earlier that evening were at fault.

Carin lay in her bed, squeezing her eyes closed tightly. Try as she might, she could not fall asleep. She would start her dreams out with anything—the dogs, the baby— and soon they would turn into dreams of Adrian and she would experience the strangest emotions. She sat up, pounded the feather pillow, and plopped back down. Just what was the matter with her?

A knock sounded at her door. Carin sat back up, her heart pounding. "Who is it?"

"It's me, Hez."

"Hez?" Carin quickly moved to light a taper. "What is the matter?"

"Are Marie and the puppies in there with you?" Hez asked.

"No," Carin called. Her heart sank. "Why?"

"I think I lost them," Hez said.

"Oh, no," Carin breathed. She sprang from the bed and threw her robe over herself. Then she grabbed a candle and ran to open the door.

Hez, small and sleepy eyed, peered up at her. "I'm sorry. I forgot ter close the door like ye told me to. Then I fell asleep. They were on my bed. But when I woke up . . ."

"Oh, dear!" Carin exclaimed. "We must find them."

"I looked in Bertha's room. But she and baby Partridge were sleeping. Bertha snores something frightful, you know? And I knocked on Miss Mumford's door, but she didn't answer. I think she's asleep too," Hez said. "Coor, if his nibs finds out, he's sure to toss them out."

"No, he won't," Carin assured him staunchly. "Only do let us find them. Where do you think they could have gone?"

Hez thought a moment. He grinned. "If I were a dog I'd go to the kitchen. Look for some chickens."

"Very good," Carin said, nodding. "See if they are there. I will search upstairs."

"Right." Hez nodded, his small face solemn. He dashed away down the hall.

Carin shook her head and moved down the hall in the other direction. As she walked she called out quietly for Marie and the pups. She decided not to concern herself with any door that was firmly closed. It was not as if Marie and the pups could open them.

She wandered into the corridor, still calling out for Marie, Napoleon, Louis, and Richelieu. The number of rooms in one town house still stunned her. Out of the many doors she had only found two ajar. She had entered and searched the rooms. The furnishings in the rooms, even by one meager candle's glow, appeared opulent.

She came to another door that was ajar. She entered the room. Her heart leapt in joy. She had found Marie and the puppies. Then her heart effected a quick reverse and plummeted.

This was no guest room. A fire remained lit in the grate, casting its own glow over a huge room. Over masculine furnishings. Over a male nightshirt upon a huge bed. Over Napoleon burrowed in that nightshirt. Over Louis nestled upon the accompanying nightcap. Over Marie lying upon the pillows of the turned-down covers with Richelieu curled up beside her.

"Marie, why?" Carin groaned. "Out of all the rooms to choose, why his?"

Marie lifted her head, let out a contented woof, and lowered her head once more.

"Oh, no, you don't!" Carin exclaimed. She hurried over to the large bed and set her candle down upon the bedside table.

"You must get down immediately!" She leaned over and shoved Marie. Marie whined. "No, you must get off the bed." Carin said, crawling onto it and wrapping her arms around the large dog. Employing all her strength, she wrestled Marie to the edge of the bed. She ruthlessly shoved her off. Marie hit the floor with a howl.

"I am sorry," Carin said, biting her lip. "But you cannot sleep here."

By this time the pups had awakened. Carin reached for Richelieu, who was closest. Richelieu yapped and, wagging his tail, attempted to scamper away from her. "Rich, please. This is not a game." The other two pups sent up merry barks as she caught Richelieu and lowered him to the carpet. "Now for you two." Carin caught Nap and Louis and rendered them the same service.

"There," Carin said, smiling in satisfaction. Her smile turned to horror as Marie promptly leapt back onto the bed.

"Marie!" Carin lunged for her, repeating her efforts. But by the time she had expelled Marie from the bed, she discovered Richelieu returning. "How . . . ?" Carin exclaimed indignantly. She sat and stared as Louis followed behind, jumping upon an ottoman, then onto the trunk at the bed's foot, and then onto the mattress itself. "Good gracious!"

Marie, with a congenial woof, joined her puppies with a bounding leap.

"I give up!" Defeated, Carin fell back upon the mattress herself. She closed her eyes. Now she was exhausted. "Thank heavens he said he would not be home for the night."

"What are you doing here?" Adrian's voice asked. It was low and hoarse.

Carin snapped her eyes open. Adrian stood beside the bed. His gaze seemed dazed. There was something else in his eyes—something that sent a shiver through Carin.

Blushing, she sat up quickly. "I am sorry."

"You should not be here," Adrian said, his tone sharp.

"I know," Carin said. "I came for the dogs."

"You should not be here," he repeated firmly.

"Yes," Carin repeated. "But the dogs—"

"Hang the dogs," Adrian said. "I do not care about them. *You* should not be here!"

"I said I know," Carin cried. Hurt welled up in her. This afternoon she had started to think he liked her, but clearly he did not. He would rather have the dogs on his bed instead of her. "I understand you do not want me here. You never wanted me here."

"I didn't mean that," Adrian said. "I meant in my room."

"Or anywhere in the house," Carin said. She scrambled to the edge of the bed.

"You don't understand!"

"I do!" Carin cried, springing up.

"No, you don't," Adrian said. He clasped her shoulders, peering down at her in anger and exasperation. "You must understand—"

"I said I do," Carin said.

"Oh, to blazes with it," Adrian said. He jerked her forward and kissed her ruthlessly. Carin gasped as wild sensations coursed through her. A stunned moan escaped her.

Adrian pulled back. "Do you understand now?"

"I—I . . ." Carin couldn't marshal her thoughts.

"You must understand," Adrian said. Clearly he took her hesitation as not understanding, for he kissed her again, this time pulling her body up against his.

Somehow, Carin understood. Indeed, the shocking, compelling, intriguing answer to the greater part of the universe became hers. She also realized her knees had turned to water.

Whether Adrian exactly comprehended her plight or not she could not be certain but they fell onto the bed. Adrian kissed her cheeks, her eyes, her lips. His hands moved fluidly across her body, sending thrilling warm chills over Carin.

"So sweet," Adrian murmured.

Oh, yes, it is so sweet, Carin thought. *Sweet and tingly and slowly aching. All of me.* She clutched Adrian's shoulders, her body arching to his, begging for his hands to touch her and teach her.

"You feel—" Adrian murmured, his lips nuzzling her ear.

"Yes. Yes, I feel," Carin answered in a daze.

"—so good." Adrian groaned as his lips traced down the column of her neck even as his hand rose to slide her robe from her shoulder.

"Yes, so very good . . ." Carin mumbled.

"You feel . . . furry!"

"Furry?" Carin's eyes snapped open just as she felt the same thing. Fur! On her neck, suspiciously close to where Adrian's lips were.

"Blast!" Adrian sputtered, lifting his head.

"What?" Carin asked.

"That infernal pup kissed me."

"Oh, dear," Carin murmured. Then reality struck. "Oh dear!"

"Go away," Adrian muttered, shoving at the pup. A sad whine sounded in Carin's ear.

"Yes, I must," Carin said, shoving at Adrian.

"I didn't mean you," Adrian exclaimed.

"I-I did," Carin said, pushing all the harder. Adrian

groaned, but rolled away from her. Carin, the minute she was free, scrambled from the bed.

"Carin, wait!" Adrian said, sitting up.

"No," Carin said, unable to look at him. "I understand. I should not be here."

"I—"

Carin dashed from the room without waiting for Adrian's words. She was frightened of what they might be. She dashed down the hall. Tears began to fall as she reached her own room.

"Miss Carin," Hez called. "They aren't in the kitchen."

Carin spun. Hez was walking down the hall. "No, I found them."

"You did?" Hez asked, his face brightening. Then he frowned. "Where are they?"

"They are in the marquise's room," Carin whispered.

"Blimey!" Hez exclaimed. "And you left them there?"

"He is there too," Carin said. A sob escaped her.

"Oh, no," Hez said. "He ain't going to toss them out, is he?"

"No," Carin said, shaking her head quickly.

"Then why are you crying?" Hez said.

"It is nothing," Carin lied.

"Ah. He came down heavy on ye, did he?" Hez asked, his tone sympathetic.

"What?" Carin gurgled.

"Raked ye over the coals about the dogs, did he?"

"Yes," Carin said. "Something like that."

They suddenly heard the sound of nails and a woof. Hez lifted his candle. Marie Antoinette trailed by her three pups came barreling down the hall.

"There you are, ye bad dogs," Hez cried. Marie wagged her tail. "Don't you go wandering orf again. And you keep clear of his nibs from now on—do ye hear?"

Marie barked happily.

Carin stifled another sob. She didn't know about

Marie, but she fully intended to stay clear of his nibs. In fact, she didn't wish to ever see him again. She was sure she wouldn't be able to look him in the eye if she did.

Chapter Four

Four Birds A-calling

"If you will excuse me now," Adrian said, rising from the breakfast table. He barely glanced at the company. He nodded to Nelson, who hovered with a teapot in his hand. "I shall be home for luncheon, Nelson." With that and only that, Adrian departed the breakfast room.

"Well!" Hez exclaimed. "If he ain't an icicle! And what I want ter know is why he's coming home fer luncheon. All he's going ter do is sit through it all silent like. He don't like me talkin' 'bout maggots, but I don't eat when he's like that."

"I—I believe I will go and see to baby Partridge," Carin said softly. She rose.

"Why?" Bertha asked, reaching across the table and spearing the last piece of toast. "That young footman Gaskins is with her. It ain't often I trust a man with a baby, but I do him."

"Yes," Nelson said. "I thought it rather . . . er . . . unusual when he asked if he could assist with the child." He moved to sit in the vacated chair. "Though I can see why he desired to change his post. There is not a footman upon the staff who wishes to greet my lord these days."

Everyone laughed, except Carin. She flushed, gazing

at the floor. "I believe I will still go and see after baby Partridge." She departed swiftly.

"I am worried about her," Meg said, frowning. "It is not common for her to be so downcast. Especially now, during Christmas."

"It's because of his nibs," Hez said hotly. "He's still in a tear 'cause he found Marie and the pups in his room. He's actin' like it's all Miss Carin's fault. It's been two days and he's still being an old curmudgeon."

"Might be," Bertha said. She grinned. "I think there's more there than we know."

"Carin will not speak of it," Meg said, sighing. "Not even to me."

" 'Course not," Bertha said, her eyes glinting. "But his mightiness is the one who should be turned over someone's knee. He's actin' like a spoilt bratling."

"I fear I must agree," Nelson said. "The entire staff is in a pelter. He is either barking at them or treating them to that frigid temper of his. Miss Knightsbridge will not hold out much longer, I believe. Though I am not particularly fond of her, she truly does have an affliction in regard to the dogs."

"What are we going ter do?" Hez asked, his face worried.

"Lad, there ain't nothing we can do," Bertha said, shaking her head. "His mightiness is the king of this castle. Ye can't tell him anything."

Hez frowned darkly. "That ain't fair."

"Hah!" Bertha said. "You and I both know life ain't fair."

Hez opened his mouth. Then he shut it. His gaze grew solemn and meditative. "*Someone* ought ter tell him."

"That's the one thing I ain't going ter do," Bertha said. She cast an amused look around the table. "Anyone else here want ter? Not that he'd listen ter us."

Hez didn't expect any of the four to answer, himself

included. He only grew more meditative. Just who should inform the marquise he was being bad? Very bad!

Adrian stumbled from the carriage, blinking as if even the moon's glow was too much.

"Can I help you, my lord?" his coachman asked from the box.

"No, no," Adrian said, straightening up as much as he could. "I-I am fine." He grinned. "Righto fine!"

"My lord?"

"I am going to go to b-bed now," Adrian said with dignity. He narrowed his eyes and made a lurching charge up the town house steps.

"Bed. By myself," he muttered and fumbled for his keys to the house. Unlike other noblemen he never required his staff to remain up awaiting his return. He was kind and considerate. Much good it did him. His staff did not appreciate it. Everyone thought him a monster.

His key clicked in the door and he tumbled into the house. "Yes, indeed. I go to b-bed by myself. I don't need servants." He slammed the door shut. "I don't need women." A cringe convulsed him. "I mean Nanette." He shivered once more. Turning, he meandered to the stairs. "Planned t-to turn her off anyway."

Adrian's head, even despite the numbing of a generous quantity of brandy, pounded in pain. Faith! No man should ever be forced to live through the scene he had just suffered. True, he had visited Nanette three nights straight. And true, all three nights he had not been able to—well, to perform in a manly fashion.

Still, did that give a woman the right to turn on a man as Nanette had? To wail and accuse? To attack a man in the worse possible way, asking deep, personal questions about what he *felt*? Faith, the one sure way to make a man deflate in his offering was to ask such questions. Did they have no delicacy? No understanding? They were said to be the frailer of the genders, yet they could broadside a man at his weakest moment without mercy.

"Frail, hah!" Adrian laughed bitterly as he stumbled up the stairs. They were no better then men. All they wanted from a man was his services. As he climbed a few more stairs, he started to wheeze. Yes, that was it: They only wanted a man to perform.

Suddenly a vision of innocent eyes dazed with passion and sudden knowledge rose before him. Eyes that turned to hurt. Adrian groaned. No, there was a woman who hadn't wanted sex. As if to be the worst traitor, as if to heap burning coals upon his head, Adrian's body sprung to life with the memory of Carin in his arms, the feel of her supple body, the taste of her soft, sweet lips.

"Blast and damn. Damn and bl-a-ast," Adrian muttered, as he finally reached the hall. Why did his body do this cursed thing? Why would it no longer respond to the charms of the sultry Nanette when it should? And why had it reacted like a randy goat with Carin when it shouldn't? Why, as drunk as he was now, did it still react to the thought of her?

"You Bluebeard," Adrian cursed himself. She was a guest in his home. Yet the chit *had* been in his room. She had worn that innocent nightgown—that flannel thing with the ribbons. What else could she expect? An embarrassed flush heated him. Clearly not what Nanette had expected and wanted.

That was the rub—the infernal, painful rub. He had been a cad. He had forced his attentions on an innocent. Now she attempted to avoid him. Her eyes were frightened when she was around him. He did not know what he could say to exonerate himself, which only made him angrier.

Adrian stumbled into his room and with determination changed into his night attire. He did not need servants for that. He stripped off his jacket and shirt and flung them upon the bed. He could do it on his own. He performed a clumsy dance, freeing himself of his boots and pantaloons, which he tossed on the bed, too. He could do everything on his own!

Shivering, he grabbed up the nightclothes laid out for him and struggled into them. Winded and dizzy, he fell onto his bed, losing all consciousness.

A small elfin figure slipped into Adrian's room. Silently and stealthily it moved toward the bed and Adrian's snoring form. It stood a moment, tense and waiting. When all remained still, it placed a large, bloated and lumpy pillowcase beside Adrian. Then it placed a placard upon the bedside table. Adrian mumbled and shifted, throwing an arm across the pillowcase. A gasp rang out and the figure turned, running from the room.

A few moments later four other dark shapes invaded the room. They converged upon the bed.

"My lord! My lord!" a voice shrilled. Adrian snorted into consciousness. Instantly his head shot pain throughout his system. The pain escalated with each time someone roared, "My lord." Slowly Adrian defined the voice. It was his valet's. Why was Marchim striving to propel Adrian into Bedlam? Surely, he must realize that a cannon shot in the morning was not good ton. Adrian lacked a decent answer.

"For God's sake, Marchim," Adrian croaked through a dry, fuzz-lined mouth, refusing to open his eyes. "What is the matter with you?"

"With me? Nothing is wrong with me, my lord!" Marchim cried. "It is you!"

"Me?" Adrian sighed, deciding he must move. He attempted to do so, but found he could not. Never had drink affected him to the point of immobility. He snapped his eyes open in fear. A groan escaped him as blinding light seared his beleaguered senses.

"What?" he whispered. His vision cleared and he discovered he could at least move his head, so he did. He came directly nose to nose with a ball of black fur. "Blast it!" He sputtered as the little beast slurped his cheek and whined a puppy greeting. "Get that infernal canine away from me!"

"Which one, my lord?" Marchim asked, his voice a sob.

"Which one?" Once again Adrian tried to sit up, only to fall back. "Confound it. I cannot move. Why the devil can I not move?"

"There . . . there is a singularly large one of *them* on top of you, my lord," Marchim said.

"You mean a dog?"

"Yes, my lord."

"Thank God," Adrian sighed. Better a dog than loss of the use of his limbs. "Move her."

"I—I can't, my lord," Marchim sniffled. "I—I am afraid of dogs. I-I have always been afraid of them. When I was a child, I—"

"Oh, be quiet," Adrian groaned. "Marie, get off of me now!" He heard a bark that shattered his senses. Then the weight was lifted. Sighing in relief, Adrian wasted no time in sitting up. Pain shot through him and he lifted a shaky hand to his forehead. He blinked. He lowered the hand back down to study it in confusion. "Marchim. My hand appears to be black. Is it black?"

"It is, my lord," Marchim said.

"Why would it be black?" Adrian murmured.

"I fear it is coal, my lord."

"Coal?" Adrian frowned. "Impossible."

"That is not the worst of it," Marchim cried.

"I have a black hand. That is not the worst of it?"

Adrian asked in bemusement. He turned his blurry gaze to Marchim. Marchim waved Adrian's jacket from the night before at him. The movement made Adrian decidedly seasick.

"Look what those dreadful creatures have done, my lord," Marchim sobbed. "They have torn holes in your jacket. They have shredded your shirt. They have gnawed your boots."

"My boots!" Adrian roared.

"And everything is black with coal!" Marchim wailed. "I cannot work under these conditions, my lord."

"You cannot?" Adrian snarled. The pain of a hangover was mild to the pain of the red-hot anger thrumming through his veins. Slowly, almost viscously, Adrian forced himself to focus upon his surroundings. There were three pups upon his bed. Each one possessed an article of his. They chewed upon them almost lovingly. Marie sat next to him.

"Woof!" Marie barked as Adrian's gaze met hers.

"Confound it!" Adrian muttered. In instinctive denial, he lowered his gaze. That was when he discovered a large pillowcase beside him. Coal spewed out of it.

Adrian cursed so fluidly that Marchim shrieked and covered his ears. "My lord, please!"

"Oh, do—" Adrian halted as something upon the bedside table caught his eye. Through a burning haze he read what was chalked upon a placard in coal.

Yer been bad. Real bad, yer nibs. Bad!

Saint Niklass

"Hez," Adrian breathed. "I am going to kill the little fiend."

"What, my lord?" Marchim asked.

"Kill him!" Adrian shouted. He jumped from the bed, swayed, then lurched toward the door.

"My lord," Marchim cried, "where are you going? You are not dressed. My lord, come back!"

Carin sat quietly, listening to the merry breakfast conversation flowing about her. She winced. It was noticeable that Adrian was absent. The others obviously took his absence as a blessing. She could only take it as a reprieve. Adrian clearly was disgusted with her. It was patently clear he disliked her all the more after that night in his room and he would rather have her gone.

In truth, she wished the same. She still could not manage to untangle the mass of emotions she had felt. Her mother had warned her never to permit a man to kiss her or touch her. It was the first step on the road to misery. Her mother had been correct. Now it was misery. Oh, but at the time, it had been bliss, earth-shattering bliss. Worse, her mind turned constantly to that moment, daydreaming about it. However, in the dreams it was something right and acceptable, something to be enjoyed.

Carin peeked at old Bertha, who was laughing at the moment. Could that be what she had been talking about when she told Carin she did not know what she would miss without marriage? Surely that was what she had meant by a man warming her at night? Carin flushed. Bertha had been polite in the use of the term *warm*.

"Hez!" A bellow sounded from outside the breakfast room. The door burst open. A towering, enraged Adrian stalked into the room. His face was as black as his anger—literally black—as was the nightshirt he sported.

"Lord love a duck," Bertha exclaimed. "What coal heap did ye fall into, m'lord?"

"I didn't," Adrian growled, stomping toward Hez. "There you are, you little devil. How dare you put coal in my bed!"

"Oh, Hez," Carin cried. "Never say you did!"

"I didn't," Hez said, shaking his head vehemently. "St. Nicholas did."

"St. Nicholas?" Carin asked, her eyes widening.

"You said he gave bad boys stockings full of coal," Hez said. His chin tilted up. "His nibs has been bad and St. Nicholas gave him coal."

"It wasn't a damn stocking," Adrian said, his eyes narrowing. "It was an entire pillowcase full."

"So?" Hez said, shrugging. "He didn't have no stocking. He used them all up on the good blokes."

"But, Hez," Carin said, frowning in distraction as she noticed Marie Antoinette and her court pad into the room. "St. Nicholas . . . er . . . doesn't come until Christmas."

"He came early," Hez said. "A special visit like 'cause the guv was being bad. Very bad."

Marie Antoinette unfortunately barked a greeting at that moment.

"Shh!" Carin whispered.

"No need for that, madam," Adrian said, his words cutting. "I know they are there. In fact, I slept with them all night. A time during which they entertained themselves by digesting my clothes and boots."

"Oh, dear," Carin sighed.

Adrian leveled a fierce look at Hez. "I suppose you are going to tell me St. Nicholas let those ravaging dogs into my room as well?"

"No. They was gone when I got back to my—" Hez gurgled to a halt.

"Aha!" Adrian cried. "You are going to get the strapping of yer life, my boy!"

"No!" Carin cried, frightened.

"Don't worry," Bertha snickered. "He ain't got a belt on him."

With a belt or not, Adrian lunged at Hez. He missed him by a hairbreadth. Hez slid down under the table and crawled out the other side. He tore out of the room, Adrian close behind him. The dogs barked and gave excited chase.

"Dear heavens, no," Carin cried, springing up.

"Let them settle it, lass," Bertha said.

Carin did not listen. She picked up her skirts and dashed after them into the foyer. Adrian must not be allowed to hurt Hez. She skittered to a halt. The scene before her was not what she had expected.

Adrian had been chasing Hez before with bloodlust in his eyes. Now Adrian stood, a swaying bulwark, while Hez swung wildly at him, shouting. His small fists never reached Adrian because Adrian held the boy off with one strong arm. Maria had the hem of Adrian's nightshirt between her teeth, and she was tugging upon it. Clearly here was another protective female. Napoleon, Richelieu, and Louis scurried between the three, yapping and nipping indiscriminately. The din of the dogs and the boy was overpowering.

"Gracious," Carin heard Meg mutter. She glanced back. Meg, Nelson and Bertha were just behind her.

"We must stop them," Carin exclaimed.

Turning, she dashed up to grab hold of Hez from behind. "Hez, stop! You must stop."

Nelson circled around to Marie, bravely attempting to pull her away from Adrian. Meg dove to scoop up Louis. Carin heard Bertha call something. She glanced over to the old woman, who was the only one remaining uninvolved.

"Someone's knocking on the door," Bertha shouted.

"What?" Carin called. "Help us."

"I said . . ." Bertha bellowed. Her hands flew up. "Never mind. I'll play butler since he's playing with the dog."

"Bertha!" Carin objected as she finally realized the woman's purpose.

Hez at that moment lunged forward. Carin, unprepared, went with him. Her added weight must have broken Adrian's stronghold, for they rammed into him. All three tumbled backward. It was a crashing of bodies and a mingling of even more bodies since Marie and Nelson too were tangled in the fall. A strangled silence fell; no doubt everyone was too stunned.

"Ye want to see his lordship?" Bertha's voice said. "What are yer names?"

"Bertha, no," Carin cried, attempting to break free from the knot of squirming dogs and wrestling limbs.

"Never mind. I reckon I know who you are," Bertha's voice said cheerfully. "And who's she? Oh, yer maid, Molly. Yer makin' this a proper call, ain't ye?"

"Bertha!" Carin heard Adrian's voice loudly. "Don't—"

"Come on in. His lordship is here somewhere," Bertha said.

Carin was the first to disengage herself. She sprung up. Bertha, with the blandest of smiles upon her face, trotted toward them. "Yer lordship, ye've got two birds come a-calling. One's a fine ladybird at that."

A diminutive brunette dressed in a brilliant emerald silk, followed by a pale servant, entered the foyer. The brunette stared at the muddle upon the floor. Then she looked at Carin.

"Who are you?" Nanette asked, her eyes narrowing.

Carin swallowed, unable to speak.

"Her name's Carin," Bertha said cheerfully. "She lives here with his lordship."

"What?" Nanette gasped.

"Pretty young thing, ain't she?" Bertha said, her tone sly.

"Nanette!" Adrian exclaimed, finally digging himself from the jumble and rising. "It is not what you think!"

"It is not?" Nanette asked, her eyes snapping as she

looked at him. Then they widened. "What happened to you? You are all black."

"St. Nicholas came early," Adrian said with a growl.

"St. Nicholas?" Nanette frowned. "What nonsense."

"It is not nonsense," Carin asserted quickly, "though it wasn't really St. Nicholas this time."

"M'lord got coal," Bertha sniggered. " 'Cause he has been bad."

Carin groaned and glared at Bertha.

"Bad!" Nanette exclaimed. "No, he has been worse than bad. Never in my life have I been played so fast and loose."

"Never?" Bertha murmured.

"And to think I came here to try and discuss our difficulties!" Nanette said, starting to cry. "When all this time—"

"Nanette, please," Adrian said, stepping toward her. Unbelievably Marie stumbled up and stood in front of him, growling.

"You have another mistress," Nanette sobbed.

"She is not my mistress," Adrian objected.

"Truly, I am not," Carin exclaimed.

"I am her chaperone," Meg said helpfully.

"Just like you've got yer maid with ye," Bertha said, winking at Nanette.

"All these nights . . ." Nanette sniffed. "All these nights when you said you were too drunk to—"

"Be quiet!" Adrian roared. He flushed. "There are children present."

"If you mean me," Hez said, "never you mind. I know the time of day, I think."

"Do go on," Bertha encouraged. "This is getting better."

Nanette did flush then. She cast Carin a vengeful look. "You have been going to her! Keeping two mistresses. I have never heard of anything so . . . so . . ."

"Bad?" Hez supplied.

"Dastardly," Nanette cried, her reproachful eyes upon Adrian. "Have I not been good to you? I loved you!"

"That's the ticket." Bertha nodded, grinning. "Ye might get a carriage from this if you work it right."

Nanette glared at her. She then turned tearful eyes back to Adrian. "I thought . . ."

A knock sounded upon the ajar door.

"Hello?" a female voice called.

"Oh, God, no!" Adrian swore.

"Best shoot your bolt," Bertha advised Nanette. "He's got more callers." Bertha turned.

"Bertha, don't you dare," Adrian shouted.

"Is anyone home?" Two ladies dressed in the highest kick of fashion tiptoed into the hall.

"No," Adrian groaned. "Please, no."

Bertha grinned. "Well, ain't this nice? Two *more* birds come a-calling. Yer a mighty popular chap, yer lordship. Four birds all at once."

The one lady's mouth fell open as she viewed the scene. "Adrian! I am sorry. My friend and I were—"

Adrian sighed in resignation. "Hello, Delilah. Do come in, since you already have. Permit me to introduce you." He pointed. "This is Nanette, my—she *was* my mistress. And her maid, Molly, of course—here to lend propriety, I believe." He waved an expansive hand. "That is Carin, Lord Worthington's daughter—legitimate daughter, I might add. This is her chaperone, Miss Mumford. She is here because she is a *real* chaperone. They are visiting until Lord Worthington can settle his affairs and make arrangements for her. He has entrusted her to my care because he believes me honorable, which I am, though I doubt you will believe that for the nonce."

"I . . ." Delilah began.

"This misbegotten urchin is Hez," Adrian continued.

"I will say no more for the moment, except there will be a reckoning between him and me."

"I . . ." Hez exclaimed.

"This is Marie Antoinette," Adrian proceeded relentlessly. "And her court. Richelieu, Napoleon, and Louis."

Marie barked and thumped her tail.

"They live with me too," Adrian said. "I do hope all of you ladies do not think dark thoughts upon that head. I am dastardly, but surely not that dastardly." Bertha chuckled. "And this beldame is Bertha, who has enjoyed playing butler far too much." He pointed. "And this is my real butler, Nelson, who I wish to God had been performing his duty this day."

"Your lord—" Nelson began.

"And I am covered in black," Adrian continued. "Because St. Nicholas came early and gave me a pillowcase full of coal, of which I slept forthwith through the night. I slept with Marie and her court as well, but once again, I do not wish to lead you to evil thoughts. I wish you all a . . . a blooming, merry Christmas. Now if you will excuse me, I believe I shall retire"—he glared at Carin—"and ponder the wonder of it all!"

He turned and stalked away.

"Anyone care for a nip?" Bertha asked. She withdrew her flask from her pocket. "It's the finest, aged Blue Ruin a body could want. We can all sit down and have a comfortable coze."

Carin watched as four ladies fluttered from the house. She doubted they would call again.

A knock sounded at the door. Adrian struggled with his cuff. "Come in!"

The door cracked open slowly and Hez entered. His face was red and frightened. "I came fer me rec . . . recko . . ."

"Reckoning," Adrian said. "Do you know what the word means?"

"No," Hez said. "But I'm thinking it's a whippin'. Or sending me back ter the orphanage."

"Come here," Adrian said.

Hez stiffened his shoulders and walked bravely to Adrian.

Adrian studied the boy. He didn't know what to say. Anger and respect, as well as a good share of guilt, warred within him. He stuck his wrist out. Hez jumped. "See if you can get this link. Marchim is lying down on his bed with heart palpitations. I doubt he will remain long."

"What?" Hez asked frowning. Drawing in a breath, he attempted to obey, his small fingers fiddling with the link.

"You know," Adrian said as calmly as he could, "if you had a complaint, you should have come and talked to me directly. That is what an honorable man does. He does not pretend to be other than what he is."

Hez looked up. "I wanted to tell you. But everyone said there was nothing I could do. They said that you was the king in this castle and you could do what you wished."

"A man does like to believe he is master in his own house," Adrian said dryly.

"Even if he is being mean to everyone?" Hez asked. "Even if you—I mean, he—makes Miss Carin cry and go about all quiet."

Adrian found himself flushing. "Perhaps not."

"I can't do this," Hez sighed. He stepped back. "I'm sorry. I'm sorry for it all. I'm sorry about pretending to be St. Nicholas. And I'm sorry about the dogs. And I'm sorry I queered it all with yer mistress."

"Now that is not something you did," Adrian confessed. "I had already queered it with her. And I am—" Adrian halted. He looked at Hez. If a boy could apologize, he decided he best do so also. "I am sorry I behaved so foully this morning. You deserved to be punished, but my behavior was not above reproach. I am supposed to be the man here, I believe."

"Ye are, guv," Hez said, shifting upon his feet. "Yer a better man than I've seen afore."

"Thank you," Adrian said, overcome. "I think we have settled everything that needed settling."

Hez gaped at him. "What? You ain't going ter . . . ?"

"No," Adrian said quickly. "I am not going to wallop you or send you back to the orphanage." Hez still stared. Adrian put on a dark enough frown. "This time, and only this time. I promise you, the next time you do anything like this, I will wallop you good. I will—"

"Beat the cinders out of me?" Hez grinned.

"Yes." Adrian nodded. He narrowed his eyes. "Especially if you ever dare to think of turning on me and fighting me like you did. Do you understand?"

"I understand." Hez nodded eagerly. He turned and scampered to the door, apparently wishing to depart before Adrian changed his mind. Only he halted. His face became frightened again. "I—I . . ."

"What?"

"Are you going to be angry with Miss Carin?"

"No," Adrian sighed. "Like you, I believe I can no longer escape my reckoning. I promise you that I will attempt to face it bravely as a man should."

"Then yer going to see her now?" Hez asked.

"You won't let any grass grow under my feet, will you?" Adrian murmured.

"Well, guv," Hez said in a knowing tone.

"I will see her now," Adrian said.

"I'll go and prepare her if you like," Hez said kindly. "Get the lay of the land fer you."

"No," Adrian said. "I would rather you did not."

"Yer sure?"

"Yes, I'm sure," Adrian said. "But thank you."

"Anytime." Hez grinned.

* * *

Carin sat in the schoolroom holding baby Partridge close. Clearly everyone thought she needed the most comforting, for to receive a turn at holding baby Partridge lately was a rare treat. Both Bertha and Gaskins hovered close. Nelson and Meg had taken up chairs. The dogs had all found feet to rest by or lie upon.

It was a subdued group. Talk was upon anything but what had transpired this morning. Everyone shied away from discussing what must now be transpiring with Hez.

A knock sounded upon the door and Adrian entered. He halted, appearing rested as he gazed at the assembled group. Indeed, he took a step back. "Pardon me."

Hez quietly appeared behind him. He grinned. "His nibs wants ter talk to Carin, don't ye?"

Carin swallowed hard, not knowing where to look.

"Yes," Adrian said. "Yes, I do."

"Private like," Hez said, casting a pregnant look to the assembled group. He waved a hand at them. Carin could have sworn she saw him wink. "We should clear out of here."

"No," Carin objected.

"That will not be necessary," Adrian said at the same time. "We could—"

He lost the opportunity to finish. Everyone, including the dogs, rose. "Of course," "Most certainly," and "Ain't no problem" were heard before they dashed from the room.

Hez alone remained holding the door. "Don't you worry none about us hearin'. I'll make sure we are . . . honorable." Grinning, he left, closing the door upon them.

Carin stared at Adrian, unable to speak. Fortunately, baby Partridge broke the silence. She gurgled and burped.

"They certainly were glad enough to run and escape," Adrian observed, a hesitant smile upon his face. He nodded toward baby Partridge, who then expounded with a chortle. "Except her, that is."

"Yes," Carin said, returning his smile nervously. "It will be some time before she knows how to run." Adrian's brow shot up. Carin gasped. "I did not mean that she would wish to run from you. Of a certain, she cannot even crawl yet, let alone run." She blinked. "Oh, dear."

Adrian laughed. "I understand what you mean."

Carin started. She looked down quickly as his eyes darkened. "I am sorry about the mishaps this morning."

"So am I," Adrian said in quick response.

She glanced up. His eyes were solemn. A fear entered her. "If you wish for me—I mean, us—to leave, we will." Baby Partridge rendered up a la-la-la-la.

"No. No, of course not," Adrian said. "I have already held this discussion with Hez. I do not wish for him to leave. Or for you to leave."

"You do not?" Carin asked. Her chest contracted.

"I fear I lost my temper," Adrian said. "It was inexcusable."

"No," Carin said. "It was understandable."

"No," Adrian said. "Hez was right. I *have* been bad."

A new and greater fear entered Carin. It now appeared he might discuss what had happened a few nights before. She was certain she would absolutely sink if he did. "No, waking up to coal in your bed and the dogs—it is understandable that you were upset."

"Not to the point."

"And for Hez to attack you . . ."

"It was a natural reaction. He has had to scrap his entire life."

"And I'm dreadfully sorry about your mistress and her misunderstanding the . . . uh . . ."

"She did not misunderstand."

Carin sucked in her breath. "I am sure if you explain to her at a more private—I mean, quiet time . . ."

"I doubt I will."

"And Bertha!" Carin exclaimed in desperation. "She was terrible. I do not understand why she wished to cause such trouble."

"She is an old woman."

"Yes, but if she had not opened the door," Carin said quickly, "none of that would have happened."

"But she did open the door."

"And the dogs," Carin said, feeling at the end of her rope. "I am sorry."

"Carin," Adrian said, his voice low.

"They should not have attacked you either."

"Carin."

"Of course, Nap, Rich, and Louis are just pups. They only followed Marie's lead."

"Carin!" Adrian's voice was sharper.

She jumped. "Yes?"

"You have apologized for everyone," Adrian said, his tone firm. "Now will you permit me to apologize as well?"

Carin flushed. "You have apologized."

"No," Adrian said, his voice gentle. "I have not apologized for the other night."

"Oh, that," Carin said, attempting a look of surprise.

"Yes, that," Adrian said dryly. "I kissed you. Do you remember?"

Carin would truly have liked the floor to open wide and give her a hole to hide in. She wished for baby Partridge to start squalling. The babe remained mute. "Yes, I do remember."

"Thank God," Adrian said, his tone rueful.

"What?" Carin asked, her eyes wide.

He smiled. "I rarely make apologies. I would rather not do so over something that has been forgotten."

"I see," Carin said.

He walked over to her. Carin tensed. He drew up a chair and sat. "That was unpardonable and I ask your forgiveness."

"I should not have been in your room."

Adrian sighed. "That was *my* excuse. You need not repeat it to me. The truth is, you are under my protection and it should not have mattered where you were." He grimaced. "I know you did not invite the kiss and I should not have forced my attentions upon you."

Carin remained silent. She had not invited the kiss, but she had enjoyed it. She felt mortified, a terrible fraud, in fact.

"I promise you," Adrian said quietly, "you need not fear that it will happen again."

Carin peeked at him, not knowing what to say. He clearly expected some response. "Uh . . . thank you?"

It must have been the correct response, for he smiled in relief. "Good. I am glad that is settled." He stood swiftly. "It was merely an unexpected happenstance for which we were not prepared. It was late. You were in my room in your nightgown. It was only natural."

"It was?" Carin asked. Relief filled her.

"Of course it was," Adrian said. He frowned. "Don't you think so?"

"I would not know," Carin said.

Adrian stilled. "What do you mean, you wouldn't know?"

"I . . ." Carin sighed. "I would not know."

Adrian sat back down. His gaze was intense. "Have you not been kissed before?"

"No," Carin said, shaking her head in embarrassment.

"I see." Adrian actually smiled. It seemed a very satisfied smile. Then he looked serious. "I find that difficult to believe."

"You do?" Carin asked. It was her turn to frown. "Why? I am not a loose woman. At least, I-I haven't been before."

"I did not mean to imply that," Adrian exclaimed. "I only meant that as beautiful as you are I would have thought one of the country boys would have stolen a kiss from you."

"No," Carin said. She flushed. "I was not acquainted with many boys. I did not socialize often."

"What did you do for entertainment then?" Adrian asked, frowning.

"Oh, there was always so very much to do," Carin said. "Mother was not often strong."

"Which means you most likely ran the household?" Adrian said in quick understanding.

"Meg and I did." Carin nodded. "Though I assure you I did not live in seclusion."

"No," Adrian said, a glimmer of a smile tipping his lips. "With your penchant for acquiring strays, I doubt it."

Carin looked away. "I meant that I did have outside interests. I assisted often at the church and its small school."

"Faith, you certainly wouldn't find men attempting to steal a kiss from you there," Adrian said. He chuckled.

"No," Carin said, gazing at him in surprise. The sound of him chuckling was stunning to her. It seemed to reverberate through her. Adrian's gaze deepened as Carin continued to stare at him. She started and attempted to refocus her thoughts. "Besides, a lady does not permit a man to steal a kiss. Mother said so."

"What?" Adrian exclaimed. The compelling look of a moment ago was replaced with one of consternation. He drew in a deep breath. "I do not wish to disagree with your mother, especially since she has passed on to her reward, but a lady can still be a lady, even if she permits a man to steal a kiss." He then flushed. "It should only be one . . . and not as involved as we became the other night, but it does happen and it should not be considered such a grave sin. It is a natural thing between a man and a woman."

"It is?" Carin asked rather hopefully. It was balm to her guilt.

"It is," Adrian said firmly. "There is always a natural desire between men and women."

"All men and women?" Carin asked. She shook her head in confusion. "I have never experienced it before."

"Well, perhaps not between all men and women," Adrian said quickly. "A woman should not want *every* man to kiss her, to be sure. For a women to give her affections to every buck and dandy would make her loose. Yet if a woman cares for a man, then the desire is quite natural, I believe. Of course, as a lady, you will reserve that for your husband."

"I see," Carin said rather eagerly. The concept was striking a deep chord of favor within her. Then her heart sank. "Only I am not going to have a husband."

"Er, yes," Adrian said. He appeared quite uncomfortable. "That can be a predicament."

"Is that why you said a woman could not be happy unless she is married?" Carin asked in a small voice.

"I—I . . ." Adrian looked confused himself. He rose. "Confound it. I am not the one who should be telling you all of this. What do I know? I am a man. We look at . . . er . . . such matters differently."

"Oh," Carin said, disheartened once more.

He drew in a breath. "I only wished to assure you that what occurred between us was natural and you should not consider yourself a wanton. It was my fault completely. I promise you it will never happen again."

"Er, yes," Carin said. The word "never" did something odd to Carin's insides. Baby Partridge suddenly gave out a loud squall, the kind Carin would have indulged in if she had not been an adult. "Shh, baby Partridge."

"Why is she crying?" Adrian asked, his tone nervous.

"I don't know. She is normally such a quiet child," Carin said. She rocked the baby and reached at the same time to see if she was wet. "No, she is dry. Do not cry, baby Partridge."

Adrian came close to peer at the squalling child. "Is she hurt or something?"

"I don't know," Carin said. "Sometimes they cry and you don't know why."

"There must be a reason," Adrian said. He frowned and peered even closer.

Baby Partridge in that instant stopped. She hiccuped and a tiny hand shot up and flailed toward Adrian.

"Good God," Adrian exclaimed, rearing back. Baby Partridge gurgled and waved her hand as if searching. Adrian, his face stunned, slowly put his finger up. Baby Partridge gripped it in her tiny fingers. "She's holding my finger."

"She likes you," Carin said, smiling. "You made her stop crying."

"I did not," Adrian said though his tone was mild and his face was filled with pleasure.

"Would you like to hold her?"

"No!" Adrian said quickly. "I must be going."

Carin noticed, however, that he withdrew his finger very gently. He stood just as slowly, his gaze watchful. Baby Partridge gurgled and *cooed*. Carin smiled as the baby offered Adrian a smile.

"Hmm, yes," Adrian murmured. He turned and all but tiptoed toward the door. To see such a large man so intent upon being quiet was, in truth, endearing. He halted then and turned. A deep frown marked his brow. "Why do you only call her "baby" or baby Partridge? Why does she not have a *real* name?"

"I do not know," Carin said, biting her lip. "The note did not say what her given name was."

"You have named the dogs," Adrian said, his tone

rather accusatory. "But she has not been given a name. That does not seem right."

"True," Carin said, surprised. Then she frowned in deep consideration. "I believe it is because none of us wishes to name her since we know she cannot stay. If we give her a name it will only make it all the harder to let her go when we must. It should be her future parents who give her a name."

Adrian remained silent a moment. He looked away. "Name the child."

"You truly mean it?" Carin asked, catching her breath.

"Yes." Adrian looked at her. What Carin saw in Adrian's eyes warmed her. It disappeared quickly, but she had seen it. "Name her . . . please."

"I will," Carin said softly.

"Very well." He took a step and then turned around once more. "What are you going to name her?"

Carin blinked. "You want me to name her now?"

"Er." Adrian shifted. "No, I suppose you will need time to consider."

A laugh escaped Carin. Her heart filled. "No, I can name her now."

"What is it?" Adrian asked.

"Joy," Carin said, smiling. "Her name is Joy."

Adrian fell silent a moment. Carin waited. She half expected for him to turn cynical, to object. Then Adrian nodded. "Joy. That is a good name."

Without looking at her or speaking another word, Adrian left the room. Carin gazed after him a moment. Feeling like both the young girl she was and a grown woman at the same time, Carin smiled and looked down. "Hello, Joy. I told you you need not worry. Uncle Adrian will not send you away to any frightful orphanage. We will find you a good home."

Chapter Five

Five Gold Rings

The following morning Adrian sat reading his newspaper and taking coffee at his club. He seemed relaxed and unaware of his surroundings. Clearly he was too involved in his reading to notice that men at the other tables glanced in his direction and talked in low voices to their comrades. Indeed, he appeared far too intent to notice as his acquaintances avoided his table and did not hail him heartily as they commonly did.

"Ah, Adrian!" a loud and cheery voice called. Adrian looked up. Gerald, his usual wide and innocent smile on his face, waved as he walked toward him. "Just got back from the country. It's good to see you, old man." Gerald plopped himself into the chair across from Adrian.

"You might not want to sit there, Gerald," Adrian said in a dry tone. "You are committing a social faux pas."

"Then you do know?" Gerald's eyebrows shot up. He shook his head. "You fooled me. I thought you were totally unaware."

"No," Adrian said, his tone slightly surprised. "I thought you were."

"I came in last night," Gerald said lowly. "Heard it all at the Reevers' ball. The cat's really out of the bag."

"The cat being Delilah," Adrian murmured.

"You can say that again," Gerald said, leaning back with a sigh, "though her friend Malissa was vouching for her veracity. According to the tantalizing morsels of gossip served up last night, they discovered you in your night-shirt involved in what sounded indubitably like an orgy with old Worthington's daughter—illegitimate daughter, mind you—and a host of low-bred others. Your mistress—excuse me, ex-mistress—included. As well as dogs?"

"She didn't miss a trick." Adrian nodded.

"Gads," Gerald exclaimed, his eyes growing wide. "You mean something did happen? I thought she must be making it up out of broadcloth. Thought you had angered her, don't you know. Just what happened?"

"I'd rather not discuss it," Adrian said. "But I assure you, it was more a debacle than an orgy."

"What are you going to do?" Gerald asked, frowning.

"What is there to do?" Adrian asked. "I intend to ignore it. Shouldn't be more than a nine days' wonder."

"You intend to ignore it? All of it? Even the dogs?" Gerald asked. He frowned at Adrian.

"I do," Adrian said. Gerald continued to frown. Adrian raised his brow. "Yes?"

"Well, I have no doubt you can brazen it out. You have always had the ability to . . ." He flushed. "Well, er . . ."

"I am a cool customer?" Adrian asked mildly.

"Yes," Gerald nodded in relief. "Exactly. I mean, there ain't a man here who'd approach you on it. They know they would catch cold at it. Frozen, to tell the truth."

"Thank you," Adrian said.

"You are welcome," Gerald said, missing Adrian's sarcastic tone entirely. "But what about the girl?"

"What about her?" Adrian asked, his tone chilling. "She does not go about in society. Nor need she do so."

"Is that her decision or yours?" Gerald asked cautiously.

"Both," Adrian said. "She told me she neither cared for society nor was in need of a reputation."

"What?"

"She does not intend to marry, you see," Adrian said. "In fact, she promised her mother on her deathbed that she wouldn't."

"Gadzooks," Gerald exclaimed.

"Therefore," Adrian said, refusing further explanation, "the best thing in this matter is to ignore it. It will blow over."

"That ain't right," Gerald objected. "I don't care what the girl says, she's too young to know what she wants. You've never had sisters, but I have. And I warn you, seventeen is their most dangerous age. If they don't have those who care watching over them, they can take missteps that ruin their lives."

"Thank you for such assurances," Adrian said.

"If you ignore this scandal and let it pass, it will be dandy for you," Gerald persisted. "There are a lot of other men who are caught in worse scandals to be sure and society forgives them. But it doesn't forgive the ladies. This girl will have no reputation left. She will never be able to enter society."

Adrian lowered his paper and sighed. "What are you proposing I do to save her reputation?"

"Bring her out into society," Gerald said. "Show them you aren't hiding anything. That it is all proper and aboveboard."

"My God," Adrian said, staring. "You are insane."

"Am I?" Gerald asked. "Force her on society now. If anyone has the brass to stare the ton down it is you. If you don't and you keep her hidden, the stories will only grow worse. Not about you because you will be there looking them in the eye. But about her because she won't be there to defend herself."

Adrian studied Gerald. His eyes darkened and his voice

was low. "You do not understand. She *is* an innocent. An honest innocent. She believes in charity and miracles and Christmas for God's sake. And she doesn't just talk about it. She does it. She goes about saving street urchins and old ladies and abandoned babies."

"She does?" Gerald's brows shot up.

"How do you think I acquired all the low-bred company Delilah is talking about? They are living with me."

"Good God," Gerald exclaimed.

"Yes," Adrian said curtly.

Gerald fell silent a moment. Then he raised a brow. "Even the dogs?"

"One bitch and three pups," Adrian said, nodding. "Some misbegotten proprietor of some discreditable dining establishment was going to kill the dog for stealing his capons for God's sake."

"What?"

"It doesn't matter," Adrian sighed. "The story was confusing and made little sense. At least not to me. But it made perfect sense to her. They needed to be saved and she saved them. She gave that mongrel bitch a bath in my own tub."

Gerald stared. He snorted. He then doubled over and hooted.

Adrian lifted a cool brow. "It is not that amusing."

"Yes, it is," Gerald said, still laughing. He brushed at his eyes. "That you . . . and . . ."

Adrian glared. "Yes?"

"Never mind," Gerald said. He sucked in his breath, sobering quickly. "She sounds like an amazing girl. It would be a pity for her chances to be ruined with society."

"Have you not been listening to me?" Adrian asked angrily. "Call her an amazing girl, but can you not see what will happen if we introduce her? The ton will eat her alive."

"B'gad," Gerald said, his voice stunned. "You want to protect her. That is it, isn't it?"

Adrian stiffened. "She was entrusted to my care. It is my duty."

"No." Gerald grinned. "You want to protect her. You, who do not believe in any such twaddle. You, whose attitude could shrivel mistletoe, want to protect her. You don't want her to become disillusioned like you are."

"Rot," Adrian said tersely.

"Then prove it," Gerald said in a challenging tone. "My sister Heather is giving a party two days from now. Bring the girl and her chaperone. It ain't a large affair. We can all act as if everything is proper and see what happens. Test the waters, so to speak."

Adrian frowned. "I will think on it."

"Good," Gerald said, nodding. He grinned. "Truth is, I'm doing this merely because I want to meet the girl."

Adrian smiled. "Now who is talking gammon? You are doing this because you are as softhearted as she is."

Adrian paced the library carpet. The door opened and Nelson entered.

"You rang, my lord?" Nelson asked.

"Yes. Yes, I did," Adrian said. "Could you please inform Miss Carin I require her attendance."

"Certainly, my lord," Nelson said, his face showing a wariness.

"No," Adrian said quickly. "No. Perhaps not."

"Perhaps not, my lord?"

"That is right," Adrian said. "Perhaps not."

"Very well, my lord," Nelson said, nodding slowly. He waited a moment. "Is that all, my lord?"

"Yes. No." Adrian ran his hand through his hair. "Blast it, I do not know. Confound Gerald and his schemes. Just because he has sisters it does not mean he knows everything."

"Er, no, my lord," Nelson said, clearly unsure of his answer.

"And Miss Carin is not my sister," Adrian said, frowning at the floor.

"Indeed not, my lord," Nelson said, his tone positive on that score.

"Oh, the devil," Adrian said, squaring his shoulders. "Bring her here."

"Very well," Nelson said. He turned and departed.

Adrian resumed his pacing. He halted abruptly when Carin entered, a worried look upon her face.

"Nelson said you wished to see me?" Carin asked. "Is something wrong?"

"No, of course not," Adrian said quickly. Then he frowned. "There isn't, is there?"

"No," Carin returned just as quickly. She flushed. "Of course not."

Adrian sighed in relief, only to tense once more as Carin looked at him inquiringly. "Please. You may sit."

"Thank you," Carin said and dutifully sat down.

Adrian cleared his throat. "My friend Gerald is having a party two days from now. I wondered if you would care to attend it. With me, that is."

"What?" Carin gasped.

Adrian sucked in his breath. "I wondered if you would care to attend. With Miss Mumford as chaperone of course."

"You would like to take me to your friend's party?" Carin asked. Her tone was clearly bewildered.

"Yes," Adrian said. "Would you care to go?"

One tense moment passed. Then a smile wreathed Carin's face and her eyes lighted. "Yes. Yes, of course. I would enjoy that."

For a moment Adrian forgot his purpose altogether. The excitement in Carin's face filled him with pleasure and no little excitement of his own. "Excellent. That is settled then."

"Yes. Yes, it is," Carin said.

They stared at each other, both smiling rather inanely. Only then Carin's face clouded.

Adrian frowned. "What is it?"

"Are you sure you wish to do this?" Carin asked. "I thought I—or we . . . or . . ." She drew in a breath. "I thought I wasn't to go out in society. That it was best if they did not know of my presence here."

Adrian swallowed, his purpose returning with a vengeance. It was a sticky issue, a crossing point. He had so enjoyed her pleasure before. He couldn't bring himself to inform her that the scene yesterday had already alerted the haute ton to her presence in his house and in the most unflattering of ways. If she were more worldly, she would have surmised it. "Er, yes. Perhaps I was overly cautious in that regard."

"Very well," Carin said, her brow lightening again. "If you are certain."

Adrian bit back a curse. Why did she seem to be giving him a second chance to come clean? He bolstered his resolve. She was indeed a young girl and there could be no purpose in telling her he might very well be inviting her into a lion's den. Nor was he sure she would approve if she knew this was a tactic to save her reputation. "I am positive."

"Then thank you," Carin said.

Adrian looked away quickly. "It will not be a large affair—merely dinner and dancing."

"Dancing?" Carin asked, her eyes widening.

"You do dance?" Adrian asked.

"Yes," Carin said, nodding eagerly. "Meg taught me. She is an excellent dancer. Only . . ."

"You did not go to many parties," Adrian finished.

"No, I didn't," Carin said.

"I would not worry about that overly much," Adrian said. "It will be recognized that you are not officially out."

"Yes, of course," Carin said, smiling in relief. Then she looked dismayed. "What do they wear to these affairs here in London?"

He cleared his throat. "Why not ask Miss Mumford. I am sure she can advise you."

"Yes," Carin said, springing up. "I shall do that. Meg will know."

Adrian watched Carin leave. He cringed. Just what had he done? Not until he said it had he realized that Carin indeed would be a young debutante in the eyes of the world. In truth, he had lost that vision of her. He could decry her innocence, but suddenly he could not decry her youth. Other girls her age would have only thoughts of parties and dresses and beaux. Carin's thoughts were for abandoned babies and orphans and streetwomen.

He walked over and poured himself a hefty brandy. Just who was responsible for Carin and who she was? Worse, who would be responsible for whom she became? He had the sinking suspicion Carin was the one responsible for who she was, and if he did not take care, as Gerald warned, he would be responsible for whom she became.

He shot the brandy back. What a damnable position. He would gladly kill her mother if that woman had not already wisely taken her parting from the earth. And if he ever saw her father again, he would wring the man's neck.

Adrian heard a cough. He started and looked up. Nelson stood within the library door.

"Yes. What is it, Nelson?" Adrian asked.

"Miss Carin informs me you are taking her to a party, my lord," Nelson said.

"Yes," Adrian said. He drank swiftly from his glass again.

"I do hope it will serve, my lord," Nelson said.

Adrian stared at Nelson. "Do you?"

"The servants talk as well as their masters," Nelson said quietly.

Adrian looked away. "She does not know why I asked her."

"I should hope not," Nelson said.

Adrian shot Nelson a rueful glance. "You do not think me a coward then?"

"I believe," Nelson said consideringly, "Miss Carin can win over even the most jaded of hearts if she is permitted to be her own pleasing self."

"Yes, that is what I thought," Adrian said, nodding. He snorted. "And this is the ton. There will be plenty of jaded hearts for her, I assure you."

"Yes, my lord," Nelson said. He smiled. "But as Miss Carin says, it is Christmas and a time for miracles."

"Why does Miss Carin have ter wear that white dress?" Hez complained as they left the modiste's shop and strolled down the street. "The red one was prettier. I thought *that* one was fine as five pence."

"Young ladies do not wear bright colors before they are officially out," Meg said, smiling. She glanced at Nelson, who walked beside her. "At least, I do not think they do."

"They do not," Nelson said, nodding.

"Carin," Meg said, "when we return home, we must practice your curtsy again. Also we must study the *Peerage* again."

"Gore. You have ter to do all that just so you can eat and dance?" Bertha said.

"Don't sound like much fun," Hez said, shaking his head.

"I know," Carin said, laughing. Still, her heart leapt in anticipation. She thought her dress beautiful and hoped

Adrian would think it so as well. "But I would not wish to embarrass Adrian, would I? It is his friend's party, you know."

"So it is, Miss Carin," Nelson said solemnly. "But you could never embarrass him. Unquestionably, you shall be the loveliest lady there."

" 'Course she will," Hez said, his tone gruff. He halted before a shop window. It glittered and sparkled with jewelry. "Look at that!"

Everyone halted and did indeed gaze upon it.

"Look at that bauble," Bertha gasped, ramming her index finger into the glass in excitement.

"That is an emerald," Nelson said. "Very expensive."

"Don't ye just know it," Bertha said, cracking a wide grin. "Thems are for the lords and ladies to sparkle about. That'd be a common man's bread fer his whole life."

Hez breathed on the glass, so close did he peer. Then he studied Carin's hand. "Miss Carin, ye don't have a ring like these here."

"I do not wear jewelry," Carin murmured as she too gazed at the display. "Mother did not believe young girls should wear it."

"But won't everyone else be sparkling at that party?" Hez asked.

"Perhaps," Carin said, smiling. "But that will not matter."

"But if they are going to be sparkling," Hez persisted, "you should too."

"I'm sorry, Hez, but I will just have to survive without sparkling," Carin said. Her face turned wistful and she pointed to a ring. "Isn't that lovely?"

Hez studied it. It was merely figured gold, delicately wrought. "That don't sparkle."

"I know," Carin said. "I like it because it is simple."

"I agree." Meg nodded. She pointed to another one beside it. "That is beautiful."

"You like that one?" Hez asked, narrowing his eyes. Then he exclaimed in awe. "Look at that tiny ring there. That could be for Joy!"

"It is tiny," Carin said, smiling.

Bertha narrowed her own eyes. "It's time to turn your peepers off all this, Hez. It could make a body think orv stealing, it could."

"Oh, no," Carin said, her eyes solemn. "Hez would not think of stealing them, would you, Hez?"

" 'Course not. I ain't going ter do that no more. I'm an honorable gent now," Hez said. "But what if I bought them for you right properly?"

"That is a very sweet thought," Carin said. Hez beamed at her. "But they are far too expensive." His face fell and Carin hid her smile, placing an arm about his shoulder. "I appreciate the thought in itself. That is a good enough gift for me. Now do let us go."

"Yes," Bertha said, her tone dry. "Missy has ter practice those curtsies."

"Perhaps we should practice my dancing," Carin said.

"That's more like it," Bertha said eagerly. "I know a jig or two fer you ter learn."

"So do I," Hez said as the party proceeded. He only glanced back once at the window.

Hez sat upon his bed. His face was blackened with coal and he wore his old ragged clothes. Marie Antoinette and her court sat upon the floor in a circle. One meager candle lit the darkened room.

"Now we've got to work hard if we are goin' to buy those rings for Christmas," Hez said solemnly. Richelieu whined and wagged his tail. Hez grinned. "I can't wait meself. We'll be giving something nice back fer all they've done for us. Now we have to earn enough of the ready fer five rings." He lifted his hand and ticked each finger. "One fer Miss Carin, one fer Mistress Meg, one fer Bertha, one fer baby Joy." He frowned a moment and then grinned. "And one fer his nibs. His will cost more I'm thinking because it'll be bigger. But then Joy's will be smaller."

Marie barked and raised her paw.

"You really want ter help?" Hez asked.

Marie cracked her healthy fangs.

"Very well," Hez said. He reached over and picked up two pillowcases strung together with a piece of rope. "Stand up."

Marie obediently stood. Hez took the tied muslin cases and placed one on either side of Marie's back, a makeshift saddlebag. Hez stepped back and observed his handiwork. "That should do fine."

He drew in his breath. "I sent a boy to Jimmy, tellin' him to come round at two o'clock. That means we have two hours of hard work ahead of us." Louis yapped and scratched his ear. "Jimmy's a friend of mine. He's the one who'll pay us honest pounds fer anything we get."

Carin sat in the coach beside Meg. Excitement coursed through her. She felt like a princess. The look of approval upon Adrian's face had warmed her. Even Hez had said she looked right fine before she had left, even if she were not sparkling. She frowned slightly. He had seemed tired and less than his jubilant self this past day. She feared he might be sick.

"We are here," Adrian said, smiling as the coach stopped. Almost in response to Carin's sudden fears, Adrian nodded. "May I say you two ladies look beautiful?"

The door burst open. A stocky, blond-haired man held the door. He grinned. "Hello, I've been waiting for you."

"That is clear," Adrian said dryly.

The man grinned. "And it's blasted cold out."

Adrian laughed. He looked to Carin. "Miss Worthington, may I present Gerald Nathan Vincent, the Viscount of Severs, to you?"

"How do you do?" Carin said, nodding.

"Good Lord," Gerald said, his eyes widening. "You are far too beautiful. We'll never manage it."

"I beg your pardon?" Carin asked, blinking.

"You must forgive Gerald," Adrian said, his tone repressive. "He is a perfect nodcock around lovely ladies."

Gerald's eyes flew to his and he flushed. "Er, that's right. Forgive me."

"However," Adrian said, gazing at Carin, "if others stare at you tonight you must not permit them to unsettle you."

"I will not," Carin stammered.

"Excellent," Adrian smiled. "I am counting upon you."

Carin flushed. She was not certain why he had said it, but when he smiled like that, she couldn't seem to worry about anything. "Thank you."

"Gerald," Adrian then murmured. "May I also present Miss Mumford, Miss Worthington's chaperone."

"Pleased to meet you." Gerald nodded to Meg, who nodded back. "Well, do let us go in. I have Heather posted . . . er . . . I mean she is waiting, too."

They alighted from the coach and Carin gasped. The large manor before her was ablaze with lights. Great boughs of evergreen decorated each of its many windows. "How beautiful."

"Heather enjoys the holiday season," Gerald said, laughing as he led them into the house. He bounded away as footmen converged upon them to take their wraps and coats. When he returned, he was leading a petite brunette. He beamed. "This is my sister, Heather."

"Hello," Heather said smiling. Her blue eyes, very

much like her brother's, widened when they fell upon Carin. "Gracious. You are far too lovely."

Carin flushed even as Adrian laughed. "Gerald has already said that."

"Well, it cannot be helped," Heather said. She smiled warmly. "Do forgive me. The old biddies are going to be clucking, I warn you."

"What?" Carin asked.

Heather blinked herself. "Er, I mean . . ."

"She is only warning you that the ladies of the ton are always curious about any newcomer," Adrian said. "However, you are here to have an enjoyable evening and nothing more."

"Indeed," Meg said. She had the oddest look upon her face. Carin watched as Meg appeared to change before her very eyes. She stood taller and her face became cooler. "I thank you for inviting us, my lady."

"Heather," Adrian said, "this is Miss Mumford."

"How do you do?" Heather said. Her look turned eager. "Are you any relations to the Devonshire Mumfords?"

"No," Meg said. She smiled slowly. "I am, however, connected to General Benton. A great-niece to be exact, though our family was not recognized by him."

"Meg?" Carin gasped. "Is that true? You never told me."

"Yes," Meg said. "But there wasn't any reason to mention it before."

"The old general passed away last year," Heather exclaimed, clapping her hands together. "How marvelous. We can make use of the connection without fear."

Meg nodded. "Indeed, he did."

"Well, now, things are definitely looking better," Heather said. She looked to Carin. "My dear, I have you and Miss Mumford seated next to Lady Dweedle for dinner. All things considered, she will be the best one to converse with." She looked at Adrian. "You, of course, must take Lady Haversham down."

"Oh, Lord," Adrian sighed. "She is such a rattle."

"It is your fault for being a marquise," Heather said lightly.

Carin swallowed, but bit her tongue. She felt totally lost, though everyone around her seemed to understand what the procedures were. Even Meg seemed to understand.

"I need not warn you, Adrian," Heather said, lifting a brow, "to remain mostly with the men for the evening. Your concern for Carin can be fatherly and indulgent."

"I know," Adrian said curtly.

"Very well," Heather said. "I believe Miss Mumford and I will do well with the ladies. And, Gerald . . ."

"Yes?" Gerald said quickly.

"You will lead Carin out for the first dance," Heather said. "Though if I don't mistake it she will not lack for partners."

"I'd be pleased," Gerald said bowing.

"Very well," Heather said. "Then we are all set. Let us proceed."

Everyone moved forward, except Carin. She remained rooted to the marble floor. The group turned.

"Carin, are you coming?" Adrian asked softly.

"What am I supposed to do?" Carin said.

"Just enjoy yourself," Adrian said, smiling.

"Yes, dear," Heather said, nodding. "We shall do the rest."

Carin swallowed. She no longer felt like a princess. She felt like a frightened mouse. Nor did she understand what "doing the rest" meant.

"So, you are Earl of Worthington's daughter?" Lady Dweedle asked loudly. She was an older, Spartan lady with a piercing eye.

"Yes, my lady," Carin said, smiling.

"Didn't know he had a daughter," Lady Dweedle said, staring at Carin almost in challenge.

"He had me," Carin said helpfully.

"Who was your mother?" Lady Dweedle asked.

"Lavinia Tarrence," Carin said dutifully.

"Tarrence?" Lady Dweedle asked. She appeared sly. "Of the Shropshire Tarrences?"

Meg, who sat beside Carin, coughed.

Carin frowned in consideration. "I do not think so. I have not met all of my mother's family, but they come from Devon," Carin said. She turned to Meg. "Do I have any relations among the Shropshire Tarrences?"

"I wouldn't think so," Meg said, gazing steadily at Lady Dweedle. "Indeed, I do not recall any Shropshire Tarrences."

Lady Dweedle cracked a grin. "So you are right. I am a forgetful old woman."

"You do remember the Devon Tarrences however?" Meg asked, smiling.

"So I do," Lady Dweedle said. "Not my cup of tea. Good blood, substantial holdings, but as grim as merchants."

"Indeed," Meg said, nodding. "They were not pleased when Lavinia Tarrence married Lord Worthington. I believe it was a scandal at the time."

"Hmm," Lady Dweedle said. Her mouth began moving as if she were chewing, but Carin knew she hadn't taken a bite. "Hah! Now I remember! Even remember the gel. Pretty young thing." She looked at Carin. "You take after your mother, to be sure."

"Thank you," Carin said.

Lady Dweedle nodded firmly. "So you are Lord Worthington's daughter."

"Yes," Carin said. Accustomed to older people, Carin

hid her sigh. Apparently now they would circle into the same conversation they had just held.

"How come we never saw your mother all those years?" Lady Dweedle asked, once again challenging.

Carin started at the new tack. "She did not care for society and preferred to remain in the country."

"Hmm. With your father racketing about here in town like he did that makes sense," Lady Dweedle said almost as if Carin had scored a point.

"Lady Lavinia was also a devoutly religious woman," Meg added.

"Hmm, an old poker like the rest of her family." Lady Dweedle nodded. Her eyes glittered. "Are you prim like her, missy?"

Carin frowned. "I am not sure."

"What?" Lady Dweedle gasped.

"I certainly wish to do good," Carin said sincerely. "But Mother always said I had too much an ease of manner and would accept any stray creature."

"Would you now?" Lady Dweedle said, starting to snicker. "And do you think the marquise a stray?"

"Gracious, no," Carin said, blinking. "He always knows his position far too well to ever be a stray."

Lady Dweedle stared and then barked a laugh.

"Are you enjoying yourself?" Adrian asked Carin, forcing a smile. Gerald had finally decreed that it was Adrian's turn to lead Carin into the acceptable second dance—a country dance—and they stood waiting for the set to begin.

Adrian had covertly watched Carin during dinner. She had apparently passed muster, for she had caused old Lady Dweedle to chuckle and nod. Gerald had reported his satisfaction with Carin's dancing when he had led her out. Apparently the many young men who had led her out had also felt satisfied. Indeed, they returned her to Meg wearing the most asinine expressions of pleasure upon their faces. "You appear to be."

"Oh, I am," Carin said, nodding her silver head eagerly. "I was nervous at first, but everyone is being so very kind."

"Including your dance partners?" Adrian asked. A feeling kin to jealousy flared through him. He assured himself it was merely his desire to protect Carin because she was so innocent.

"Oh, yes," Carin said. Her brow wrinkled in perplexity.

"What is it?" Adrian asked, his eyes narrowing.

"It is nothing really," Carin said. "Though if you had not warned me before, I think I might have been overset."

"Warned you?" Adrian asked cautiously.

"Yes, about people staring," Carin said, "which I have noticed they do. But when they also make comments about one's looks, it is difficult to know what to say."

"Indeed?"

"Do not misunderstand me," Carin said quickly. "I am sure they wish to be kind."

"I have no doubt," Adrian said dryly.

"But it grows embarrassing," Carin confessed.

"Good," muttered Adrian. Carin's eyes widened. He clenched his teeth. "Forgive me. I do not wish for you to be embarrassed, but do not let them turn your head with all their flattery."

"No, I shan't," Carin said, pink rising to her cheeks.

"You cannot trust what these men say," Adrian said, unable to stop himself. "They will lie to you."

"They will?" Carin asked, her voice small.

"Yes," Adrian said. He stiffened, realizing his connotation. "I am not saying that you are not beautiful. You are. Very beautiful."

"You truly think so?" Carin asked, her face brightening

and her eyes eager. There was no embarrassment there this time.

It was Adrian who felt embarrassed. "Er, yes. And that is why you shouldn't let these men turn your head because . . ."

"Because why?"

Adrian strove for a lighter tone, though he wanted to growl. "The next thing they will do will be to try and steal a kiss from you. You wouldn't want that." He gazed into her blue eyes deeply. Then, unwillingly, his gaze turned to her lips. He swallowed hard as she licked them nervously. "Would you?"

"Yes," Carin whispered.

"What!" Adrian exclaimed. The thought of any other man discovering the sweet pleasure of her lips knotted his insides.

Carin blinked. "What did I say?"

"You said yes," Adrian frowned. "Do you want them to steal a kiss from you?"

"No. Oh, no," Carin said quickly. "I wouldn't want them to do that. I won't let that happen."

"Good," Adrian said rather viciously. The music began and no doubt it was a good thing the dance's steps separated them. Only Adrian was torn between smiling whenever he held Carin's hand for a figure and frowning at the other men as she passed to them for the next.

Carin permitted yet another partner to return her to Meg. She was exhausted. Meg appeared deep in conversation with the matron sitting beside her. Carin bit her lip. The sudden notion of escaping from the crowded room overtook her. To be alone for a few moments would be heavenly.

"I am going to the retiring room," Carin announced

in a soft tone. Then she departed, not waiting for Meg's response.

That Meg no doubt had not heard her did not weigh on Carin's mind too much. Smiling she wended her way toward the grand doors and stepped out into a hall. She peered about. It was deserted. She should have asked for directions, but she never doubted she would find a servant soon.

She drifted down the hall, fanning her face with her hands. She saw a man approaching. It was a young man whom she had danced with much earlier in the evening. She believed his name was Lord Munson. She cast him a polite smile, intending to pass him.

"Ah, Mish Worthington," Lord Munson slurred. He offered her a wide grin. "We meet again."

"Yes, we do," Carin said. She frowned. His words had not been slurred when she had danced with him before. Nor had his eyes held the feverish look he now bent upon her.

"It ish fate," Lord Munson said. His fair complexion deepened to a bright red.

"Fate?" Carin asked, perplexed. "I am sorry. I am looking for the retiring room."

"No, no," Lord Munson said, shaking his head vehemently. "It's fate. I wanted to talk to you again." He swayed toward her. "B-been wanting to all night."

"You have?" Carin murmured, stepping back hastily. She recognized the smell on his breath. It was not Bertha's Blue Ruin, but it was certainly alcohol. "Why?"

"B-because," Lord Munson stammered, "I didn't t-tell you everything I wanted to."

"I am sure you did," Carin said, slightly alarmed.

"Did I?" Lord Munson appeared surprised. He frowned. "D-did I tell you you are the most b-beautiful girl I have ever s-seen."

"Yes," Carin said quickly. She flushed. Actually he had

merely mumbled that she looked fetching. "Or I'm sure you told me something like that."

"Oh," Lord Munson said, looking deflated. He peered at her. "Did I tell you"—he halted a moment in thought—"that the marquise de Chambert is too old? A relic, in fact."

"No," Carin said honestly. "That you did not."

"Well, he is!" Lord Munson shouted.

"Very well," Carin said nervously.

"Me! I am the right age," Lord Munson declared.

"For what?" Carin asked despite herself.

"For you!" Lord Munson said. He stretched out his arms, and before Carin could guess his intent, he lunged at her—or perhaps more correctly fell at her—wrapping his arms about her.

"Oh, what . . . ?"

"Me!" Lord Munson whispered. He slobbered a kiss upon Carin's open, unsuspecting mouth.

Carin sputtered in surprise. Then she choked and clamped her lips tightly together in disgust. Squirming, she shoved at the drunken lord. Fortunately, he was not prepared for her action and he stumbled back readily.

"Do not come near me," Carin said. Instinctively her fists clenched. Borrowing a tactic from Hez, she raised them in what she hoped was an off-putting manner.

"Please don't deny me," Lord Munson cried. He leapt forward—right into Carin's fist.

"Ouch!" he cried. His hand flew to his nose. "You hit me."

"No, you hit my fist," Carin objected.

"You hit me," he cried again. His voice was muffled and nasal from his clamping both hands over his nose.

"Yes, in a manner I did," Carin admitted. She noticed blood trickling between his fingers. "Oh dear . . ."

"Carin!" a voice cracked from down the hall.

Carin turned. Adrian, his face thunderous, strode toward them.

"My lord," Carin exclaimed.

"What?" Lord Munson exclaimed, turning. He then emitted the oddest gurgling sounds.

"What happened?" Adrian asked, his gray eyes turning black in anger.

"Lord Munson tried to steal a kiss," Carin said, guilt ridden. "And I fear . . ."

"He what?" Adrian growled.

"I didn't," Lord Munson said, shaking his head.

"I'm afraid I—" Carin continued her confession.

"You bastard," Adrian growled. He stepped forward. His fist shot out like lightning, cracking into Lord Munson's jaw.

"—hit him," Carin finished in a murmur as Lord Munson groaned and toppled stiffly back, like a tree felled in the forest.

"Are you all right?" Adrian asked.

"Yes?" Carin stammered, blinking as Adrian put his arm protectively around her shoulder.

"He didn't hurt you?"

"No," Carin said. She gazed up at him, still confused. "I hit him."

"And you should have," Adrian said. "I'm proud of you."

"You are?" Carin asked. Her guilt fled immediately.

"Yes," Adrian said. "He shouldn't have tried to kiss you."

"He kissed me once," Carin murmured, staring raptly up at Adrian. "It was dreadful."

"Hush," Adrian murmured, bending his head closer. "You are safe now. Do not think about it."

Adrian's lips then covered hers warmly. Carin immediately forgot about Lord Munson. Indeed, she forgot about everything as she drowned in the marvelous sensations of Adrian holding her and kissing her.

"Good God!" a voice exclaimed. "What are you doing?"

Adrian sprung back from Carin. Carin blinked. Gerald was coming down the hall. His face was worried and he kept peering about. He halted as his gaze fell upon the prone Lord Munson. "Rather, what did you do?"

"I . . ." Adrian said.

Carin flushed. "Lord Munson tried to steal a kiss and I'm afraid I hit him."

"*You* floored him like that?" Gerald exclaimed, his blue eyes popping.

"No," Adrian said. "I hit him as well."

"Oh. That makes more sense," Gerald said with a sigh of relief. Then he frowned. "No, it doesn't. You shouldn't have hit him here in the middle of a party. Bad ton, old man. That's not like you at all, Adrian."

"He tried to kiss, Carin," Adrian said, stiffening.

"And what were you doing?" Gerald accused.

"I . . ." Adrian halted. He stiffened all the more. "I was merely comforting her."

"If she had already hit the fellow, it doesn't seem to me she needed—" Gerald suddenly stopped. A twinkle entered his eyes. "Very well, you were comforting her."

"It was only natural," Adrian said.

"Oh, yes," Gerald said, nodding his head. "To be sure."

Relief filled Carin. "Yes, it was only natural, wasn't it?"

"Yes," Gerald said. His gaze narrowed as he looked at Adrian. "This one time."

"Of course," Adrian said, his chin lifting.

"I'm sure it won't happen again," Carin said. She flushed. "It isn't as if I will have men stealing kisses from me often."

Gerald snorted. Adrian glared at him. Gerald's face

washed to innocence. "Well, one thing is certain. I don't think Lord Munson will try it again."

"I should hope not," Carin said vehemently.

Gerald's eyes twinkled even more as Adrian growled. "Well, we better not stand about. Everyone will be wondering where we all are. That is why I came out here in the first place. It is fortunate I did rather than someone else. Miss Worthington, you must go back in and act as if nothing happened. Not a word to anyone." He looked to Adrian. "I'd advise you to go somewhere. Go outside and cool your . . . er . . . temper off." He looked to the fallen Munson and sighed. "I'll bundle the fellow up and have a servant take him home. With luck, he'll think it was his front stoop that did that to him."

Chapter Six

Six Geese Who Shouldn't Have Been A-laying . . .

"Just what is so important that made you arrive here at this godforsaken early hour?" Adrian asked Gerald, who reclined comfortably against the headboard of the marquise's bed. Marchim was just then adding the finishing touches to Adrian's cravat.

"I've been thinking," Gerald said.

"Yes?" Adrian asked.

Gerald's face flushed. "Er . . . would like to talk to you in private?"

Adrian snorted. "You are in my bedchamber, Gerald. What could be more private?"

"You know what I mean," Gerald said, his gaze upon Marchim.

"Ah . . . yes," Adrian said. "That will be all, Marchim."

"Certainly, my lord." Marchim said. He sniffed and left the room.

"You have offended my valet, old man," Adrian said with a sigh.

"You are concerned about what your servants think?" Gerald asked, his eyes wide.

Adrian grimaced. "Yes. A sad state of affairs, I own. Yet I am reduced to treading lightly with them. Marchim still suffers shattered nerves over the coal debacle. Mrs. Knightsbridge goes sniffing and crying about."

"Gads!" Gerald exclaimed.

"She's allergic to dogs," Adrian said dryly, "and to many other of the inhabitants in the house, if I'm not mistaken."

"Then let her go," Gerald said.

"And with whom would I replace her?" Adrian asked. "I fear I am no longer the employer most desired by the lower orders."

"You are bamming me," Gerald said.

Adrian grimaced. "Forgive me. What is it you wished to discuss?"

"Oh, yes," Gerald murmured. He grew serious. "I talked to Heather last night after the party. I'd say we all made a good showing—except for you hitting Lord Munson. I wouldn't think he'd care to talk about it."

"He'd best not," Adrian said, his temper flaring.

"He'd look the fool," Gerald said quickly. "However, I think it best if we acknowledge the fact."

"What fact?" Adrian asked cautiously.

Gerald flushed. "That Carin needs a different chaperone."

"Why?" Adrian asked, narrowing his eyes.

"Do not mistake me," Gerald said. "Miss Mumford does well. That she is related to the old general is marvelous. Still— Well, there is no way to wrap it up in clean linen. Carin is too blasted pretty. All the young bucks will be after her. She'd be better under the auspice of a stronger and more prominent lady."

"Who would you have in mind?" Adrian asked.

"Heather and I thought Grandmother Vincent would be a good candidate," Gerald said in a rush.

"What?" Adrian exclaimed. "That Tartar!"

Gerald flushed. "Her bark is worse then her bite."

"To you perhaps," Adrian said.

"Confound it," Gerald said. "So she is a shrew, but that is part of the plan. You must admit there won't be many chaps brave enough to dally with Carin if Grandmother is around."

"Faith, no. And I'm one of those chaps," Adrian said. He frowned. "What I mean to say is, I'm not brave enough to have her living under my roof either."

"If you don't," Gerald said, "you had best be prepared to be fending off every blade in town. And considering your manner of fending them off, there will be bloodshed before the end."

Adrian glared at Gerald. Then he sighed. "What did I ever do to deserve this infernal situation?"

"I can't fathom," Gerald said, his eyes twinkling. "It's confounding what the Almight . . . er . . . life will dish out to a poor, unsuspecting fellow."

"You do not know the half of it," Adrian said.

"I don't think I need to know," Gerald said, his tone embarrassed. "What has gone on between you and Carin is just between the two of you."

"Nothing has—" Adrian halted. He could not lie to his best friend. He found himself flushing. "Just how do you propose we go about engaging your grandmother as Carin's chaperone?"

"She's residing at my country estate at present," Gerald said. "Heather and I thought that, if we made it a weekend party there, everyone could meet and see if it will . . . er . . . work."

"Just why would I suddenly wish to go to a weekend house party?"

Gerald widened his eyes. "You need a tree, old man. And evergreen boughs and holly and mistletoe. Can't get that here, old chum."

"Oh, God, no," Adrian said, rolling his eyes.

"Yes, you do," Gerald said, nodding his head seriously. He grinned. "It will be fun, you old humbugger."

"Fun? Your notion of fun and mine are far different."

"Simple pleasures, don't you know," Gerald said. He grinned. "Besides it will kill two birds at once."

"Don't talk to me of birds," Adrian growled.

"What?" Gerald asked, showing confusion.

"Never mind," Adrian said. "And what two birds are we killing this time?"

"Carin and Grandmother can meet," Gerald said in a satisfied voice. "And if Lord Munson is foolish enough to start talking, it is best to be out of town for the nonce."

"I see," Adrian said stiffly. A sudden thought crossed his mind. "Faith, I wasn't thinking. Carin will not leave. Not without everyone else."

"Of course not. They are invited as well," Gerald said. He grinned. "The more the merrier is what I always say."

Adrian smiled wickedly. "You haven't met the more yet."

Constable Moral scratched his head and frowned at his notepad as he walked down the elegant square. He was far out of his ken and his pride was wounded. He knew the case he had been given, though it dealt with the highest of high brows, was the lowest insult. He had been given the case because the chief constable would not have thought to give it to anyone of importance.

"But it is important," he told himself to bolster his flagging spirits. These great houses he visited had suffered from thievery. Thievery of the most unnatural order. The items stolen ranged from the family silver to trinkets and even odder items. One house swore the larder had been ravaged the most. Another complained they did not care as much that the gold plate had been taken, but that their vase of some dynasty or other had been left shattered upon the carpet. Constable Moral wasn't sure what that meant, but the lord had assured him the vase itself was of far greater value then the gold plate could ever be. No great jewels were stolen or anything of that sort from the bedrooms.

"Must be a lower-story man," Constable Moral murmured. Then he flushed. That was the rub. There was no sign of a man. All signs were of dogs. As impossible as it sounded, his notes verified it. Lord Rutherford avowed to nefarious muddy paw prints around his broken vase. Lady Freemont's butler expounded upon the outrage of not only having the silver tea set gone, but having skidded upon a puddle of opprobrious origin. When questioned further, the butler declared he knew bloody well what it was because there had been other leavings close to that as well.

"The Canine Caper," was what Chief Constable called it in a raucous way. Constable Moral's peers jeered. There was no denying the world was going to the dogs. At least this square of the world was doing so.

Constable Moral halted before an elegant town house. He studied it. He had received no report of thievery from it as yet. Houses upon both sides of it had reported incidents of thievery, but this house had not. Scratching his head, Constable Moral walked up to the front door. He employed the brass knocker.

The door was instantly opened. A swollen-eyed woman peered at him. "Praise the Lord," the woman said, sniffing. "I thought it was them returning."

"Beg pardon?" Constable Moral asked cautiously.

"Forgive me," the lady said. Her gaze darted past him in fright.

Constable Moral drew himself up. "Is the lord or lady of the house at home?"

"No!" the lady exclaimed. She appeared to jump at

her own vehemence and then said in a calmer voice, "They just left for a stay in the country an hour ago."

"They did?" Constable Moral asked.

"Yes," the lady said. "They are gone. All of them."

"I see." Constable Moral nodded. "I have only one more question, ma'am. Has anything been stolen from this residence in the last few days?"

"Not that I know of," the woman said, sniffing. "Yet in this household, one could never tell."

"Ma'am?" Constable Moral asked, frowning.

"Everything is at sixes and sevens. What with that baby and the old lady"—she shivered—"and that thieving boy and his dogs."

"What?" Constable Moral yelped.

"It is dreadful," the lady said, appearing as if she were ready to burst into tears. "You do not understand how very dreadful it is. But his lordship will not see reason."

"Please, ma'am," Constable Moral said, grabbing for his pencil and thumbing to a new page in his pad eagerly. "Please tell me about the thieving boy and his dogs."

The woman looked at him in sudden suspicion. "Why do you want to know about them?"

Constable Moral stood at attention. "I am an officer of the law, ma'am. I am investigating the burglaries that have been happening in this neighborhood."

"Burglaries?" the woman's eyes widened.

"Yes . . . er . . . Miss?"

"Mrs. Knightsbridge," the woman said, still appearing stunned.

"I believe you have very important information," Constable Moral said eagerly.

"I do?" Mrs. Knightsbridge asked, sniffing.

"Yes," Constable Moral said, nodding. "Information which you as a conscientious citizen should impart to me."

"About the boy and the dogs?" Mrs. Knightsbridge asked, her gaze turning meditative.

"Yes," Constable Moral said, "in the service of justice."

"Justice?" Mrs. Knightsbridge's face brightened. "I knew it. That boy is nothing but trouble and those dogs are beasts that should never be found in a proper household."

"Tell me all you know," Constable Moral said eagerly.

"I will," Mrs. Knightsbridge said. She looked back and then stepped out, closing the door. "We must beware of Mr. Nelson, the butler. He is on their side."

"Is he now?"

"Yes." Mrs. Knightsbridge nodded.

She then began to speak much quicker than Constable Moral could write. Almost. Her sniffs and sneezes, however, offered him the pauses he required.

"I don't see why we got to go visit these toffs," Hez said, kicking his leg against the squabs of the carriage. He clutched a satchel to him. "A body should be in London now."

Carin smiled to herself. Hez was holding the satchel to him as if it were life itself. Clearly he was frightened of a new place and different surroundings. "You have never been to the country, have you?"

" 'Course not," Hez said in scorn. "I'm a man of the city and proud of it. I ain't no hayseed."

"You will enjoy the country," Carin assured him. She peered closer. He still seemed pale and tired. "The fresh air will be healthy for you."

As she rocked a sleeping Joy, Bertha said, "It's bloody cold air and I've been to the country afore. Ain't anything good in it."

"But we will be hunting for a Christmas tree," Carin said with excitement. "It will be fun."

We'd Like to Invite You to Subscribe to Zebra's Regency Romance Book Club and Give You a Gift of 4 Free Books as Your Introduction! (Worth $19.96!)

If you're a Regency lover, imagine the joy of getting **4 FREE Zebra Regency Romances** and then the chance to have thes lovely stories delivered to your home each month at the lowest prices available! Well, that's our offer to you and here's how you benefit by becoming a Zebra Home Subscription Service subscriber:

- **4 FREE** Introductory Regency Romances are delivered to your doorste|
- **4 BRAND NEW** Regencies are then delivered each month (usually before they're available in bookstores)
- Subscribers save almost $4.00 every month
- Home delivery is always **FREE**
- You also receive a **FREE** monthly newsletter, *Zebra/ Pinnacle Romanc* *News* which features author profiles, contests, subscriber benefits, bool previews and more
- No risks or obligations...in other words you can cancel whenever you wish with no questions asked

Join the thousands of readers who enjoy the savings and convenience offered to Regency Romance subscribers. After your initial introductory shipment, you receive 4 brand-new Zebra Regency Romances each month to examine for 10 days. Then, if you decide to keep the books, you'll pay the preferred subscriber's price of just $4.00 per title. That's only $16.00 for all 4 books and there's never an extra charge for shipping and handling.

It's a no-lose proposition, so return the FREE BOOK CERTIFICATE today!

Say Yes to 4 Free Books!
Complete and return the order card to receive this $19.96 value, ABSOLUTELY FREE!

(If the certificate is missing below, write to:)
Zebra Home Subscription Service, Inc.,
120 Brighton Road, P.O. Box 5214, Clifton, New Jersey 07015-5214
or call TOLL-FREE 1-888-345-BOOK

Check out our website at www.kensingtonbooks.com.

FREE BOOK CERTIFICATE

YES! Please rush me 4 Zebra Regency Romances without cost or obligation. I understand that each month thereafter I will be able to preview 4 brand-new Regency Romances FREE for 10 days. Then, if I should decide to keep them, I will pay the money-saving preferred subscriber's price of just $16.00 for all 4...that's a savings of almost $4 off the publisher's price with no additional charge for shipping and handling. I may return any shipment within 10 days and owe nothing, and I may cancel this subscription at any time. My 4 FREE books will be mine to keep in any case.

Name _____

Address _____ Apt. _____

City _____ State_____ Zip _____

Telephone ( ) _____

Signature _____ RNH9A
(If under 18, parent or guardian must sign.)

AFFIX
STAMP
HERE

ZEBRA HOME SUBSCRIPTION SERVICE, INC.

120 BRIGHTON ROAD

P.O. BOX 5214

CLIFTON, NEW JERSEY 07015-5214

"I don't understand," Hez said. "Why does his nibs want to go doing something like this? He don't believe in Christmas."

Carin tried to hide her pleasure. "Perhaps he is . . . is changing."

"Not bloomin' likely," Bertha snorted.

"I agree," Hez said. "He ain't the type to get all moony and suddenly want to go chop a tree down."

"He did permit you to bring Marie and her pups," Meg said from her corner of the carriage.

"Yes, but he's making them ride in the cart with the luggage," Hez said.

"There *is* no room in here for them," Carin said reasonably.

"I know," Hez admitted sullenly.

Carin frowned. "Hez, is anything wrong? Are you feeling well?"

" 'Course I am," Hez said. He flushed. "I just didn't want ter leave London. I have lots of things ter do before Christmas."

Carin started to ask exactly what he meant when the carriage came to a halt. The door opened and Adrian stuck his head inside.

"We have arrived," Adrian said, smiling. His hair was tousled from riding outside and his features ruddy from the cold. Carin caught herself staring at him. He was so exceptionally handsome.

A shout sounded from behind. Adrian looked back. He shook his head. "Gerald's been waiting for us again. Do let us hurry. He's rather blue."

He stepped back and everyone clambered from the carriage. Carin was the last to alight and by that time it appeared there was a race between Gerald and the dogs as to who would reach them first.

"Gads," Gerald exclaimed, his blue eyes bulging.

"You said the more the merrier, old man," Adrian said, an odd smile twitching his lips.

"Er . . . yes," Gerald said, swallowing. "But the dogs?"

"What's wrong with dogs?" Hez asked belligerently.

"Nothing," Gerald said. "I like them myself. But Grandmother . . ." He sighed. "We'd best go into the house. Heather sent a message her family will not be able to come. Little Beth came down sick."

"I'm sorry to hear that," Carin said with sympathy.

Gerald smiled weakly as he gazed at the group. "It appears we have enough for a house party regardless. Let us go in to Grandmother. She is waiting. We—we can make the introductions where it is warm."

They entered the house as a group and immediately stopped. When Gerald said his grandmother was waiting for them, he had not overstated. A tall, regal lady stood directly in the middle of the foyer, both hands resting upon a cane.

"You are late," she decreed in a stern voice. "We expected you at noon."

"Forgive us, Lady Vincent," Adrian said quickly. "We had—"

"What are those?" she exclaimed as Marie and the pups cleared the doorway.

"Dogs," Hez said. He frowned. "Haven't you ever seen dogs afore?"

"I have, young man," Lady Vincent said, her tone steely, "but never within my house." She waved her hand at a retinue of footmen who stood waiting. "Take those creatures to the barn."

"The barn!" Hez yelped.

"Yes," Lady Vincent said, lifting her brow. "That is where they belong."

"No, they—" Hez began.

"Hez," Carin said, her tone reproving. "If Lady Vincent does not wish to have the dogs in her house that is her right."

"The barn is a fine place for dogs," Gerald said in a jovial tone. "They will enjoy themselves. They can play with the other animals. And hunt for mice. There is plenty of hay for them as well. It will be warm and cozy. In fact—"

"Gerald," Lady Vincent said, "do stop. You are rattling on like a want wit."

"I think I'd like to go to the barn with the dogs," Hez muttered.

Carin gasped. Gerald gurgled. Adrian laughed outright. Lady Vincent turned a piercing gaze upon Adrian. "You find that amusing?"

"No, my lady," Adrian said, though his eyes were suspiciously bright. "But you must own, Gerald was painting a rather alluring picture."

"As I said, he is acting like a ninnyhammer," Lady Vincent said, her tone dry. She gave Adrian a look that assured him she thought the same of his behavior. She then looked back to Hez. "And you, young man—where you wish to go is your choice. Indeed, if you wish to sleep with the dogs, you may."

Hez's face flushed a bright red. As if in sympathy, baby Joy sent up a wail from within Bertha's arms.

"Gracious," Lady Vincent exclaimed. Her gaze swiveled to Bertha and narrowed. "What . . . ?"

"This here is a baby," Bertha said, stepping firmly forward with a militant glint in her own eye. "Her name is Joy. Little Lady Joy Partridge. And I ain't taking her to the barn nohow."

Lady Vincent stiffened. "Gerald, who *is* this person?"

"Forgive me," Gerald stammered. "We haven't gotten to proper introductions as yet."

"This person," Bertha said, glaring, "is Bertha. Bertha

Hammersham, plain and simple. I don't have any proper title in front of me name."

"There is no need to explain," Lady Vincent said tartly, "that which is eminently obvious."

"I thought I'd just warn ye like"—Bertha smirked—"'cause I take care of me own."

"So do I," Lady Vincent said. Her eyes flared in challenge. "And though I *do* possess the proper title of Lady Mildred Vincent, viscountess of Severs, it does not hinder me in the process one jot."

Bertha, laughing, mimicked, "That is eminently obvious."

"Ah, yes," Gerald said, shifting on his feet. "Perhaps we'd best move on with the other introductions."

Baby Joy cried out again. Lady Vincent did not even spare a glance at Gerald. "If you are so very good at looking after your own, Bertha Plain and Simple, then do let us take the baby out of this drafty hall and closer to a fire before it catches its death of cold."

"I was just about ter suggest that," Bertha said, stepping forward to follow as Lady Vincent turned and walked away. "Only *someone* was causing a frightful dustup over some poor dogs and I was too polite ter interrupt."

"Polite?" Lady Vincent barked out a laugh as they disappeared from the foyer. "I doubt you understand the term."

Gerald stared after them. "Well I'll be—"

"Gut foundered." Hez nodded.

Gerald jumped. He cast Carin and Meg a sheepish glance. "I'm sorry about that. I didn't have a chance to introduce you."

"That is all right," Carin said, with a trembling smile.

"Indeed," Adrian said, his tone dry. "Carin will gladly await her turn, I have no doubt."

* * *

"For once I quite agree with Lady Vincent," Adrian said as they walked toward the forest, the snow crunching beneath their feet. "The servants can do this."

"Oh, no," Carin said, laughing up at him. "That would destroy all the fun."

"So Bertha was quick to inform her," Adrian grinned. "Something about us blue bloods being too mollycoddled?"

"Gads, yes," Gerald hooted as he followed behind with Meg. "My grandmother is a Tartar, but your Bertha is no piker, not by half."

"It is frightening," Adrian said. "They are perfect complements to each other. Not that one will hear ought but insults from either."

"I think they enjoy it," Carin said, frowning in consideration.

"Well, I'm glad they didn't come with us," Hez said as he skipped ahead.

Carin smiled. For a boy who hadn't wanted to come, he was showing immense enjoyment. He had even become resigned to the confinement of Marie and the pups to the barnyard, once he discovered they did indeed have a warm barn and the most excellent company of sundry farm animals.

"No," Adrian said. "They are cozily by the fire, happily scrapping with each other. While we are out here tromping through the woods and ogling trees."

"But that is part of having a Christmas tree," Carin said. "It is very important to discover the most perfect one . . . for that year."

"Could we not have at least sent the servants out to scout first?" Adrian asked reasonably.

" 'Course not, old man. That would be cheating. It wouldn't be tradition either," Gerald said. "If you don't do it yourself, then it ain't your tradition. It would be the servants' tradition instead."

Adrian lifted his brow and looked down at Carin. "You actually do this every year?"

"Yes." Carin nodded eagerly. "Meg and I do."

"And do you chop the tree down yourself?" Adrian asked, his tone teasing.

"Go on with ye, guv." Hez giggled. "She's a woman. They don't chop trees."

"Did you?" Adrian persisted.

Carin flushed. "No. We did have the servants do that."

Adrian halted. He looked offended. "Are you saying I am doing the servants' work?"

"Oh, no," Carin exclaimed horrified. "I didn't mean that!"

"How I have fallen in the world," Adrian said, shaking his head. A twinkle entered his eyes. "I am just my lady's lackey now, fit only to carry her ax. Well, have Gerald carry it, that is."

Carin's own eyes widened. "You are teasing me."

He grinned. "I never tease, my lady."

"You are," Carin said, laughing.

"No," Adrian said. His tone deepened and he bowed. "I am pleased to be my lady's servant."

"Yuck," Hez said, scornfully. "Mush."

"And rot," Carin said. Then she flushed since she had borrowed the term from Bertha.

Adrian hooted. "Do you hear that, Gerald? I attempt to be pleasing and this is what I am offered in return."

"Don't come to me for sympathy," Gerald said. "I may be carrying the ax, but you are chopping down the tree."

Adrian blinked. "And why am I doing that?"

"It is tradition," Gerald said, grinning.

"A very convenient tradition," Adrian said dryly.

"No," Gerald said. "The man of the household cuts the tree down."

Adrian looked at Carin. "This is true?"

"Yes." Carin nodded. She bit her lip. "We only had the servants do it because Papa was never there."

"I see," Adrian said, his tone gentle. Carin gazed up at him, losing her breath. His look was steady upon her. He drew in a breath—the one Carin evidently was missing—and turned his gaze to Gerald. "Well, Gerald, I must take your word for it then upon this tradition business. Carin's father was always absent and I doubt my parents even knew a tree and Christmas could be in the same sentence."

"That's why yer such an old curmudgeon," Hez said.

"I am not," Adrian said, stiffening.

"You don't believe in Christmas," Hez said. "That makes you a curmudgeon."

"And what of you, young cawker?" Adrian asked. "You said you didn't believe in it either. You've turned traitor."

"No, I've just changed my mind," Hez said with dignity. He then grinned wickedly and scooped up a handful of snow. "And I ain't no traitor."

"Don't you—" Adrian said. Hez threw the ball at him before he could finish. It slammed into his chest. Adrian growled. "Didn't I warn you about attacking me?"

"Oh, dear," Carin breathed as Adrian bolted at Hez. Hez squealed as Adrian tackled him. Frightened, Carin rushed over. "Please do not fight."

She heard Hez giggle and her eyes widened. Adrian was tickling the boy unmercifully.

"Did you hear the woman?" Adrian laughed, halting. "She's telling us men what to do. We cannot permit that."

"Sure can't, guv," Hez said.

Before Carin assimilated it all, the two rolled directly at her. She toppled into the snow. That she did assimilate. Laughing, she began tossing snow into their faces.

Thurstead, Lady Vincent's butler, was passing through the great hall when he heard a scratching and barking at the door. He halted. Once again he heard a bark. His brow rising, he strode over to the door and opened it.

He peered down. He swallowed. "Good God!"

He slammed the door shut. Now a full bay arose. He jerked open the door. He looked down sternly. "You do not wish me to take this to her ladyship, I assure you. My advice is to bury it." He closed the door sharply. Once more a shrill bark came. This time he cracked the door open and hissed, "Very well, if you persist. Let it be on your head."

He closed the door. Squaring his shoulders he walked from the hall and entered the parlor. Lady Vincent was employed at her needlepoint. Bertha was darning a sock. Baby Joy cooed and gurgled in a rosewood crib brought down from the attic.

Thurstead cleared his throat. "Excuse me, my lady."

"Yes, what is it?" Lady Vincent asked.

"You have a visitor at the front door."

"Who is it?" Lady Vincent asked, frowning.

"I would rather not say, my lady."

"I do not care what you would rather do," Lady Vincent said sharply. "You surely must have gotten the name."

"No, I did not get the name," Thurstead said, flushing.

"Do not harangue the poor man," Bertha said, pulling on a thread. "If he didn't get the name, he didn't get the name."

"Oh, very well. Show him in," Lady Vincent said.

"I do not know if it is a him," Thurstead said. "And I do not think you wish for me to do so."

"If I tell you to show him in—" Lady Vincent said.

"Oh, do cut line," Bertha said, tossing down her sewing and rising. "If you won't take care of your visitor, I will. You can't leave him standing in the cold. Or perhaps *you* can."

"Would you, my lady . . . I mean, madam?" Thurstead asked in a relieved tone.

"No," Lady Vincent said, rising majestically and grabbing up her cane. "He is my visitor. I shall attend to him."

Poor Thurstead was pressed to scramble aside as the two old ladies pounded by him. He knew they did not race toward something good. Growing suddenly religious, he crossed himself and followed the two competitors into the foyer.

Bertha apparently came in first. She opened the door. Her reaction was similar to Thurstead's.

"Bloody hell," she muttered and slammed the door shut.

"Who is it?" Lady Vincent panted as she came in a close second.

"It ain't anybody," Bertha said. She sighed. "All right, if ye must know it is Marie Antoinette."

"Marie Antoinette?" Lady Vincent said. "Do not be ridiculous. She is dead."

"Er . . . no," Bertha said. "Marie Antoinette is the dog. You know, the one you sent to the barn."

"A dog is my visitor?" Lady Vincent asked, her brows shooting up.

"Yes," Bertha said. "And I think Marie means ter try and butter you up. She's come bearing you a gift."

Lady Vincent narrowed her eyes. "Open the door."

Bertha, rolling her eyes, opened the door. "Marie brought you a duck. She likes birds."

Lady Vincent stared at Marie, who wagged her tail and laid before her a limp offering, its long neck twisted. The dog barked a greeting. "That is not a duck. That is a goose. My goose!"

"A goose?" Bertha peered down in interest. "So that's what it is. It is a Christmas gift then."

"Oh, God," Lady Vincent cried. She stomped out the

door, just barely sidestepping Marie Antoinette and the dead fowl.

"Where're you going?" Bertha asked, trailing behind. "It's cold out here and you don't have no coat. Why don't you let yer servant do this?"

Lady Vincent stopped a goodly number of yards from the house, apparently finding what she sought.

Bertha came up from behind. She said with forced cheerfulness, "Well, now. Look at that. Little Richelieu is bringing you a goose, too. What a strong little pup he is. And trying ter be nice, he is."

"Nice, my—" Lady Vincent growled.

"Yer a lady, remember," Bertha said quickly. "You don't swear."

She winced as Lady Vincent showed her just how fluently a lady could swear. The variation of curses took them another number of steps.

"Ah, Louis got you a gift as well," Bertha said, her voice strained. "Imagine that!" A yap sounded not far away. The two ladies peered into the distance. "And Napoleon is dragging . . . er . . . bringing you another a gift. Blimey, there're a lot of geese."

"There are six of them," Lady Vincent said.

"Were six," Bertha said, reaching into her pocket and drawing out a flask. "I suppose ye wouldn't like a drink?"

Lady Vincent cast her a loathing stare and stomped away, her cane poking holes into the snow.

"Didn't think so," Bertha said, shaking her head. She uncapped the flask. "Guess I'll have ter have it fer her."

Cold and starry-eyed, Carin entered the house with the rest of the party. She could not remember a more fantastic day. The sheer amount of laughter and teasing filled her heart. Adrian had appeared a totally changed man, not only approachable, but open. A warmth in her blood chased away any chill. He must like her, truly like her.

Her eyes alighted upon Bertha, who sat upon a chair in the foyer. A rosewood crib stood beside. Joy's vocals could be heard coming forth.

"Bertha," Carin said with excitement, "we found the most perfect tree."

"It is quite . . . noble," Meg said, her eyes glinting.

"A big, fat one too," Hez nodded.

"And Adrian felled it like a man," Gerald said, laughing.

"It is a tradition"—Adrian smiled lazily—"though these two at least drew the line at asking me to carry it back on my shoulders. That at least the servants are permitted to attend."

"Sh-sh!" Bertha said, lifting a finger to her lips. She stood and rushed over to them.

"Oh, Bertha, no," Carin sighed as the pungent aroma of Blue Ruin filled her nostrils. "You have been drinking again."

"Just a few nips. Thought it best if one of us kept our spirits up." She burped. "Must tell you . . . our goose is cooked. No, truth is, our geese are cooked. Or *hers* is, unless she wants them ter go ter waste."

"What are you talking about?" Carin asked, bemused.

"I don't like the sound of this," Meg murmured.

"You are talking about birds again," Adrian said, eyes narrowed.

"Dead ones." Bertha nodded her head vehemently. "Six this time."

"What?" Gerald asked, his blue eyes bulging.

"The Christmas geese got killed a mite early," Bertha said. She swiveled her head, peering around blurrily. A waft of gin passed by them as she exhaled. "Been waiting fer you. Wanted to head you off. She's in the parlor having a proper fit. Told her to have a drink, but she's too niffy-naffy. She's a-stewin' and a-boilin', she is."

"There you are," a chilled voice said. Everyone turned. Lady Vincent entered the foyer from the parlor. Her cane cracked the marble floor as she approached. "I imagine Bertha has told you what has occurred."

"Some of it?" Gerald offered.

"You didn't let me get it finished," Bertha said, shrugging.

"Then I will finish it," Lady Vincent said stiffly. She turned her gaze to Adrian. "I will tell you now, Lord Hazard, I will most certainly not accept the onerous task of being Miss Worthington's chaperone. You could ask and ask until the Thames freezes over and I would not consider it. I would not care to live within the vicinity of you and yours."

"Grandmother!" Gerald exclaimed.

"What?" Carin's eyes widened and she looked at Adrian. "What is she talking about? Why would you ask her to be my chaperone? Meg is my chaperone."

"That's right," Bertha said belligerently. "She has Meg. What would she need you for?"

"I understand," Meg said softly, turning pale. "I had suspected at the party, but I was not certain."

"She would only need me," Lady Vincent said coolly, "if she were to save her reputation as well as that of Hazard's. Though Miss Mumford has some connections, she certainly does not possess enough power to scotch the gossip."

"What gossip?" Carin whispered.

Adrian's eyes were regretful. "I did not wish to worry you about it."

"Balderdash," Lady Vincent said. "Gerald told me. You think her too innocent to face the truth. Or accept the consequences of her situation. Though if she can live with this ramshackle crew and those murderous dogs, facing mere scandal should be a stroll in the park for her."

"What situation?" Carin asked.

Lady Vincent snorted. "Why the situation of you being a beautiful young girl living under a bachelor's roof. A situation Delilah Randels has cried out to the ton—and in no small detail."

"She did?" Carin gasped.

"Yes," Adrian said.

"You all were perfect noddies to think you would get by with it," Lady Vincent said rather viciously.

"Grandmother," Gerald objected.

"No," Lady Vincent said, raising her hand. "I was leery of your scheme before. Yet because you asked it of me, I permitted you to bring the child here to see if I thought I could help."

"That is why we are here?" Carin asked, her eyes flying to Adrian. The pain of betrayal sliced through her. "Not for the Christmas tree?"

"What is a Christmas tree," Lady Vincent asked, "when both your reputations are on the brink of ruination? My advice to you two is to cease your air dreaming and naive idiocy. Accept the situation gracefully and get married."

"Married! No!" Carin cried.

"Out of the question," Adrian said sharply.

The two stared at each other. Both were pictures of wounded pride.

"Blast it, Lady Vincent," Bertha muttered. "Now look what ye done? I told ye ter have a drink. Instead, ye've let yer spleen turn ye nasty and cruel."

Although Lady Vincent lifted her chin, her voice was more hesitant. "There is nothing cruel in telling them they must marry."

"I will never marry," Carin said. "Never."

"She promised her ma on her deathbed," Bertha whispered aside and heaved a great sigh.

"Good gracious," Lady Vincent said. "Well, that was before her reputation was ruined."

"I do not care about my reputation," Carin said, her throat dry. "Lord Hazard knew that. And that is why he did not inform me of these schemes." She bit her lip. "I thought that he was just being nice."

"Well, for God's sake," Lady Vincent said, frowning, "he is being nice. And damn honorable to boot. What more could a girl want in a husband? And he's tolerated all these . . . friends of yours. Never thought I'd see the day Adrian Hazard, marquise de Chambert, did something like that. You two would make a wonderful match."

"Shut yer yapper, Mildred," Bertha ordered. She stalked over and shoved her flask at Lady Vincent. "If you keep going on like this you'll be joining yer precious geese in the pot."

Lady Vincent blinked, but she took the flask and remained silent.

"Does this mean we are going back ter London?" Hez finally asked.

Carin lowered her eyes as Adrian looked searchingly at her.

"Yes, it does. This very instant in fact," he said, his tone clipped. He turned to Lady Vincent. "Forgive us if we do not stay for dinner, my lady."

"But—" Lady Vincent began.

"What did I just tell yer, Mildred?" Bertha warned.

Mildred shut her yapper once more. She only opened it to take a hearty swig of Bertha's gin.

Chapter Seven

Seven Swans . . . Running

Constable Moral eagerly received the letter from the boy when he heard it came from the marquise de Chambert's household. He tore it open.

> *Dear Constable Moral,*
>   They *returned home last night. The boy and the dogs are back.*
>
>   *A conscientious citizen*

Grinning, Constable Moral glanced around. Everyone bustled by. No one appeared to take note. Of course, the sad truth was they never took note of him, unless it was to jeer at him. He would change that tonight.

Pretending indifference, he pocketed the missive. Tonight he would single-handedly catch the nefarious boy and those thieving dogs. He would gain the honor and recognition he deserved!

"Hmm, yes. Thank you, Nelson," Adrian said, staring down at the cards in his hand.

"Yes, my lord," Nelson said. Receiving no answer he

cleared his throat. "How was your stay at Lady Vincent's, my lord? It was rather . . . ah . . . brief, was it not?"

"I do not wish to talk about it," Adrian said stiffly. He glanced at the cards in his hand. "No, confound it. I do!"

"You do?" Nelson asked, his tone eager.

"Yes," Adrian said, his jaw clenching. "Please inform Miss Worthington I request an interview with her."

Nelson's face deflated. "Yes, my lord."

He turned and departed. Adrian slapped the cards in his hand and then went to sit at his desk and wait. When Carin entered, pale and dark eyed, he straightened up in his chair, grateful for the security of the officious desk between them.

"Nelson said you wished to speak to me," Carin said.

"Yes," Adrian said, clearing his throat. He purposely nodded toward the chair in front of his desk. It reinforced the sense of business. "Please sit down."

"What did you wish to speak to me about?" Carin said. Her tone was astoundingly contained, as if during the short stay at Lady Vincent's she had taken lessons from that fearsome lady.

"While we were at Lady Vincent's *finding a Christmas tree,*" Adrian said firmly, holding out the cards, "you had several callers. Most of them gentlemen. They left their cards."

"I see," Carin said. She clasped her hands primly in her lap.

Adrian frowned. "Are you not going to take them?"

"No," Carin said. "It was never my intention to enter society when I came here. Nor do I wish to do so now."

"Take them," Adrian growled.

"No," Carin said, shaking her head. "I do not wish to have anything to do with men. They are not trustworthy."

Adrian stiffened. "No doubt that remark was made for my benefit."

"No, it wasn't," Carin said, tilting her chin defiantly, though her eyes told him differently.

"Yes, it was," Adrian said. "But I am not going to apologize this time, confound it. I did nothing wrong. I was attempting to do the right thing and protect you." He lifted his own chin. "Even Lady Vincent noticed that, if you did not."

"You told me you wished to take me to the party to meet your friends because you wanted my company," Carin said in a small voice, "not because you wanted to save our reputations. You told me we were going to Gerald's to find a Christmas tree and mistletoe. I thought you were changing. That you were starting to care . . . about Christmas and people."

Adrian swallowed. He realized he was changing. He was starting to care. It galled him all the more. "Then I guess you were wrong. I am still the old curmudgeon you know. The cool customer. An untrustworthy man who was wicked enough to try and help protect your reputation."

"And yours," Carin retorted.

Anger, pure red, shot through Adrian. "Faith, you are naive. I have but to ignore this and it will blow over for me. I will not be ostracized. I need not bow to society. You make me out to be some society sycophant who will do anything to please the ton. Next you will be thinking I want to marry you."

Carin's eyes flew to his, hurt and haunted. Actually haunted. Adrian flushed. It was the last subject he should have ever tendered.

"No," Carin said. "I may be innocent about many things, but I am not so deluded as to sink into thinking that."

It was Adrian's turn to feel the knife's cut. That he did confused him. "I would never marry you for society's sake." His eyes widened as Carin looked swiftly away, flushing. Both pride and the strongest of male instincts flared within him. He sprung up, running his hand through his hair. "I meant I do not wish to marry anyone."

"Neither do I," Carin said, her head crooking at a defiant angle.

"I like my life just as it is," Adrian said to cap it off royally. "I mean, as it was."

"I understand," Carin said. "We have been a disruptive force in your life." Adrian snorted. Carin flushed. "However, you need not concern yourself so greatly. Your sense of honor is great, but if you wish to go about your regular life, I promise you I shall try to ensure we do not interrupt it anymore."

Adrian stiffened. She was saying clearly, "Here's your hat. You may go now." And after all he had done for her.

"Excellent," Adrian said viciously. "I am so glad to know I will not be needed in the future or be caught up in all the imbroglios of this household."

Carin appeared rather stunned at his temper. She rose swiftly. "May I leave now?"

"No," Adrian said contrarily.

"Why may I not?"

Adrian blinked. He wasn't sure. Perhaps because the fight seemed unfinished. He wasn't prepared for her to leave. What should be left to say, he didn't rightly know. "Because you need to take those cards."

"I told you I do not want them," Carin said, lowering her eyes.

"You will take them," Adrian said, irrationally angered. He stalked over and snatched up the stack of cards. He approached a stiff Carin, grabbed her hand, and pushed them into her palm. "They are your responsibility."

"I don't want them," Carin said. She raised her eyes to his. They shimmered with tears. "I do not want anything to do with men."

Adrian's heart sank as a string of blinding thoughts

struck him. The first was that he had been a fool not to have permitted the argument to end when it should have instead of forcing the issue further. The second was that the hand he held was smooth and fragile and trembling. The third was that he wanted to kiss those tears away. If he didn't leave he knew he would lose the fight. "I'm going to my club."

He dropped her hand and bolted past her. He heard her choked response. He halted. Blast it! He had already lost the fight. Somewhere between yesterday and the fun in the snow when she had looked at him with joy and now when she looked at him with tears, he had lost. Lost before he even knew what the fight was about. Worse, he still didn't know its source.

He turned around. Stalking back he spun her to face him. He lowered his lips to hers and kissed her ruthlessly. Her lips were warm with surprise. Unable to stop himself, he kissed her cheeks, her eyes. He kissed those tears away as he had wanted to do.

Then he pushed her limp form back. The slightest satisfaction engulfed him. She gazed up at him with dazed, stunned eyes. Yet the tears were gone.

"You are correct," Adrian said. "You cannot trust us men. We cannot even trust ourselves. *Now* I am going to the club."

He rotated on his heel and beat a hasty retreat.

It was teatime when a sharp rap sounded at the town house's front door. Nelson, just leaving the parlor, walked across and opened the door. He stiffened as he recognized Lady Vincent before him, flanked by two footmen, who strained under cumbersome trunks. He peered past her. Two more carriages lined the street. They were piled high with more capacious trunks. "Good afternoon, my lady."

"Well, don't just stand there," Lady Vincent rapped out. "Step aside, my good man. My footmen will expire soon if not permitted to unburden themselves." With a prod of her cane, she marched Nelson backward and waved her footmen forward.

"Is my lord expecting you, my lady?" Nelson asked, alarm escaping into his voice as the footmen clunked their trunks to the marble floor. Others were streaming in behind them.

"Of course not," Lady Vincent said. Her brow arched. "You are a good butler. If you have failed to discover all the details of the past day, I make no doubt you shall rectify the deficiency promptly. Now employ your excellence and find me a suitable chamber. Preferably one that is large and away from the street. And away from those infernal dogs."

"Aha!" Bertha said from the parlor doorway. "Should have known by the commotion what was happening. Had a bad notion we hadn't seen the last of you, Mildred."

"Really?" Lady Vincent asked, stomping over to her. "I would have imagined you would have thought those beastly dogs to have felled a passing pedestrian only to drag it home to you as a gift."

Bertha grinned. "Got to hand it to ye, Mildred. Yer just in times fer tea."

"Thank God for small mercies. I am parched and famished," Lady Vincent said. She flung over her shoulder to Nelson. "Oh, Butler, you may—"

"His name's Nelson," Bertha said querulously.

Lady Vincent turned. "Nelson. Forgive me. Order my footmen to bring you the two baskets in the first carriage. There is an excellent goose liver pâté in it that I wish for tea." Bertha cracked a laugh. "And bring me sherry." She turned to Bertha with a frown. "I refuse to drink that rot of yours."

"Do what she says, Nelson," Bertha chuckled as Nelson

hesitated. "This fine lady here has come to lend us her god-awful but mighty presence. Don't fret about his nibs. He'll stomach her in the end, I've no doubt."

"As well as goose liver pâté and goose pie and goose something or other according to the creativity of your chef." Nelson gurgled.

Lady Vincent frowned. "Go about your business, man. His lordship won't toss me out. If he can take in the street riffraff as he has, then he can stomach me as well."

"Miss Carin took us in, not his lordship," Bertha said. "And you've set them at loggerheads."

"Of course I have," Lady Vincent said tartly. "My nitwit but well-meaning grandson didn't inform me they were in love. I knew he was attempting to be sly and hold something back. His ears always turn red. Humph. He probably didn't think I knew about romance at my age. Which is totty headed. If I hadn't known anything about romance, his father wouldn't have been born, nor would he have. So lay the blame on his doorstep and not mine. Now I want a drink."

"Yes, my lady," Nelson said, a slow grin crossing his face. "I shall have you settled directly."

"Thank you . . . er . . . ?" Lady Vincent said.

"Nelson. His name is Nelson," Bertha said, turning to lead Lady Vincent to the parlor. "Fer goodness' sake, can't ye remember a body's name fer more than a blink?"

"I remember every name and rank in the peerage," Lady Vincent retorted. "That is more then you can say, I am sure."

"That's not something I would want ter say," Bertha snorted. "But we best do our talking while we're alone. It was just me and Joy, but we'll accept you."

Carin and Meg returned from their walk. Carin felt terribly uncomfortable, for try as she might, she found she could not discuss this morning with Meg. Just as she couldn't discuss any of her feelings. She was too confused. Too embarrassed.

They heard voices from the parlor and both looked at each other before making their way to that room. Carin and Meg both stopped.

"Lady Vincent?" Carin asked, surprised to discover that dame sitting cozily upon the settee with a wineglass in her hand. Bertha sat across from her, pouring the contents of her scratched and dented pewter flask politely into a demitasse.

"Ah, there you are, my dear girl," Lady Vincent greeted. She stood and grabbed her cane. She then halted, her eyes narrowing. "Where are the boy and dog?"

Carin's eyes widened and she looked to Bertha. "I thought they were here."

"Good God, no," Lady Vincent exclaimed.

"They ain't," Bertha said. She shook her head. "Hez said he changed his mind and he and the dogs were wanting to go with you."

"He didn't," Meg said, frowning.

"Then the lad's playing truant," Bertha said in a cheery tone. "He's of that age."

"Truant," Lady Vincent said. "That boy is—"

"Leave the lad out of this," Bertha said, her eyes glinting. Her brows waggled in the oddest manner. "Don't ye have something to tell Miss Carin, Mildred?"

"Yes, I was getting to that," Lady Vincent said, her tone sharp as she looked at Bertha. When she turned her gaze to Carin, her entire demeanor changed. Her eyes teared and her voice grew weak. "Can you ever forgive an old lady her temper? I was dreadful yesterday. Just dreadful."

Carin's heart went out to Lady Vincent as the old woman leaned heavily upon her cane and stepped haltingly forward. "Of course, I can. Marie and the pups did behave abominably."

"You are a dear, sweet girl," Lady Vincent said. She then looked to Meg. "And my dear Miss Mumford, I fear the rash things I said yesterday made it appear I did not respect your abilities. I never meant it in that fashion. It is clear you have raised Carin to be a proper young lady."

Bertha whispered, "Don't overplay." Carin glanced at her. Bertha broke into coughs. She then offered an innocent look. "Sorry, I might be catching an ague or something."

Meg studied Bertha. She then turned a curious look upon Lady Vincent. "Thank you, my lady, for your kind words."

"You can call me Mildred," Lady Vincent said, her face cracking somewhat. "And you too, dear Carin."

"Er, thank you," Carin said. The thought of doing so was impossible, but she smiled politely.

"I have come to make amends," Lady Vincent said quickly. "I hope you will forgive me and permit me to chaperone you along with Miss Mumford."

Carin felt all at sea and sinking fast at that. "It truly is not necessary, my lady."

"You ought to hear Mildred out," Bertha said.

"Please do." Lady Vincent sighed heavily. "I will not feel forgiven unless you permit me to assist you in entering society smoothly."

"I have no need to enter society," Carin said stubbornly.

"You might wish to listen," Meg said, her eyes starting to twinkle. "It is only polite to do so."

"Very well," Carin conceded.

"Mildred and I were thinking," Bertha said quickly. "You say you don't intend to enter society now. But you plan to live with your father when he returns, don't ye? He ain't the type to live in the country. He entertains society. If yer his hostess, ye best be on good terms with his friends."

"That is good," Meg exclaimed, her voice awed.

"Thanks," Bertha said, grinning.

"In truth," Mildred said, glaring at Bertha, "I thought of it."

Carin, baffled, looked at all the ladies. "No, I had not thought of that."

"Well, you should," Lady Vincent said firmly. "You'll need a reputation for that and I'm the one to help you."

"I don't know," Carin said. Helplessness overwhelmed her, though that useless feeling had trailed her since this morning.

"What is there to know?" Lady Vincent asked. "You would be doing me the favor if you permitted me to come and reside here. If you would let me go with you out into society. Otherwise I will be so lonely for Christmas."

"Will you?" Meg asked, her tone amused.

"Meg," Carin exclaimed, shocked at Meg's odd callousness.

"It is the season for charity," Bertha said, her voice wheedling. "True, Mildred is a Tartar—"

"Do not press it," Lady Vincent hissed.

"But you wouldn't want her to feel unforgiven," Bertha said hastily, "or as if she ain't of any use. You heard her: The poor dear will be all alone fer Christmas elsewise."

"I am so very sorry," Carin stammered, gazing sincerely at Lady Vincent, who sniffed. "But I truly do not have a say in the matter. It is the marquise de Chambert's residence. It will have to be his decision."

"What is my decision?" Adrian asked from behind.

Carin jumped. "What are you doing here?"

"Yes," Bertha said, frowning. "We thought you'd be at your club for the next year. Er, I meant—"

"I know what you meant," Adrian said, his eyes darkening. "Nelson sent a message to White's. He at least still realizes it *is* my house and I should have some say as to who resides here."

"To be sure," Lady Vincent said. "Only I am sorry for yesterday, and I do wish to help you."

Adrian stiffened. He frowned heavily at Carin. "It has been decided that we need no help."

Bertha snorted. Adrian glared at her. She lifted her hand. "Everybody could use a little help now and again."

"Yes," Lady Vincent said in a wise tone. "It is clear you two will never marry. Faith, you ought not marry. Surely, Carin's stay here will be brief."

Adrian appeared stunned. "Er, yes. Perhaps. But that has not been ascertained. We do not know where her father is."

"I know her father," Lady Vincent said. She waved airily. "Worthington may be suffering setbacks presently, but that man will always land on his feet. Look how he finagled you into taking Carin in for him. And you, above all people, are not an easy mark."

"True," Adrian said, his tone mollified.

"So it stands to reason," Lady Vincent said firmly, "that if you two will but make a push now to deal with your own difficulties, your rewards will be great. You two will part quite unencumbered and unscathed from your acquaintance and can go your merry way."

"My lord would like that," Carin said.

Adrian glared at her. "So would you. Do not lay it at my door this time. Do what you wish, for I shall not press you in this matter."

Carin lifted her chin. "I merely did not wish to interrupt your life once more."

"Aha!" Adrian said. "You are hoping to make me out a curmudgeon again." He looked to Lady Vincent, his gray eyes molten. "Please do stay. I will be at your disposal for whatever you ask. I am amenable to whatever you deem necessary for us to do to release us from our difficulties."

"Excellent." Lady Vincent nodded, smiling. "We shall begin with the ballet tomorrow night."

"So soon?" Carin gasped.

"There is nothing like the present," Lady Vincent answered.

"I shall be there," Adrian said curtly. He bowed. "Now I shall be going out for the evening."

Carin watched him depart with both trepidation and confusion. She then peeked at the ladies. They watched her closely. "I believe I shall look at my wardrobe."

"You do that, dear," Lady Vincent said kindly. "It is always important to look your best."

Carin nodded and departed swiftly.

"That was almost too easy," Lady Vincent said, smirking.

"Carin turned the trick in the end," Bertha laughed.

Meg lifted her brow. "As a co-chaperone, may I be permitted to join this matchmaking endeavor?"

"Certainly." Bertha grinned.

"She's a quick one," Lady Vincent observed.

"That she is." Bertha nodded. She pointed to the chair. "Sit down and tell us what Carin's said."

"Nothing," Meg said. "She will not discuss Adrian."

"She is in love," Lady Vincent said. She frowned. "If she is not speaking, that means there are things she is not confessing."

" 'Course not," Bertha said scornfully. "You said yourself you remembered how it was when you were young."

"Yes," Lady Vincent said. "And that is why I am here. The trick is to get those two to the altar while Carin is still a virgin."

Meg gasped. "Carin would never . . . and Adrian is honorable . . ."

Bertha grinned. "Me, I ain't so niffy naffy about that.

I've known many a fine couple who started together 'cause they had a bundle on the way."

"Well, that will not happen to Carin," Meg said firmly.

"I suppose not," Bertha said, sighing. "That would be too simple. I'll just have ter wait to be a grandmother."

It was a moonless night. Nor did the stars shine. Only the Dog Star glimmered, but very dimly. Sailors would curse such a black evening with nothing to steer by. Hez was in fine fettle.

"Gore, Jimmy," Hez breathed as he stared at the hackney cab drawn up to the side of a gracious town house, "why didn't I thinks of this? We got so much more this way than having only Marie hauling it."

"Ah, it weren't nothing," Jimmy said. "Ye've been workin' hard. And when ye told me only the servants were here and the toffs have gone fer Christmas, I figured it'd be a shame not to take what's offered."

"I'll lay ye odds this here will do it fer me," Hez said, his tone eager. "I can buy those rings fer Christmas."

"Ye won't be doin' this no more?"

"I'm straight now," Hez said proudly. "I haven't picked a pocket since Miss Carin's. Well, I picked his nibs's in the beginning, but I always slipped it right back. It was just ter wean me off of it, ye see. Get the itch out of me fingers."

Jimmy shook his head, his face awed. "Yer gone straight. You workin' this hard fer honest pay ter get gifts fer yer loved ones—if that ain't plain bloody noble, I don't know what is."

"I'm going ter be a proper gent," Hez boasted. "Ye best take off now. I've got ter call Marie and the pups off from guarding. I'll come round tomorrow fer me pay."

Jimmy nodded and backed the horses up. Hez crept back along the side of the house. He reached the open kitchen door. He stuck his head in and whispered, "Yer off duty. Come." He then proceeded to walk away in a casual manner. He'd take the long way home.

Constable Moral remained posted outside the marquise de Chambert's town house in the shadows, or what would be shadows if there were a moon to create them. He fidgeted and scratched his head. Instinct told him he must have missed his quarry. Sighing, he stepped out of the shadow that wasn't and stood on the street beneath the lamplight.

He suddenly noticed a hansom cab pull out from the side of a house four doors away. It looked like the cabby was driving right on the grass.

"Drunken fellow," Constable Moral muttered. He proceeded to walk down the street, scratching his head and ruminating on how he could have missed the boy and his dogs. He knew he had been tardy to his post, but the chief had thrown another late duty upon him. He'd told the chief he was hot on the trail of the canine thieves, but the chief had only laughed and ordered him to chase the dog's tail after his shift.

"I get no respect," Constable Moral sighed as he reached the house. He frowned. He had been right. That cabby had indeed driven upon the grass. "Should have booked the chap. Driving when bosky. Dangerous."

He thought he heard a dog's bark. One lone woof. Constable Moral peered into the darkness, his heart catching. It must be the nefarious canine thieves. He was going to catch them right in the act. Crouching, he ran across the yard and along the house. He spied an open door.

"Aha!" Constable Moral cried. He stepped into the kitchen. He peered around. He spied a puppy. "Got you!" Constable Moral grinned. He stepped toward the pup. His foot skidded upon something wet upon the floor. Howling in shock, he crashed to the floor.

The wind gone from his sails, as well as his chest, Constable Moral pushed himself to his feet. He blinked, seeing stars. Undaunted, he searched for the puppy. He rammed into a table. A clatter of disturbed pans echoed. "Where are you, you thievin' cur?"

A noise sounded to the side of him. He spun. He winced as a bright light supplanted the stars in his eyes. A shriek arose just as Constable Moral's vision cleared.

He gurgled. A frightful woman in cap and gown charged down upon him, her arm raised with a vase in her hand.

That was the last of his painful sensations.

Carin attempted to smile as she sat in Gerald's box. The theater before her glittered. The myriad candelabras could not match the brilliance of the assemblage taking their places to supposedly watch the performance of the ballet.

"There is Lady Wetherford." Lady Vincent nodded and waved.

She had not stopped waving at people since they arrived. As was everyone else. It appeared the ton enjoyed the spectacle of greeting each other before the curtain's rise more than the performance itself.

"Faith, it is good to be in society again," she said, well satisfied.

"To be sure," Adrian drawled from where he sat. He appeared far too handsome in his dress attire. He also appeared totally bored.

"Only wait, Carin," Lady Vincent murmured. "We shall have the ton at your feet in no time."

"I must say," Gerald said, smiling at her with open approval, "Grandmother is right. You are very beautiful to-night. That is a very fetching dress."

"Thank you," Carin murmured. It had only taken an entire day of shopping with Lady Vincent to discover it. An exhausting day at that.

"Indeed," Adrian said, his tone cool. "From the glances you are receiving from the young bucks in the pit, it will take just this evening to have them drooling . . . at your feet."

"I am not here for that purpose," Carin said, flushing.

"Forgive me. I quite forgot," Adrian drawled. "Men are unnecessary creatures to you. Imagine, half the world's population is *de trop* in your books."

"Adrian," Lady Vincent snapped, "that was entirely un-called for."

Carin bit her lip, but her spirit rebelled. "No, my lady. He only speaks the truth. Men *are de trop*. Some more then others."

"Carin," Meg gasped this time. "That was not polite. Especially after everything Lord Hazard has done for us."

"Do not worry, Miss Mumford," Adrian said, his voice dry. "I have not done anything that was not to further my own selfish purposes. I care so much for my good standing, you understand?"

Carin's gaze flew to his. His eyes narrowed. She flushed. "No, indeed. I am well aware that we have been a trial to his lordship."

"Cease," Lady Vincent said sternly. "If you two continue to bicker like this, nothing will ever be accomplished. If strangers were to overhear this conversation they might very well mistake it for a lover's tiff."

"I . . ." Carin began.

"I . . ." Adrian said.

"No," Lady Vincent said. "Be quiet. The performance is about to begin. Thank God."

* * *

"Did ye have fun t'day?" Bertha asked Hez as she dealt out cards to him and Nelson. A fire crackled merrily in the fireplace. Baby Joy gurgled and cooed in her crib beside them. Marie and the pups were dozing in the corners of the room.

"Coor, but I did," Hez said, grinning. "Ye wouldn't believe my day. It was the best ever."

"I noticed ye are disappearing a lot," Bertha said. "Miss Carin is worried. I told her you weren't doing anything you oughtn't."

"I've gone straight, I have," Hez said.

"Then where have you been going?" Bertha asked point-blank as she led off the play.

Hez's eyes twinkled. "Yer not suppose ter ask things like that afore Christmas, ye know."

"Ah." Bertha nodded.

Hez sighed. "Miss Carin and Meg sure looked fine as five pence tonight, didn't they?"

"They did," Bertha nodded. She shook her head. "Ye got to hand it to Mildred, she does know how to fancify a girl. Though poor Miss Carin was lookin' burnt to the socket from all the shopping they did ter day."

Hez frowned. "What kind of play are they seeing tonight?"

"It's not a play," Bertha said, snorting. "It's the ballet. All they do is prance around from what I've heard."

"Lady Vincent said it would be special. It's going to have swans in it, too." Hez sighed. "I'd like ter see the swans."

"I doubt there will be real swans on stage," Nelson said, frowning.

"She said it was going ter be original," Hez objected.

"No," Nelson said. "Original means someone has just

written the ballet or it's being performed for the first time, which in my experience is never true."

"Oh," Hez said. He grinned. "I'm glad I'm here then."

A commotion sounded outside the door and it burst open. A constable of the law marched in, flanked by two assistants. Mrs. Knightsbridge came sniffing and fluttering in behind them, with a rather vindictive glaze to her weeping eyes.

"My name is Constable Moral," the man said, puffing out his chest. His air of consequence was diluted by a large white bandage about his head. "These here are my assistants." The two assistants nodded in embarrassment. "I am here to arrest one person named Hez and his band of nefarious thieving dogs."

"What?" Hez jumped up. "I ain't done nothing wrong."

"Haven't you?" Constable Moral all but growled, which made Marie stand up and growl. Constable Moral reached into his pocket and drew out a box with a flare of melodrama. "Then how'd you get these?"

"Those are mine!" Hez shouted.

"Loot from the houses you've been stealing from," Constable Moral snorted. He snapped the case open. Five golden rings glittered.

"No, I bought them fair and square," Hez shouted. "You give them back to me."

"I told you he'd lie," Mrs. Knightsbridge sniffed. "He—" She sneezed.

"Mrs. Knightsbridge," Nelson said in a stern tone, "what have you done?"

"I am only being a good citizen," Mrs. Knightsbridge said, sniffing.

"You are dismissed from service immediately," Nelson said.

"Give them back to me," Hez said. His face turned red and he charged at the constable.

"Here now!" Constable Moral cried as Hez threw himself on the man, pummeling him. "You're resisting arrest! That's . . . *oof* . . . another charge." He cuffed Hez, causing the boy to shake his head in a daze.

"Sir," Nelson said, stalking toward the constable, "that was unnecessary."

"Oh yeah? This here is a dangerous—Ouch!" Constable Moral cried as Hez saw clear enough to wallop him in the stomach again. "Help me, you two!" Constable Moral cried to his assistants, who stood gaping.

Hez did not need to call out. Nelson was already stepping forward as were Marie and her court. Bertha would have too, but baby Joy cried out and she went to her.

"Arrest them," Constable Moral cried, "for striking an officer of the law. *Yowl!* And for biting an officer of the law!"

Marie bayed and bayed. Bertha gripped the rope she had tied around Marie as they stood outside the impressive entrance of the theater. "Don't you worry, old girl," she said. "We'll get them back. Miss Carin and his lordship will see ter that, I hope."

"But how?" Gaskins said as he stood beside Bertha holding baby Joy tightly to him. "They wouldn't permit us entrance to see my lord."

"Coldhearted bastards," Bertha muttered. The theater attendants—upon viewing an old woman, a whining dog, and a footman with a baby in his arms—had swiftly denied them entrance. At Bertha's assurance that his lordship would wish to see them and that it was of bloody importance, for couldn't they see there was a grieving mother here, they had indeed rushed Gaskins and Bertha down the very steps of the theater. Marie had only whined and cried all the more.

"Well, I've never seen the front entrance of a theater

afore, but I know the back. Come on. But, Marie, if you don't stop yer caterwauling, we'll never get to his lordship. You should be happy you got free." Marie whined, but then subsided.

Bertha, with a sublime knowledge, led them to the back alley and the back door of the theater.

"We can't just walk in," Gaskins gasped.

"Yes, ye can," Bertha said. "I've often nipped in here on cold nights. Theater people never notice you when they are doing a performance. Too busy. Besides, they're good people. Just act as if yer supposed ter be here and we'll scrape by. It's finding the bloody door ter the front that will be difficult."

They entered the back door, and true to Bertha's word, they wandered down a warren of corridors, receiving glances from harried stagehands but not much more. Only when they came upon the stage entrance itself did Gaskins whisper, "We shouldn't be here."

"Shh," Bertha murmured as they tiptoed closer. Her gaze was upon the dancing ballerinas on the stage. "My, ain't they pretty," she whispered.

Seven ballerinas in fluttering gowns of white, with beautifully crafted wings twirled and drifted across the stage. It was indeed a spellbinding moment, for everyone offstage stood hushed and watching, which was a compliment of the first order from one performer to another.

"Ah, my swans," A lone voice whispered in excitement. "See how they glide."

Bertha wanted to tell the speaker to be quiet as she moved closer, mesmerized.

"This will make me famous," the speaker—a thin, overdressed man—exclaimed. "My *Swan River* will be renowned. See how they float."

"And my costumes," a man beside him sighed. "Magnificent. When you asked for feathers, I was not sure."

"Feathers?" Bertha frowned, peering closer at the wings.

At that moment Marie bayed and Bertha's relaxed fingers lost hold of the rope. As Marie loped forward, Bertha sighed. "Feathers. Blast that dog and birds!"

Then she lifted her skirts as the gliding ballerinas, finding a large black mastiff jumping and snapping at their wings, no longer glided, but shrieked and crashed into each other in a frenzy to escape.

"Marie, come back here," Bertha shouted as she shoved through the swans reverted into terrified women. "They ain't real birds, you ninnyhammer!"

Gaskins was directly behind her, though how he could assist, holding baby Joy, who shrieked, was questionable.

Suddenly Bertha was grabbed by two stagehands. Realizing that she had failed in her purpose, she struggled. She attempted to see into the audience, but the lights made it a blur. "Miss Carin! Lord Adrian! Are ye out there?"

"Bertha!"

"Help! They arrested Hez!" The stagehands cursed and began dragging Bertha from the stage. Bertha added, "Think they got me, too."

She heard laughter from the audience. She heard Joy's crying and Marie's barking and growling. She heard also another wail. "My *Swan River.* They have destroyed it. I am ruined."

Chapter Eight

Eight Maids . . .

"Do you dare to tell me that you arrested this young man upon these flimsy charges?" Adrian asked in a cutting voice.

"They aren't flimsy," Constable Moral said staunchly.

Carin could only stare in awe. Adrian's icy rage should have weakened the man. She would have buckled herself. Indeed, she shivered, though it might be because they stood at the moment outside the bailey cell—a cell where Hez, Nelson, and the three puppies were incarcerated.

Two guards, looking the worse for wear, stood posted. Only she and Adrian had been permitted to view the prisoners. She shivered once more at the thought.

"I have the goods," Constable Moral said. "I can also testify to the fact that one of those nefarious dogs was at the scene of a burglary last night."

"I didn't steal them," Hez said, his small hands gripping the bars. "Honest, guv. I bought them with the real thing."

"Be quiet, Hez," Adrian said, glaring.

"Yes, guv," Hez said.

Richelieu yapped.

"You too," Adrian said.

Richelieu wined.

At that moment the outer door opened and an officious man of stocky build entered. He slammed the door shut. "Jesus." His face was dark. "This is a bloody police station, not an asylum for the insane. Do they think this is bloody Bedlam?"

"My thoughts exactly," Adrian said coolly.

The man flushed and cleared his throat. "I am sorry. You must be the marquise de Chambert."

"Yes." Adrian nodded. "Can I hope that you are the chief constable?"

"Officer Trump at your service," the man said, nodding. "I came the minute my man notified me." He glared at Moral. "Now what seems to be the matter."

"There is nothing wrong, Chief," Constable Moral said, standing at attention.

"I have been called here at this hour," Officer Trump said. "The place is overrun with the quality." He flushed. "Forgive me, my lord."

"Certainly." Adrian nodded. "We do not care to be here any more than you wish us here, I assure you."

"So what the bloody hell did you do this time, Moral?" Officer Trump barked.

"Only my duty, Chief," Constable Moral said, nodding toward the cell. "I apprehended this boy and his nefarious band of dog thieves."

"Oh, God," Officer Trump exclaimed as he finally noted Hez and the pups in the cell. "You great looby, you've got dogs in my cell."

"They are the culprits, Chief," Constable Moral said rather doggedly.

"And who is he?" Officer Trump nodded toward Nelson.

"He is my butler," Adrian said.

"I have word that he is one of them," Constable Moral said. "He also attacked an officer of the law."

"Something I am very close to doing myself," Officer Trump growled with a look of disgust at Moral. He sighed. "Just what proof do you have, Moral?"

"This, Chief," Moral said in an important tone. He drew out a box.

"Don't show them!" Hez cried.

"See," Officer Moral said. "He doesn't want you to view the goods."

"No," Hez shouted again. "I want them to be a surprise for Christmas."

"Open it," Adrian said curtly.

Moral snapped the lid open and held the box out for display. Carin, like all the rest, moved close. Five golden rings lay on a velvet lining.

"Oh, Hez," Carin gasped. The ring she had remembered liking was there. So was the ring Meg had admired. The tiny ring could only be for Joy. There was another gold ring with a small green stone and then a larger gold one, clearly a man's. "Oh, dear."

"I bought them, Miss Carin, just today," Hez said quickly. "I didn't steal them. I got a paper saying that, too. The store lady gave it ter me."

"Moral," Officer Trump said in a low growl. "Were you aware of that?"

"No, Chief," Moral said. "The boy and dogs attacked me directly. And he's got to be lying. These here are expensive rings."

"It doesn't matter, you idiot," Officer Trump said through gritted teeth. "If they were not part of the stolen goods from the residences in question then it doesn't matter if they are expensive."

Carin bit her lip even as a pain entered her. It did matter and she worried over it.

"But how can a boy have bought them?" Constable Moral asked, sticking to his guns.

"I tell you," Officer Trump said, looking quickly at

Adrian, "it doesn't matter. There isn't any proof of a crime. Release them, for God's sake."

"Even the dogs?" Constable Moral objected. "I can testify that I saw the boy's nefarious dog at the scene of a crime last night."

"So were you, you bleeding fool," Officer Trump gritted. "And we let you off."

"What do you mean?" Carin asked.

"Constable Moral entered a house that was burglarized last night," Officer Trump said. "He swears he saw a puppy."

"I was going to apprehend him," Constable Moral said stiffly. "But he got away. And then I was attacked."

"By the housekeeper who by that time was roused," Officer Trump sighed. "It has taken an entire day to untangle the matter, since Moral was out cold for a couple of hours and thereafter rather confused." He glared at the officer. "I assumed after the day he had he would have gone home and let the matter alone. I was not aware of his actions this evening."

Carin could only stare. She glanced at Constable Moral and then looked away. She could not look him in the eye at the moment. Nor would she dare look at Hez.

"Release them," Officer Trump ordered again. "The dogs as well."

"But—" Constable Moral began.

"You said you saw a puppy," Adrian said softly. He nodded to the cell. "Just which one of *my* dogs did you see?"

"Your dogs?" Constable Moral exclaimed. "I had it on authority that they were the boy's."

"Don't argue with his lordship," Officer Trump ordered.

Constable Moral flushed. "They all look alike. But I know I saw one of them."

"If they all look alike," Adrian said, "then I am sure there are other puppies that look similar. Furthermore,

Officer Trump says you passed out and were confused for an extended amount of time."

"I saw one of those dogs at the crime scene," Constable Moral said more desperately.

"Let it go, Constable," Officer Trump said. "It is only your word that you saw the dog there." He frowned a warning. "That or your word against the marquise's dog, I should say. And I'm afraid the pup is smarter than you."

"But—"

Officer Trump sighed. "You are relieved of duty as of now."

"But—"

"No more discussion," Officer Trump roared. "Get out."

Constable Moral flushed, and amidst a strong silence, he departed. Officer Trump shook his head. "Forgive me, my lord. He was never bright. I'm sorry he doesn't know when to leave sleeping dogs lie, as it were."

Carin sat on the edge of her bed. She had already donned her nightgown and drawn the covers down. Everything was prepared. She should go to sleep. She could only stare into the candle's flame. She did not want to blow it out. She did not want the darkness. Sleep would be impossible.

A pain coiled through her. Hez had remained silent upon the ride home. So had she. Bertha and Meg had merely kept up a steady stream of conversation, Bertha appearing excited about the fine show she had seen before being carted off the stage. Meg had dutifully *oohed* and *aahed* over her story.

Everyone ignored the fact that the marquise had not said a word to anyone since leaving Officer Trump, who had escorted them out. He and Grandmother Vincent and Gerald were returning in Gerald's carriage.

They had returned to the house. A lower footman had greeted them at the door. Carin thought it was due to the fact that both Nelson and Gaskins had been with the party and not at their posts. However, the young footman was quick to inform Nelson that Mrs. Knightsbridge had not only gone, but so had the entire staff of maids underneath her. Adrian had not appeared surprised. Indeed, he said that he had been expecting it.

A knock sounded at the door. Carin started slightly. "Who is it?"

"It's me," Hez said, his voice low. "Can I come in?"

The hurt in Carin welled up. She did not want to hear his story. She could not face it. "Can it not wait until the morning?"

"Please." Hez's voice was barely audible through the door. In truth Carin was uncertain if she truly heard it or if she heard it in her mind. Her heart battled with the hurt. She rose slowly. "I am coming."

She walked over to the door and opened it. Hez stood in the hallway, Marie and her court surrounding him. Hez looked at Carin. "I came to apologize." Hez's lower lip trembled. He looked away from her. He blinked. "I-I am sorry."

Carin's heart won over her hurt. She choked out. "Oh, Hez, so am I."

Hez's shoulders shook. Then suddenly he let out a wail and he flung himself into Carin's arms. Carin, for a moment, stood stunned. She had seen Hez scrapping, pugnacious, always the fighter. She folded him in her arms, knowing she held Hez the boy now. Hez, the boy without a surname or a childhood. "Shh, dear. It is all right."

"No, it ain't," Hez said, shaking his head and sobbing. "It ain't."

Marie woofed. Even as Carin held Hez tight and let him cry, she felt paws upon her skirts and heard yaps of concern. She chuckled through the tears forming in her own eyes. "Hez, do let us sit down before we are pawed down."

Hez backed off, scrubbing at his eyes. "Coor. Look at me, actin' like a baby."

"No, I believe you are acting like a boy growing up," Carin said softly. She took him by the hand and led him over to the bed. They managed to sit before Marie jumped up and licked Hez's face quickly.

"Lay off, Marie," Hez said, his tone embarrassed. He then gazed at Carin, misery in his eyes. "I never meant ter do all this. I only wanted ter buy you all nice gifts, something to give back ter you for all ye've done fer me." Even before Carin could speak, Hez grimaced. "Instead, I landed meself in jail. And Nelson and"—his voice broke—"even the pups. They would have had Marie too, but she bit too hard."

"I know," Carin said, her tone gentle.

Hez flushed, looking away. "I heard how Bertha came and got ye at the ballet. Coor, it must orv embarrassed the guv somethin' frightful."

Carin smiled to herself. Hez's manner of speech was daily improving from that of the urchin he had been. Yet, at times, when he was at his most ardent, the Cockney accent could be cut with a knife. Carin collected her thoughts. "Yes," Carin said, flushing herself. "But I don't think that the guv's potential embarrassment is what matters."

"No," Hez said, gulping. "What matters is that I stole."

Once again the pain shot through Carin. She could not hide her disappointment. "Why did you do it, Hez? You promised you were not going to steal anymore."

Hez shrugged, regaining some of his natural bravado. "I didn't think of it as stealing. I wanted ter buy the rings and I knew this fellow Jimmy who'd pay a bloke money fer whatever he brought him. I just thought of it as me work."

"Oh, Hez," Carin said at a loss to understand.

"Even Jimmy thought I was noble," Hez said. "I was givin' him the things and he was payin' me and I wasn't using it fer meself. It was going ter buy gifts fer you." He shook his head, while Carin still attempted to unravel his reasoning. "But I was just lying. Mean, in my heart like. All I've ever known how ter do is steal. Then you took me in and I wanted ter change. Become a gent. Only I still wanted ter do it the way I knew how ter."

"I see," Carin said in both respect and awe. Hez had looked into himself and discovered something she could never have divined.

"And 'cause of me," Hez said, his voice small and tight, "I hurt you. I made Marie and the puppies thieves. They could 'ave been locked up forever. And"—he sucked in his breath—"made a real lady and gent lie fer me."

Carin's eyes widened. "What?"

Hez flushed again. "I saw yer face when you heard that constable say he saw Richelieu in the house. I knew I'd disappointed you. But you didn't say nothin' against me. And then his nibs lifted his nose like he does and claimed Richelieu was his dog. He don't even like them. He said that 'cause he was makin' sure they wouldn't get me."

"Yes," Carin said, nodding. "He did."

"What do yer think he's going ter do ter me?" Hez asked.

He asked the question Carin had refused to consider all night. "I don't know."

Hez sighed. "He might send me back ter the orphanage. He promised he wouldn't afore, but that *was* afore this."

"I'm sure he wouldn't do that," Carin said in a bracing tone.

"Wells, whatever he does, he will be right in doing it."

"We must wait and see," Carin said, trembling slightly. Sometimes right didn't always seem right. She bit her lip. She feared she was more like Hez than not. Her wishes colored her views.

Carin came down late to breakfast. It had taken hours for her to sleep. And when she did, her dreams had been odd and tormented. In them, Hez had not been sent back to the orphanage by Adrian. Rather, Adrian had sent *her* to the orphanage. He had left her to Friday-faced Fenton and Brutus, who held out bowls of gruel crawling with maggots. Her sense of abandonment and grief had been overpowering.

She shook off the terrible feelings that still lingered as she entered the breakfast room. Meg, Hez, and Bertha were still seated at the table. Lady Vincent was rising from the table at that moment.

"I shall go with you, Nelson," she said. Her tone was sharp.

Nelson, who was posted with a teapot in his hand, seemed to start. "I do not believe that will be necessary, my lady."

"Of course it is," Lady Vincent said.

"Oh, sit down, Mildred," Bertha said, her own tone querulous. "In the bloody fractious temper yer in this morn, you'll only queer it fer us."

"I most certainly will not," Lady Vincent said. "My prominence will be respected. Indeed, all things considered, after your performance last evening, Nelson will require my assistance in commandeering a decent staff."

"Not bloomin' likely," Bertha shot back. "Ye'll probably turn all niffy-naffy and set their backs up. If you got any reputation with them it'll be as a hard one ter please."

"Come, Nelson," Lady Vincent said, sniffing. "When we return we will have a full staff of maids once more."

"I'm telling you, Mildred," Bertha said, "ye shouldn't go. I'd be more likely to get yer a staff than you."

"You! Ha!" Lady Vincent barked. "Ridiculous. It is your fault we are in this predicament."

"Very well. Go," Bertha said. "I'll lay odds you'll come back empty-handed."

Lady Vincent turned and swept out of the room. She did not even notice Carin, who upon viewing her fierce face was only too glad she hadn't. Nelson set down the teapot and followed slowly. He did not notice Carin either. His face was that of a man treading up the stairs to the hangman.

"What is happening?" Carin asked the moment she felt it safe to speak.

"You do not want to know, dear," Meg said, her face wry. "Come and have some tea. That we do have, at least."

"Ye've missed a bloody fine morning," Bertha snorted as Carin took her place.

"His nibs has already left," Hez said, his eyes large.

"Did he say anything to you?" Carin asked, her nerves jangling.

"No," Hez said. His face blanched. "But he said he'd be back fer tea."

"Oh, dear," Carin murmured.

"You do not know the full of it," Meg said, sighing.

"He only got tea and toast this morning," Hez said, looking miserable.

"That French chef swore he couldn't cook without the kitchen maids," Bertha said. "He's a chef and won't dirty his hands with nothin' else."

"He says he will only wait until noon for a new staff," Meg said. "If not . . ."

Bertha grinned. "He's takin' French leave."

"And none of the fires have been lit," Hez said.

Carin shivered. "I thought it was cold."

"His valet left as well," Meg said.

"M'lord was wearing a hankie round his neck this morning," Bertha chuckled.

"A Belcher tie," Meg informed her.

"Oh, dear," Carin said.

"That cheeky fellow waited last night ter tell his lordship he wouldn't work in a house where the butler was a criminal and in jail," Bertha added.

"His nibs said Nelson would stay, and *he* could pack his sack," Hez said proudly.

"I see," Carin said, swallowing hard. A pregnant pause ensued. "Is there anything else?"

"The rest ye've heard," Bertha said. "Mildred is going with Nelson to get us maids. Fool thing ter do. She's been riding rusty all morning over what happened last night. Said we've ruined all she was workin' fer. Said I made you all laughingstocks."

"But we had to know," Carin objected. "You only did what you could."

"She didn't see it that way," Bertha said, looking embarrassed.

"She said even the servants won't want ter work here," Hez said, his eyes wide. "And his nibs will be home fer tea. If we still don't have them maids, he'll be in a frightful tear."

"Yes, I fear he will," Carin said.

"I'll be back at old Friday-faced Fenton's fer sure," Hez moaned.

Carin shivered as her dream returned to her.

An hour had passed. Bertha, Meg, Carin, and Hez sat in the parlor. They had all given up even the pretense of conversation. They merely waited. When they heard the slam of a door outside in the foyer, they jumped up. As a group they reached the door and dashed into the foyer.

Carin, the last one out the door, arrived just in time to view Lady Vincent stalking across the foyer, her cane rapping out a sharp staccato.

"What happened, Mildred?" Bertha called.

"Where are the maids?" Hez asked.

Lady Vincent did not speak. She did not even halt. She disappeared from sight.

"Nelson, what happened?" Carin gasped, turning her attention to the butler.

He stood in the center of the foyer. He appeared shell-shocked, with a dazed look in his eyes and his body swaying slightly.

"Nelson, are you all right?" Carin cried, rushing over to him.

He turned a rather blank stare on her. "It was quite painful, Miss Carin."

"We don't have any maids," Hez sighed.

"Never mind that," Bertha said gruffly. She bustled over to Nelson. "Come on in ter the parlor."

"Yes," Meg said, her tone gentle with concern.

They took Nelson by the arms and guided him into the parlor.

"Now sit," Bertha barked.

Nelson crumpled onto the settee.

"What happened?" Hez asked, jumping up and down.

"I have never been to war," Nelson murmured. He trembled. "It could not have been worse."

"Yes, yes." Bertha nodded. She reached into her pocket and drew out her flask. She uncapped it and held it out to Nelson. "Thought Mildred would muff it."

"Muff it?" Nelson ripped the flask from her hand. He swigged from it. Nelson lowered the flask and coughed. "Mrs. Grange of the employment service had already heard the stories."

"Already?" Carin gasped.

"She placed Mrs. Knightsbridge and all our maids. She

said she had a reputation for servicing respectable house-holds and ours was not in that category." He took a swig. This time he did not cough. "Lady Vincent said it was of no significance. She would be present."

"Oh, dear," Meg said.

"Mrs. Grange said that wouldn't fadge. She had heard accounts about Lady Vincent as well," Nelson said. "That is when Lady Vincent . . . er . . ."

"Gave her what for?" Hez supplied.

"Lady Vincent possesses an extensive vocabulary," Nelson replied. He resorted to the flask. "Lady Grange vowed to notify all the services to beware of Lady Vincent."

"She didn't," Carin groaned.

"She called in a messenger for that purpose," Nelson said. A sweat broke out on his brow. "Lady Vincent inca-pacitated him with her cane and then called for Mrs. Grange to bring the next one on."

"Gracious," Carin murmured in awe.

"We were escorted out by the next messengers," Nelson said.

"Escorted?" Hez frowned. "What's that?"

"They were tossed out on their bums," Bertha trans-lated.

"Correct, madam." Nelson nodded. He lifted the flask and drank once more.

"She's a fighter, she is," Bertha laughed. "Crusty old biddy."

"But what are we going ter do now?" Hez wailed. "His nibs is coming home for tea. He'll be in a devil of a tear. And I'll be tossed out on my bum!"

"No yer won't," Bertha said. She pried the flask from Nelson's fingers. "That's enough fer you. A reviving drink is one thing—getting tap-hacket is another." She looked at Carin. "That French chef wants help. You go help him. Make him stay." She looked at Hez. "You start all the fires."

She swigged from her flask and pocketed it. "If you'll excuse me, I'm going out."

"Where are ye going?" Hez asked.

"Never you mind," Bertha said, moving toward the door. "Told Mildred I'd have a better chance than her."

Carin stirred the batter before her. Chef Andre stood close beside her, whispering in French. She assumed he was instructing her upon how to stir the batter, but since he inched closer and closer, she was unsure. Apparently she wasn't getting the right wrist action. He scooted closer. She scooted farther away. They had already covered half the length of the kitchen.

She glanced up, hoping for assistance. Meg, however, was too involved with the task of peeling potatoes. Nelson was buried up to his arms in brussels sprouts.

"Psst, Miss Carin." Carin looked up. Bertha stood in the kitchen doorway. She cracked a grin. "Come with me."

Carin blinked. She turned to Andre. "Excuse me for a minute." She walked to Bertha. "What is it?"

"Where is Mildred?" Bertha asked, clutching her by the arm and dragging her along.

"In her room, I believe," Carin said.

"Still sulking? Good," Bertha said. "She's already got her nose out of joint. I don't want her havin' a fit when she sees I've succeeded."

"Succeeded?" Carin asked as Bertha steered her through the house.

"Yes, I've got them," Bertha said.

"Them?" Carin asked.

"The maids," Bertha said. "Eight of them, in fact. Four for the household and four for the French chef."

"You do? Eight?" Carin exclaimed. "Oh, Bertha. Thank heaven. But how ever did you do that?"

Bertha dragged her into the entry hall. Carin halted. Eight ladies stood crowded into the chamber. Carin's eyes widened. All but two had a clearly common trait. Carin turned her stunned gaze to Bertha.

Bertha grinned. "If you ever want experienced maids, ye'll always find them at a house fer unwed mothers."

Carin's gaze skittered to the only two thin women. They were brightly dressed in cherry pink and grass green. Actually the two colors were an integral theme in both outfits—only one was in stripes and the other in dots.

Bertha caught her gaze. She shrugged. "They were sisters to one of them. She was a milkmaid at one time and asked me if they could be maids." Her face grew solemn. "Milkmaids are important, ain't they?"

Adrian entered the house. He had suffered a foul day. Beginning it with no valet, no daily papers, and nothing more than toast and tea had been minor. The roasting he had received from those who dared approached him was slight.

He frowned a moment. His circle of friends—actually, he must consider them acquaintances now, to be sure—had not approached him. Yet those he had counted as mere acquaintances—some who were, in truth, more Gerald's friends and some who were not—were the ones who dared to approach him.

They had roasted him. Who else would have had the oddity of an old lady destroying a performance to cry out for him and a Miss Carin? And who was this Hez who was arrested? He deemed them the curious, the sightseers of life. Yet some of them, especially Gerald's friends, seemed actually interested. Some nodded in approval as he had said coolly that it was of no significance, but that he had settled the matter in a manner in which all were safe and settled.

No, what weighed most on his mind and ruined his day was deciding what was to be done about Hez. He must do something with the lad, and though he had come to a decision, he still did not know what to do with Carin.

Drawing in his breath, he entered the parlor, highly doubting that he would discover anything more this hour than what he had enjoyed this morning.

He started back. Carin alone sat in the parlor. She wore a beautiful sprig muslin dress patterned with blue periwinkles. Matching blue satin ribbons crossed the Empire waist just below the gathered bodice of the frock accenting her young figure. Adrian stood a moment merely gazing at her. Drinking his fill of her would be the common expression—only he wasn't sure that with Carin a man could actually do it.

She stared back at him, sitting on the edge of the settee. Her blue eyes were deep and turbulent. "Hello, my lord."

"Hello," he said, walking as calmly as he could over to a chair and lowering himself onto it. He tore his gaze away. "Where is everyone? It is teatime."

"Yes," Carin said. He could not help but notice she drew in a deep breath. "They are occupied at the moment."

"Are they?" Adrian asked, raising his brow. "I do hope Hez has not taken the dogs out to visit the neighbors."

A deep flush spread across Carin's cheeks. "No, not at all."

Adrian gritted his teeth. The comment had come forth from him before he had thought. "I am glad to hear it."

Carin shifted in her chair. "I wish to thank you for what you did last night."

She licked her lips in nervousness. Her action fascinated him. It caused him to halt in his response. A response of the nature that mayhap she need not think

him a *de trop* male after all. He settled for a raised brow
and a cynical smile. "Yes?"

Carin's eyes widened, but they were still as deep as the
ocean. "Hez is very sorry for what he did. I—"

At that moment the parlor door opened. A lovely girl
entered. She wore a maid's apron; her dress beneath it
was drab gray. Adrian's eyes narrowed in observation.

The young girl walked over with her gaze lowered and
she set a silver tray down upon the table before Carin.
She dipped a curtsy. "Your tea, my lord and Miss
Worthington. Shall I serve or would you wish to, Miss
Worthington?"

"I shall," Carin said, quickly moving to pick up the
teapot.

The girl nodded and departed most properly. So properly did she do so that Adrian felt it impossible to ask
the question he wished to ask, a most impolite question
indeed. He merely said, "A new maid, I see?"

The teapot shook in Carin's hand. "Yes. We acquired
new help." She lifted her gaze to his. "She has excellent
references . . . ah . . . I have been informed. She served
at Lord Bennington's establishment."

"Did she?" Adrian asked. Lord Bennington was recognized within the clubs—indeed throughout the ton—to
be a philanderer of the worst degree. Clearly, the question he wished to ask was moot. "Yes. He is very prominent in political circles. A Whig, I believe."

Carin blinked. "Is he? I did not know. He has not been
described to me."

"That is a political party," Adrian offered.

"I see," Carin said, pouring the tea. Her brow fur-
rowed. "I have never had time to study politics."

Adrian found himself smiling despite himself. "No, you
have been too busy."

He halted as the door opened once again. Another girl
entered. She was dressed in the same manner as the other

servant: a maid's apron with a drab gray dress beneath. She carried another tray. She held the tray out farther from herself than the first had. An obvious necessity.

"My lord and Miss Worthington," she said, dipping a proper curtsy. She trod over and set a tray of the most delicious buttery scones and crystal bowls of fruit jams down upon the table. She dipped another curtsy and departed.

But Adrian had lost his appetite. He swallowed. "Another new maid?"

"Yes," Carin said. She rose and walked over to offer him his cup of tea. It rattled in the saucer. "She comes with—"

"Excellent references, I have no doubt," Adrian murmured, intent upon taking the saucer and cup before they slid onto his lap.

"Yes," Carin said. She turned and dashed back to the settee to sit, rather like a man diving over an embankment to take safety from cannon fire. "She served in Lady Eagleston's residence."

"Of course," Adrian said. Lady Eagleston was a dowager duchess who thought the sun rose and set on her two young sons. The ton knew them as wild hellions and, indeed, had all but barred them from Almack's, deeming them a threat to their daughters, fair or otherwise.

"What were you saying?" Carin said. "Do try the scones."

"I was saying," Adrian said, reaching for a scone out of nerves rather than from appetite. Frowning, he searched for the thread of conversation. Preoccupied, he bit into the scone. "Hmm, this is excellent."

"I am glad you like them," Carin said. "We have new maids for the kitchen also. Four to be exact. One is even a milkmaid. Bertha said it is important to have a milkmaid."

Adrian choked on the scone. A terrible premonition

overcame him. "Do tell me those maids are not in the same condition as the two I have just seen."

"Ah, yes," Carin said. She attempted a look of innocence. "I believe they are."

"Good God," Adrian murmured, dropping his scone. He closed his eyes. "Just how many maids are there?"

"Eight," Carin said in a small voice. "But only six are in an . . . ah . . . interesting condition."

Adrian stared in dumbfounded amazement. "Just how the devil could you find so many pregnant maids at one time?"

"Bertha found them," Carin said, her eyes looking miserable.

"Bertha?" Adrian asked, his brow shooting up. "You mean you did not do this?"

"No, we were having difficulty finding servants. Lady Vincent had an altercation with the employment service and Bertha found us maids. It seems there are always plenty at the home for unwed mothers."

Adrian swallowed hard. "I see."

"I did not know what to do," Carin stammered. Her gaze was lowered and her face turned a fiery red.

An unworthy chuckle escaped Adrian.

"I knew you might not wish to have . . ." Carin continued.

The chuckle turned into a laugh, full and loud. Adrian could not help himself or, for that matter, stop himself.

Carin's gaze flew to him. The bewilderment stamping her face made him howl. "You are laughing? What are you laughing about?"

"You," Adrian chuckled.

"Me?" Carin asked, her voice indignant.

"How does it feel with the tables turned?" Adrian asked in sheer amusement.

Carin's eyes widened. She lifted her chin. "I do not know what you mean."

"Yes, you do," Adrian chuckled. "You feel over-whelmed, don't you? Exactly how I felt when you appeared on my doorstep with a baby. And then Bertha and Hez. And the dogs. Only this time Bertha did it to you."

"Oh, dear," Carin said. "I see."

"Yes," Adrian murmured, amused.

"I am sorry," Carin said, her eyes stricken.

"No, you are not," Adrian said, gently chuckling. Carin appeared depressed, and for the first time, Adrian noticed the dark shadows beneath her eyes. He rose and walked over, looking down upon her. "You will live with all these pregnant maids. So shall I."

"You will?" Carin asked, her eyes still worried.

"I know I shall rue it," Adrian said wryly. Unable to resist, he touched her cheek gently. "But they may stay. Now do not worry so."

"Thank you," Carin said, relief washing over her face.

"Oh, my. I'm sorry to interrupt," a young female voice said. "But I brought some biscuits."

Adrian jumped, drawing his hand back. He noticed Carin's alarm and turned quickly. He sucked in his breath. A young brunette stood before them, wearing the usual maid's frock of drab gray, but this one was of a decidedly different cut. This was the most abbreviated of a French maids ensemble. Truly, the bit of lace that was the apron was just that. A bit of lace. And, yes, the frock was the conventional drab gray, but it appeared to be of a smoky hue as if it was made of velvet. Adrian bit his lip. Carin had said there were two maids who were not pregnant. This one surely was one of them.

"Hello."

"Hello," the girl said, sashaying over to set the tray down upon the table, crowding the scones and tea set. She stood and winked at Adrian. "There you are, my lord."

Adrian heard Carin gasp. He hid his smile. "Thank you . . . ?"

"Sally, my lord," the girl said merrily.

"Yes, Sally," Adrian said. "I notice you are not wearing the same uniform as the others."

"No, my lord. They were short on aprons, and I had my own costume from my other job." She smiled coquettishly. "Do you like it?"

"Yes," Adrian said, his eyes twinkling.

"My lord!" Carin exclaimed.

He schooled his expression. "However, I fear you might grow cold in it. Drafts, you know. Do see Nelson about a different uniform."

"Yes, my lord." Sally's face fell. Without curtsying, she departed.

"Just what were *her* references?" Adrian asked, turning to look at Carin in amusement.

"Her sister Teresa vouched for her," Carin said, a look of consternation crossing her face, "as well as for her other sister."

Adrian laughed. "I'm sure she was being very truthful. Sally at least appears very proficient at what she does."

Chapter Nine

Nine "Ladies" Dancing

"Come in and sit down, Hez," Adrian said from his position behind the desk. "Close the door first."

"Yes, guv," Hez said. He shut it and almost tiptoed across the room to take his seat in the large leather wing-back chair. He appeared small and lost in it; his feet barely touched the floor. He offered up a brave smile, however. *"Whew."*

"Whew?" Adrian asked, lifting a brow. "You almost sound relieved."

"I am, sort of," Hez said. "What with what's been going on ter day I thought you might not get ter talk ter me."

"Yes," Adrian murmured. "You all have been busy from what I gather."

"We tried," Hez nodded. "Are you . . . are you happy we got you the maids?"

"I appreciate all your efforts."

"Good, we are sorry that we ran the other ones off."

"It is of no significance." Adrian waved his hand. "I am sure these will be just as efficient."

"Glad ter hear it, guv," Hez said. He shook his head. "Between you and me, it gives me the jangles, havin' all those ladies who're going ter be birthing runnin' about the place. Don't know why, but it does."

"Between you and me, it gives me the 'jangles' as well," Adrian admitted. "But just between you and me."

"Right, guv." Hez nodded, grinning. "Man ter man."

"Right," Adrian said. He drew in his breath. "Now, down to business."

"Yes," Hez said, squaring his shoulders. "Are ye going ter send me back ter the orphanage?"

"No," Adrian said quickly. He frowned. "However, you must know what you did was wrong."

"Yes, guv," Hez said, flushing. "I want ter change, but this becoming honorable is confusin'. It's the very devil."

"Yes." Adrian smiled. "And it never changes."

"Never?" Hez asked in astonishment. "Even with you?"

"Of course," Adrian said. "You yourself told me when I was being bad.

"Yes, but bad is one thing," Hez said. "Honorable is another. You ain't a thief."

"No," Adrian said. He drew in his breath. "But that comes with learning. That is why I have decided to send you to a boarding school."

Hez paled. "Is that another orphanage?"

"No, no, of course not," Adrian said. "It is a school where you and boys your age will be taught. You will learn how to be honorable."

"Couldn't you teach me that?" Hez asked in a small voice. "I mean, I didn't learn quickly afore. But I will now. I'll try harder."

Adrian sighed. "There are other things that they will teach you. They will educate you so you can have an occupation. You will be able to earn the real rhino without stealing in any manner."

"But I'd have ter go away fer that," Hez choked out.

"Yes," Adrian said firmly.

Hez blinked and blinked again. "I understand."

"It will be good for you, Hez," Adrian said. "I was raised in a boarding school."

"You were?"

"Yes," Adrian said. "All Englishmen of quality are."

Hez drew in a breath. "Well, then, if you want, I will go."

"Excellent," Adrian said. Suddenly the memory of those lonely years came back to Adrian. He pushed them aside, though a quelling feeling invaded him. He shook his head. He had considered the issue before them all day. He was right. He rose. "Very well. They will be waiting for us at dinner."

"Yes," Hez said, sliding from his chair. He kicked his toe upon the Aubusson carpet. "What should I do with the rings now?"

Adrian winced. "I have thought about that. There is no way we can make restitution to the houses you have stolen from, not without bringing attention to us. We do not want that. Fortunately, the households on this street will not truly suffer from your actions."

"I'm glad of that, guv."

"You meant to give those rings to us with a good heart," Adrian said. "And you do have a good heart. I know if I am blessed to receive such a gift upon Christmas I will cherish it."

Hez's face lit up. "Will ye, guv?"

"Yes," Adrian said. He cleared his throat. Fortunately, Hez hadn't noticed how completely mawkish his words had been. Only he did. Worse, he had spoken them with heartfelt truth.

Carin looked up from the table as Adrian and Hez entered the dining room. The table was well embellished. No doubt Chief Andre had decided to forgive all past traumas and to excel with his new staff. Sally was bustling about. Fortunately she no longer wore her French maid costume, but a full-length maid's apron. Unfortunately, a bright emerald satin was beneath it, a six-inch satin flounce at the hem contrasting sharply with the white baize fabric above. The satin sleeves extending out from under the apron bodice were puffed at the shoulders and gathered at the elbows with a band of Scottish plaid. Atop her bouncing brunette curls was perched a wide plaid turban with a brocade of quail feathers perched jauntily on one side. Her sister Teresa, admittedly far into her pregnancy, managed with care to pour the wine.

"Toast to ye, Mildred," Bertha was saying with a grin. "His lordship still needs a valet. Do yer wants ter see who finds one first tomorrow?"

"Oh, do be quiet," sniffed Lady Vincent, who had finally come down to dinner. Her gaze was narrowed upon the two servants. Carin shivered to think when the dame would give vent. She had not as yet, though Bertha was crowing far too loudly about finding the maids when Mildred had not only failed but had been escorted from the premises.

"My lordship and Hez," Bertha gasped, her glass raised in midair. She quickly lowered it as both silently seated themselves.

Carin tensed, looking first at Hez's pale face, then at Adrian's cool one. No, perhaps it was not cool. It was unreadable. She bit her lip, fear rising in her throat, stopping her from asking the most important question.

"Well, m'lord," Bertha said as everyone else remained silent. "What will yer do with our boy?"

Carin choked, amazed Bertha had been able to ask the question. Not even Lady Vincent had dared to ask it. Then she noticed the older woman's eyes. They were sharp and filled with a defiant fear. It was only slightly hazed with her usual Blue Ruin. Carin nodded. It was a look she had seen in both Hez's and Bertha's eyes. Of course, they had seen more. They would ask.

"You must ask Hez," Adrian said in a firm tone. He looked at Hez very levelly. "I have told him what I will do." His brow rose slightly. "It is still his choice. He can either do it . . . or run away."

"Here now," Bertha exclaimed sharply.

"My lord," Carin cried.

Both exclamations might have well been sheaves in the wind for their notice. Adrian's gaze and Hez's were locked.

Hez paled all the more. Then a grin cracked his face. "Give over, your nibs. Did you think I'd rat?"

"It is always an option," Adrian said. The confounding man actually smiled, sending Carin into an upheaval of anger. "It was something we did not discuss."

"No, guv," Hez said, actually beaming with an unfathomable pride. At least to Carin it was unfathomable. "I ain't never been one ter run. I've been tossed out, but I ain't never run."

Adrian nodded. "Forgive me."

Just that seemed to be enough for Hez. He turned to look at Bertha and then at Carin. His chin rose and his lip trembled the slightest bit. His look was but a younger version of Bertha's before. "I've got to go to boarding school."

"After Christmas," Adrian said quickly.

Hez's eyes widened in gratitude. "After Christmas."

Carin's mouth dropped open. Then she clamped it shut. A tremble passed through her. It opened again without her intention. "No!"

"What?" Adrian asked, his brows snapping down.

"What?" Hez asked, his voice stunned.

"No," Carin said. She blinked once. Then the emotions welling within her boiled over. "No. Hez shall not go to boarding school. He has been in enough institutions. He needs a family."

"He needs an education," Adrian retorted.

"He will get one, but he does not need to leave us," Carin shot back.

"He needs a formal education, in the company of other young lads," Adrian responded. "He needs discipline and direction."

"I think he has had enough *bloody* discipline," Carin shouted, enraged like she had never been before.

"Miss Carin!" Hez cried, dropping his fork.

"Softly now," Bertha said. "Don't fight in front of the child."

"Always fatal." Lady Vincent nodded.

"What did you say?" Adrian roared, springing up from the table. He slammed his fist upon it, rattling the china.

"I said," Carin repeated, shooting up and throwing her napkin down, "he's had enough *bloody* discipline!"

"I'll go," Hez exclaimed in fright. "You don't have—"

"Be quiet," Lady Vincent ordered. "Don't interrupt your parents when they are fighting."

"What!" Adrian snapped, his gaze veering to Lady Vincent.

"What?" Carin gasped, staring.

"What?" Hez asked, his eyes suddenly shining like the moon.

"Tore it there, Mildred," Bertha murmured, reaching for her wineglass.

Lady Vincent's mouth opened and shut. Looking at none of the participants, she said to Sally, "You there, hussy. Fill my glass of wine. It is empty."

"I have the wine, my lady," Teresa offered, scuttling over.

"Then have the hussy pour it," Lady Vincent snapped, still refusing to look at the frozen combatants. "And do get off your feet before you have your child on the table before us. We have enough trouble on our hands."

Teresa burst into tears. Sally huffed.

"I am going to my club," Adrian bit out, turning to stalk toward the door.

"You've got to stop running, m'lord," Bertha called. "Hez doesn't and he's younger than . . ." But Adrian had disappeared. "Oh, never mind."

Carin stared after Adrian. She was shaking. Lady Vincent's last words rang in her ears. *Parents.*

"Don't fash yourself," Bertha said in a kind tone. "Raising a child is always difficult. You'll have fights."

"It is only natural." Lady Vincent nodded.

Carin gurgled. She had heard that before—*It is only natural*—only in a different context. She lowered her gaze. "If you will excuse me . . ."

She sped hastily from the room.

"Miss Carin," she heard Hez cry.

"What did I tell you, boy?" Lady Vincent hissed.

"I know," Hez said eagerly. "Don't speak when yer parents are fighting."

Adrian woke the next morning. He shut his eyes. The light hurt. His mouth felt and tasted as if it were lined with dried leaves, and his head thrummed angrily at the interruption of unconsciousness.

Shot the cat last night again! If he didn't slow his pace he'd be dead before the next year. *Yes,* a voice whispered, *but you wouldn't be a parent at least.*

"My lord?" a soft voice whispered.

He frowned. Never had he heard such tones from Marchim. His beleaguered brain churned. His eyes shot open. Marchim had deserted him.

"Hello," a lovely brunette murmured.

Adrian, cursing, bolted up. Then he crawled back upon

the mattress until he banged his head upon the headboard. Through a haze, he defined the lovely brunette as Sally, one of the new maids. She sported her abbreviated French maid costume and waved a feather duster.

"What are you doing here?" he asked.

"I heard last night you were looking for a valet," Sally giggled, fluttering his chin with the feather duster. "I'm here to ask for the position."

"Do you know what a valet is?" Adrian asked, frowning.

"I sure enough do," Sally said, leaning forward and fluttering her lashes. "A valet helps a gentleman dress . . . and undress himself."

Adrian shook his head. Pain responded. "You are to be a maid."

"I'd rather be a valet," Sally grinned. "They make a lot more money, don't they?"

"A valet is known as a gentleman's gentleman," Adrian said sternly. "You, miss, are no gentleman"—his jaw clenched—"or lady for that matter."

Sally shrugged. "So I'm no gentleman—or lady. I still can help undress you."

Adrian stared at her. "Your sister vouched for you as a maid. What in blazes are you about?"

"She wants me to reform." Sally shrugged. "Ever since she got knocked up, she wants everyone to reform. She even has my sister reforming."

"But not you," Adrian muttered, eyes narrowed.

"I tried it," Sally said, shrugging again. Adrian detested that. Even in his weakened state he wished to reach out and grip those shoulders before they could flippantly twitch once more. "For a whole day and night. I don't like it. You didn't like my uniform." Her gaze grew pettish. "And that old tart called me a hussy."

"Tartar," Adrian corrected angrily. "Lady Vincent is a Tartar, but no tart."

"You remember what she said," Sally said breathlessly.

She managed to shimmy while sitting down. "Wasn't she cruel?"

"Apparently not," Adrian said, his head hurting all the more.

Sally stiffened a moment and then she relaxed. Her lashes fluttered again and her lips pouted. "If you won't let me be your valet, then can I be your mistress?" She smiled slyly. "I heard that position is open as well."

"What!" Adrian exclaimed. He winced at his own vehemence.

"I heard," Sally said, flicking him once more with the duster, "that you can be a naughty boy. Your last mistress didn't like sharing you with that whey-faced girl."

"Carin! You call her whey faced?"

Sally performed that frightful shrug. "What else? Pretending to be a namby-pamby do-gooder. She has everyone fooled. Even my sister."

"Shut up!"

Sally's brown eyes widened. "Then that boy is really your son?"

"Confound it, no!"

"Are you a parent?" Sally giggled. "I didn't think so last night."

"I am no parent," Adrian growled. He had drunk an entire bottle of brandy last night to wash away that word.

"Then take me as your mistress," Sally breathed. Her gaze grew starry-eyed. "The Cyprians' Christmas Ball is tonight. I've never been there. Above my touch they are. I've just been a working girl." She turned a feverish gaze upon him. "Please take me. I want to be a gentleman's mistress."

"You ungrateful wench," Adrian growled. "First you want to reform; then you want to be a mistress. Your sister vouched for you. Bertha brought you here. Carin took you in." He struggled forward. Sally was the one to skitter back on the mattress. "They offered you a chance to re-form. Love and redemption, for God's sake. Instead, you betray them, you *turncoat.*"

Sally screeched and jumped up. "What's that I am?"

Adrian jerked the covers back and jumped from the bed enraged. "You're an infernal traitor. Just you wait. You'll have to see the blasted hurt and disappointment in their eyes. Dammit," Adrian muttered. "You don't want that."

Sally stared at him, her gaze roaming the lines of his form beneath the voluminous nightshirt. "I don't?"

"No," Adrian growled. He stalked toward her. "Now you can damn well reform. You started it. Led those poor innocents on to believe in you. Finish it. You'll not be-come an unwed mother beneath this roof. And that I swear."

"Yes, my lord," Sally said. A sob escaped her.

"And not a word to anyone of this," Adrian shouted as she turned and ran from the room. Adrian sighed. Of a certain, it was fortunate that with the advent of so much commotion in his household he had taken to wearing a nightshirt.

Carin walked hesitantly down the hall to the maids' quarters. It had not been a good day. In fact, it had been a terrible day. Adrian appeared at breakfast quite un-kempt. He had informed them in a growling tone that he would brook no argument, that he would find himself a valet upon his own, and if anyone dared to attempt to meddle in the affair, there would be hell to pay.

Carin, after another sleepless night, could only con-sider him the most heartless man she had ever met. Hon-estly, his concern was solely for his dress and a servant to care for it. Apparently the fact that he had determined to send poor Hez away to another institution held no importance whatsoever.

Every instinct demanded she confront him once more. Yet the other issue that had caused her to toss and turn last night was Lady Vincent's reference of "parents" in regard to Adrian and her. It was shocking. There was no connection between Adrian and herself in that sense. Nor could there ever be. She had vowed never to marry, vowed it to her mother upon her deathbed.

Therefore she had bitten her tongue and watched Adrian when he left in a foul mood because he lacked a valet. She'd also watched while Hez bravely attempted to accept his sentence—and she experienced the worst kind of guilt and fear as she refrained from speaking.

It had caused her to be unkind, absolutely testy in fact, during the day. She had snapped at Sally when the maid had appeared in her costume again. She had been worse to Teresa, Sally's sister, when she had dropped a vase before her. Teresa had fled in tears.

Guilt ridden, Carin was treading down the hall to the servants' quarters. She must apologize. She approached a room she thought was Teresa's. The door was ajar.

"Teresa," Carin said. She knocked on the cracked door and it swung wide. Her eyes widened. "Teresa, why are you dressed like that?" Teresa, her extended stomach cloaked by a gray domino, looked up. A black mask dangled from her hand.

"Why are all of you dressed like that?" Carin asked as she noted a crowd of maids within the room. All of them were shrouded in varying colors and sizes of dominoes.

"Miss Carin," Teresa exclaimed. "What are you doing here?"

"I came to apologize for my unkind behavior today," Carin said, entering the room cautiously. "I should not have been sharp to you merely because you dropped a vase."

"Thank you, miss," Teresa said, bursting into tears.

"Please do not cry," Carin said, hurrying over to her. "I do not mean to make you cry."

"She's not crying because of you, Miss Carin," the maid Lizzy—at least Carin thought her name was Lizzy—said. "She's crying because her jade of a little sister Sally is running off to the Cyprians' Ball."

"She's not a jade," Teresa cried. "She is too young to understand what she is doing."

"We are bad examples to her," Sarah, the other sister, said. Her domino was satin pink with white rosettes. "Me the worst. I helped get her into the business. I am sorry for it now."

"I don't understand," Carin said. "Why is it bad that she is going to a ball?"

"The Cyprians' Ball," Lizzy said, biting her lip, "is a ball where ladies—well, where we go to try and find a patron."

"Patron?"

"She wants to become a gentleman's mistress," Teresa sobbed.

"She's trying to set out on her own, no abbess to help her," Sarah said. She shook her head. "She's not ready to be a high flyer. She's just a babe."

"I thought she was going to reform," Teresa said. "This chance you have given her was an answer to my prayers. But she says she doesn't like being a maid."

"Oh, dear," Carin said. "It must be because I was so unkind to her today."

"Oh, no, miss," Lizzy said. "It wasn't—" She received a pinch from Jane next to her. "Ouch. Never mind."

"I must apologize to her," Carin said. "We must stop her."

"That's what we are planning to do," Lizzy said. "We'll bring her back. Er . . . you don't have to go with us."

"But I do," Carin exclaimed. "It is all my fault. I must go with you."

Adrian stood next to Gerald upon the crowded sideline of the ballroom. Figures twirled and danced and laughed. Indeed, the volume was already loud and raucous. The slightest tension ran between the two friends.

Gerald had appeared surprised to see Adrian at the ball. In truth, Adrian had forgotten that the Cyprians' Ball was tonight. Not until that hussy of a maid asked him, had he remembered it. Faith, it showed how far gone he was.

The Cyprians' Christmas Ball, given strictly by the demimonde strictly for the men of the ton, was one of the greatest social affairs of the year. It rivaled any Christmas gala of Prinny's. A man of the ton, if he were to uphold any reputation at all, did not miss the event. Even Gerald—who rarely ever took a mistress and was far too serious over them when he did, in Adrian's opinion—attended the ball.

"So you are sending Hez to boarding school?" Gerald murmured as they watched the dancers.

"Yes," Adrian gritted out. "But do let us not talk about it." He had come to the ball to forget about the family difficulties. He cursed. What was the matter with him? He in his own mind was becoming a turncoat and employing such frightful words as "family."

"Gadzooks, look at that girl dancing with Ferdie," Gerald exclaimed, pointing to a friend of his. "I know he likes them plump, but she looks—"

"Pregnant," Adrian supplied. Then he cursed.

"She does, don't she?" Gerald said, peering closer. "Do you think . . . ?"

"No, of course not," Adrian said curtly.

"You're right," Gerald said. "Guess it's because you were telling me about all your maids."

"Let us forget that as well," Adrian said. "It is time to dance with these lovely women. Who knows, I might find a new mistress tonight."

"Would you really . . . ?" Gerald bit his lip as Adrian lifted a brow. "Of course. Well, I think I'm going to join Dickey and the fellows over there first. Get me some more bottled courage before I dance. We have commanded a table if you wish to join us."

"No, thank you," Adrian said coolly. "I am prepared to dance now."

"Er, yes." Gerald nodded and left.

Adrian shook his head as he watched Gerald move toward the back of the room. He hated to admit it, but his friend was the male version of a wallflower. Gerald and his friends—friends Adrian now admitted to be good-hearted—would most likely drink and talk the evening through, all leaving without a glimmer of hope of attaching high flyers to their arms.

He turned his gaze back to the crowded floor with determination. Gerald's question of whether he would really take a mistress rankled. Why shouldn't he take a mistress? Was he so involved with Carin and her menagerie that Gerald thought him ready to . . . ? Adrian refused to finish the question.

He saw another woman dance by. Blast, if she didn't look pregnant to him, too. He shook his head to clear it and focused on seeing if he could discover a lady to attract. He straightened up as he noticed a diminutive girl in a blue domino and mask wending her way through the dancing couples. She appeared to be searching for someone. Her figure was trim and alluring. Adrian smiled. He actually felt a pulse of interest leap in him. Good, very good.

Grinning, he merged into the dancing throng and

weaved his way toward this alluring object. He had not reached her when another man in a green domino beat him to her.

"Looking for someone, sweetheart?" the man slurred. "I can be him."

Adrian frowned. That was going to be his clever line.

"I am sorry," a sweet voice said. "But I am looking for a woman, sir. Have you—"

"A woman!" the man gurgled. Then he grinned. "You like threesomes, do you? You're a dream come true."

"She doesn't like threesomes," Adrian growled, stalking up. He knew that sweet voice too well. Blast, he should have known by his reaction alone who it was. That fleeting thought passed quickly as anger replaced it. He took hold of her arm. "What the devil are you doing here?"

"My lord," Carin gasped.

"Here now," the man objected. "I saw her first."

"Forget it," Adrian said curtly, glaring at the man. "She's my mistress."

"My lord!" Carin gasped again.

"Seems to me if she's here," the man said, swaying, "she might be looking for someone new."

"She's not," Adrian bit out.

"I am looking for Sally," Carin interjected.

"What?" Adrian asked. He noticed the man still standing and swaying. He dragged her away from him, putting a protective arm around her as he guided her through the dancers. The man drifted behind them, but at a distance. Adrian didn't have time for the fellow. He looked down at Carin, her blue eyes the color of midnight beneath her mask. "Now what in blazes are you doing here? Why are you looking for Sally?"

"I fear I was unkind to her today," Carin said, biting her lip. "And because of me, she has decided to become a mistress."

"You didn't have anything to do with that hussy coming

here. Oh, never mind," Adrian said quickly. He was insane in attempting to clarify the matter. Of course, she was insane to be here, but that too was useless to address as well. "You mustn't be here. I am taking you home. Sally can take care of herself."

"No. Sarah says she is just a babe," Carin said.

"Who is Sarah?" Adrian sighed, looking about fiercely. The green domino was hovering in the background. Deciding whether to fight for Carin, no doubt. Adrian's rage flared higher.

"Sarah is her sister," Carin said.

"I thought Teresa was." Adrian frowned, distracted.

"Sarah is her other sister," Carin said. "She's the other . . . er . . . prostitute. Former prostitute, that is."

"Very well," Adrian replied. "No matter what she says, you are still leaving now."

"I cannot—"

"Yes, you can," Adrian said tersely. "I promise you, Sally will be able to fend for herself—far better than you, I vow."

"But what of the others?"

"Others?" Adrian's brow snapped down. "What others?"

"The other maids," Carin said in a worried tone. "I have lost them, too."

"Lost them, too?" Adrian gurgled. "How could you have—" He halted. "God, they are here, aren't they? I wasn't imagining it."

"Then you've seen them?" Carin asked, her tone relieved. "We all parted to look for Sally, and I've lost them."

"That's because they are dancing," Adrian muttered, his mind boggling. His pregnant maids were here at the Cyprians' Ball. Once again, he wondered what he had done to be so cursed.

"Oh." Carin nodded. "It is difficult not to do so. I

danced with one gentleman myself because it seemed the only polite thing to do."

"What!" It was bad enough to have his pregnant staff of maids dancing at the Cyprians' Ball, but that Carin had was the outside of enough. "We are leaving *now.*"

"We cannot leave the others," Carin gasped. "We cannot leave Sally."

"Blast, I suppose not," Adrian said, gritting his teeth. They would have to wait it out. "Where are you ladies going to rendezvous? And when? Please tell me you planned it before the unmasking."

"What do you mean?" Carin asked, a confused expression upon her face.

Adrian stared. "You did make plans to meet back together, didn't you? You surely did not just leave each other in this crowd without proper plans."

"I—we . . ." Carin's voice was small.

"Oh, Lord," Adrian sighed. He thought deeply. There was no help for it. He needed recruits. "Come with me." He tugged on her hand and Carin followed, permitting him to lead her over to where Gerald and the rest of his reticent friends were celebrating in their own fashion.

"Ah, Adrian." Gerald nodded at their approach. He stood quickly. "Hello, madam. How do you do this fine evening?"

"It is Carin, Gerald," Adrian said.

"Miss Worthington," Gerald exclaimed. He flushed deeply. "Forgive me."

"For what?" Carin frowned. "I can understand how you did not recognize me."

"I didn't." Gerald nodded. "And it's not what it looks like."

"What do you mean?" Carin asked. It was Adrian's question as well.

"Er . . ." Gerald blushed. "I only come here for the

dancing. That is all. I am not hanging out for a mistress, I promise you."

Adrian bit his lip. How and why Gerald had to bring that to her attention he didn't know.

"Oh, yes," Carin said, biting her lip. Her gaze flickered to Adrian and then away. "I am sure you are not."

Adrian studiously ignored the play. He looked at Gerald. His pride pricked him. No, actually it pained him severely. Yet pride would not help him take Carin away from here. That objective for some reason overrode everything else. "I believe I need your help—and the help of any other man here who is willing to volunteer. Do you remember the girl who was dancing with Ferdie? The one you thought appeared pregnant?"

"Yes." Gerald nodded.

"Well, she is," Adrian said, briskly. "She is one of my maids."

"Zounds," Gerald breathed.

"In fact, *all* of my maids are here," Adrian said. "They are looking for Sally, whom they wish to save from taking a patron." Gerald gabbled, but Adrian interrupted. "Please do not ask for explanations. I'm sure it is involved and would take all night. We do not have the time. There will inevitably be the unmasking and you know how wild that becomes. Suffice it to say, Carin will not leave without them and none of them made arrangements to meet."

"I see," Gerald said. He turned to his friends. "Did you hear that?"

"Indeed," Lord Swallow—or Dickey to his friends—nodded. Adrian recognized his excessive overbite, which of course a mask could not hide. "The ladies didn't think. Could be haring about all night, even after the unmasking."

"We need to find them," Gerald said. He swallowed and said manfully, "They are easy to recognize. They are all in an interesting condition."

"Two are not," Carin supplied earnestly. "One is wearing a pink satin domino with white rosettes. The other is wearing a black domino, but it has a red lining and a tear in it. At least, that is what we think she is wearing. They checked her wardrobe."

The men goggled at her. Adrian attempted to keep his mind to the task. "This will be our base of operations. Carin and I will remain here. Once you find one of my maids, bring her here directly. There are eight in total."

"Tallyho," Lord Trevor cried. He was clearly lit. "It's a hunt, b'gads! I'll lay you a monkey I can find more of those interesting maids than any other of you chaps."

It was a burst of activity, the chairs all but flying as Gerald's friends found a better occupation than before. Rather than hunting mistresses, they were hunting interesting maids. It was Dickey who actually brought the first one, Gertrude, back in. He grinned rather shyly when Carin exclaimed and breathed a thank-you and said only to tell Lord Trevor. He was going out again, but would report back within fifteen minutes. A very conscientious soldier.

Baron Harding appeared next. He beamed as he led a waddling Missy to the table. Whether he beamed from his success or from the fact that he held Missy's hand was in question. His face-splitting grin, when Missy gave him an open buss upon the cheek, settled the question.

"I'm sorry, Miss Carin," Missy said, flushing as she fell into a chair. "That's what got me into this trouble in the first place. But I was getting hot and my feet are swelling and I was growing dizzy. What they are doing out there is shocking, just shocking."

Lord Trevor reeled back at that moment. "Blast. I haven't caught one of them yet." He reached for a glass on the table and shot the wine down. "But I got slapped by one lady. Could have sworn she was pregnant." Refurbished, he stumbled back out.

Adrian paced back and forth, circling the table as Gerald and his friends brought back maid after maid. Within a half an hour they had brought six of them back. They were only missing Sarah of the pink domino and Sally, the cause of all the trouble. Teresa had been retrieved. She sat quietly crying.

Fortunately, Gerald and his friends remained. With six pregnant women at one table, they were receiving far too much notice.

"Thank you, Gerald," Adrian said tensely.

"Think nothing of it," Gerald said. He was stiff and aware. "Don't like the feel of it, old man."

"Yes," Adrian murmured. "The green domino over there is still watching. I think he wishes to fight me. He thinks I took Carin away from him."

"Hmm, yes." Gerald nodded. "In truth, he doesn't worry me as much as some of the women's looks around here. Do you think they know these maids aren't supposed to be here?"

Adrian snorted. "I would imagine so. They might cast a damper on business, don't you know."

"Hello," Lord Trevor called. Everyone looked up. Then those sitting jumped up.

"Do I win?" Lord Trevor shouted. He had Sarah of the pink domino by one arm and Sally of the black domino, red lining, and tear in it by the other.

"Blast, but you do," Gerald approved.

"Huzzah" and every other compliment arose from the men as if they themselves had conquered a country.

"We'd better be going," Adrian said, taking Carin's hand. "Let us move quietly toward the doors."

"I am not going," Sally cried, tearing out of Lord Trevor's hold.

"Yes, you are," Sarah cried, jerking out of his clasp. She stalked up to her sister. "I have had more than enough from you. All of us have."

With that, she hauled back and slapped Sally.

Adrian groaned. It was as simple as that. The first blow had been delivered.

Chapter Ten

Ten Lords A-leaping

"We thank you all so very much," Carin said warmly. She stood upon the walk outside the town house. Adrian, his clothes ripped and his face bloodied, stood next to her. Behind her were her eight maids. Except for Sally and Sarah, all were safe and unharmed.

Not so the group of men before her. Gerald and his friends were all as battered and bloodied as Adrian. She still could not determine how such a brawl had broken out.

She remembered Sarah slapping Sally. Then the man in the green domino had charged at Adrian. Then some ladies had attacked from around them. Gerald and his friends had fended them off. At that juncture, those women's escorts had joined in the fray. After that, it appeared many jumped in without reason.

That she and most of her maids stood unscathed was merely due to the men's protection. They had managed to get them out of the ballroom and all had leapt into the carriages. Adrian had shouted to meet at the town house. She swallowed hard, a lump of gratitude in her throat. "If you would come into the house, we would be pleased to tend—"

"No," Adrian said, swaying. "That is impossible."

"What?" Carin asked, even as the maids murmured behind her.

"Gads, no," Gerald exclaimed. He was squinting from one swelling eye. "You wake Grandmother and there will be hell to pay."

"Your grandmother is here?" Dickey yelped. He had taken off his cravat and wrapped it around his wounded head. "Gads, no. Not up to it at the moment. We thank you, but no."

This time the group of lords murmured and exclaimed.

"But we would like to repay you in some manner," Carin said, still feeling an overwhelming sense of duty to them. She heard the consent of all the maids. A brilliant thought struck her like lightning. "Would you care to come to a party tomorrow evening in your honor—for your bravery?"

"Carin," Adrian murmured.

"Oh, yes," Gertrude or Lizzy said. "Please do."

The men's eyes flared in excitement. "Sounds famous" and other words to that measure rang forth.

Carin nodded in pleasure. "Very well. Tomorrow evening around eight."

"Carin," Adrian murmured.

"Yes?" Carin asked, looking at him in concern.

"Never mind," Adrian sighed. "I would like to go into the house now."

"Of course, old man," Gerald said quickly. He turned to his friends. "We'd best go now."

After many words of appreciation upon all sides, Gerald and his friends departed in their carriages. The marquise's party slipped quietly into the house. The foyer was silent and dim, lit by only two sconces.

"I never knew how important it was not to have servants wait up," Adrian said. He groaned wryly. "It is ever so much easier to bring them home with you."

"We must tend to your wounds," Carin said, worried.

"I do not—"

"No," Carin said, rather stunned at her own stubbornness. "I must know you are not hurt—too badly, that is."

"Perhaps we should leave you now," Maria said, her voice exhausted.

"Sure, we will," Sarah said. She winked. "You take care of his lordship, Miss Carin. Show him our appreciation. Come on, Sally," she said to her sister, who was quiet and very bruised. "Girls. Let's clear out before we *do* wake that . . . er . . . grandmother."

It was all she needed to say. The eight maids vanished like so many shadows.

"We should go to the kitchen," Carin said, feeling both a determination and a new breathlessness.

"Should we?" Adrian asked, his tone amazingly mild. "Very well."

Her hands shaking, Carin took up a taper and lit it from the sconce. They then silently walked through the house and into the kitchen.

"Please sit down," Carin said, nodding toward the table and chairs around it. She busied herself finding soap, a bowl of water, and bandages. She returned to discover Adrian sprawled in the chair in the most relaxed attitude she had ever seen him present. However, when he looked up, his eyes were dark and enigmatic.

"I am very sorry about tonight," Carin said.

"I know you are," Adrian said in a wry tone. He shook his head and promptly winced. "You always are when things go awry."

"We only wished to—"

"Save Sally." Adrian nodded, but cautiously. "I think you will fail there, Carin."

Carin started at the warm use of her name. The bowl almost slipped through her fingers. She quickly put it on the table. "One shouldn't give up hope."

"You cannot win every time," Adrian murmured, "especially against hardened cases."

"But she is young." Carin frowned. She drew in a breath and, after dipping a cloth in the water, moved forward to stand close to him.

"And you are ancient?" Adrian said.

"I did not mean that," Carin objected. She reached out toward the largest cut upon his face and brushed it with the cloth.

"Confound it," Adrian said, sitting straight with a drawn breath.

"Forgive me," Carin said, placing a hand upon his shoulder in concern. "I did not mean to hurt you."

"I know," Adrian said. His arm slipped about her waist.

"My lord!" Carin gasped.

"No. Call me Adrian," Adrian said. He smiled slightly. "After all. We've been to the Cyprians' Ball together."

Carin looked down as memory reasserted itself. His arm about her was very pleasing. "I am sorry if I destroyed your evening, my—"

"Adrian."

"Adrian," Carin said dutifully.

"And what you are saying"—Adrian smiled—"is that you are sorry if you interrupted my search for a mistress."

"I . . ." Carin looked up, then down again. The warm amusement in his eyes confused her greatly.

"Do not let it concern you," Adrian said. He chuckled. "I believe I am giving up that endeavor. I have had the worst luck in that regard lately. I am a beaten man and I concede."

"My—"

"Adrian," he murmured, drawing her closer. "Since I am one of the wounded, one of those definitely down on his fortune, will you not be kind to me?"

"What?" Carin could only stare.

"You are kind to so many," Adrian murmured. Slowly,

very slowly, he drew her onto his lap. Carin only gazed
at him in wonderment. She felt like a rag doll as she
permitted him to fold her in the crook of his arm. "I
need that kindness too."

He kissed her. Carin sighed in pleasure. If it was a kindness rendered, it was a kindness received as their lips
melded. Tears tingled at the corner of Carin's eyes.
Adrian's lips, his touch, and his hold were tender. That
tenderness was her undoing.

Adrian groaned and drew back. He gazed at her one
long, solemn moment. "I must apologize for that."

Carin started. She sat up quickly. "No, of course not.
It was only natural after all. You were comforting me. Or
I was comforting you."

His arms held her tightly, though his voice was soft.
"No, Carin. It is not only natural anymore, is it?"

"I do not know what you mean," Carin murmured, her
heart beating fast.

"It is much more than just a natural attraction between
a man and woman," Adrian said. His breath was gentle
upon her cheek. "It is between you and me—solely between you and me."

His lips found hers once more. Yet his kiss frightened
Carin this time, as his words had.

"No," Carin cried, tearing her lips from him. "You cannot be right."

She shoved away from him and sprang up, then fled
across the kitchen.

"Carin!" Adrian called.

She stopped, compelled to do so. She fought the com-
pulsion, however, by refusing to turn around. "Yes?"

"I went to the ball determined to force myself to find
a mistress." His voice was low. "I was grateful when I saw
a girl in a blue domino. Grateful because I felt an instant
attraction. Grateful that it was for someone other than

you. Yet it was you. Out of an entire ballroom, it still was you."

Carin choked back a sob. This time she picked up her skirts and fled before he could say another word, fled before she could weaken.

"A good mead." Dickey nodded, sipping from a silver cup.

"Not as good as my recipe," Lord Trevor objected.

Carin winced in the chair she had retreated to for the moment. Her gaze was slightly misty or perhaps muzzy. She had been unable to sleep last night. Indeed, the effort to deny the last scene with Adrian had drained her to numbness. Then the entire day had been hectic with the maids of the household all twittering over the upcoming party.

Lady Vincent, of course, had gotten wind of it in the morning. Her blast of fury had finally subsided. Bertha had been the anchor, warning Mildred in no uncertain terms that they were *her* maids and not to run them off with her shrewish tongue. Youth was for learning, which meant they did doltish and dangerous things and still lived to talk about it. In this case, even to celebrate about it.

Lady Vincent had resorted in waspishly vowing the day long that, whatever had happened the night before, Carin and her maids would be disappointed. Men of the ton would not appear at a party thrown with a combination of maids and blue bloods.

Carin grinned. Lady Vincent had not counted upon the chivalry of Gerald's friends or perhaps their simple good natures. She could count ten of those kind gentlemen standing about the bowl of mead, with her maids interspersed.

She shook her head to clear it. Actually, it was the third

holiday bowl of mead. It appeared the men took their recipes for mead straight to heart, each having a secret and special one. The maids had quickly added suggestions, many having learned them from the households they had served. Therefore they were on the third concoction. Carin was amazed, for the men were indeed jolly, but only Lord Trevor seemed excessively affected. Carin herself had sipped from the first two offerings. It was more than enough. She had felt a warmth flash through her that had nothing to do with a hot poker placed in the concoction.

"When is his nibs coming home?" Hez asked, his chin on his hand as he sat slouched in his chair. Marie and the pups lay at his feet, for the moment well sated with stolen morsels. He had not taken kindly to the fact he was not permitted to test the drink. It made no difference that he was included with most of the maids. Lady Vincent had vowed she would not permit them to drink alcohol in their condition. She declared they were mercurial enough during these times, without more spirits. Heaven only knew what sort of tearful scenes might occur.

"He said he would return in time for the celebration," Carin said, sighing. Indeed, he had said that this morning.

She knew he had watched her closely during breakfast. She had been unable to meet his gaze. He had risen first from the table, his eyes intent and questioning. She had been only able to glance at him once; then she had looked away. She had felt a coward. He had bowed to the table at large and said he would not interrupt a busy day, but promised to return for the party.

"Then it's past time," Hez said with a frown.

"Yes." Carin nodded. Feeling very relaxed and quite brave, she frowned. He really should be here. She could look him in the eye far more easily at this moment.

"He won't come if he is wiser than the rest of us," Lady Vincent bit out from where she burrowed in a barrel-back chair.

"Still miffed, Mildred?" Bertha grinned. She waved her silver cup. "Go have some of that brew. Me, I like the first one." She shook her head. "Mighty potent Christmas drink. Warms the cockles of yer heart."

"Even better than your Blue Ruin?" Lady Vincent asked spitefully.

"It's a Christmas drink," Bertha laughed, her face flushed. She sprung up and shouted, "A toast!" The lords and maids at the table turned to her. "A toast to Christmas. To a warm place ter stay with a fire." The men nodded in polite approval. The maids cheered more heartily. "To brave, good souls who've come ter the aid of women." The men flushed happily as the maids cheered even more. Bertha then gazed at Carin. "To a dear, sweet child who gave an old lady love again when she thought there wasn't any left fer her." Bertha swiped at her eyes. The room had fallen solemnly silent.

"Blimey," Bertha hiccuped. "What's the matter with ye, lads and lasses? Why are ye staring? Ain't it time ter dance?" The men immediately fell back at that suggestion. Bertha, with one more sniff, raised her voice and belted out a bar song. She held forth her hand and waved it in clear demand of a partner.

"Hear, hear!" Lord Trevor cried. He stumbled over and clasped Bertha. They performed a quick whirl of a ridiculous nature. That appeared enough for the maids, however, if not for the men. The maids all drew partners, willy-nilly. Yet with the giggles and laughter, the shy lords with three variations of Christmas mead thrumming in their veins promptly joined in the spirit of the thing. They leapt to new choreographical heights. No doubt the complete lack of form or proper steps added to their sudden release of reserve.

Despite herself, Carin chortled. Dickey held Teresa out at arm's length, clearly from necessity, and steered her in a formal circle. Sarah and her lord cut such a vigorous jig about the table they made Carin's head spin. Hez had sprung up and, with a show of cleverness, had gained Sally's hand. The pups jumped and yapped about their feet as prostitute and street urchin lifted legs and skirts in a wild fling.

"Oh, for pity's sake," Lady Vincent cried, snatching up her cane and standing. The jumping room ceased a second. "Your timing is off, Bertha." She thwacked her cane sharply upon the floor in a stronger, faster beat. "This is how it goes!"

"Thank ye, Mildred," Bertha wheezed from Lord Trevor's arms. "Someone else sing."

Gerald, who had hung back, circled over to stand beside his grandmother. He cleared his throat and sang a merry verse, his voice a fine, strong tenor. Carin clapped her hands as the dancers resumed whatever twirl, sashay, kick, or jig they were performing. Her hands totally missed each other as she noticed Nelson and Meg join in this time with a modified version of a minuet.

"Faith," a deep voice murmured beside Carin. "What have you done now?"

Carin gasped and looked up. "Adrian!"

He stood beside her chair as if by magic. His lovely gray eyes were alight. "Yes, Carin?"

"You are here," Carin said. A wide smile crossed her face. "Aren't you?"

"Yes." Adrian nodded. His eyes turned questing. "Have I remained away long enough?"

Carin flushed. "I did not see you enter."

"No," Adrian said. He looked up and shook his head. "I doubt anyone did, even the three dancing in the foyer. It appears you are throwing a positive bacchanalia."

"A what?" Carin frowned. "They are only dancing."

Adrian lifted a brow. "Dancing? Is that what it is? It appears more of a tribal ritual—or what I hear the American savages do. That you even have these particular gentlemen capering about as they are is amazing."

"I did not do it," Carin said quickly. She flushed. "I believe the mead . . . meads did it."

"Meads?" Adrian asked. "No, I do not wish to know. Would you care to dance?"

"Yes," Carin breathed. She shot up like an arrow. Embarrassed at her eagerness, she turned her gaze to the company, unsure just which step Adrian intended to employ.

Adrian, smiling deeply, stepped forward and put his arms about her. Carin flushed. "A waltz?"

"I am sure the patronesses of Almack's will never know," Adrian murmured, pulling her very close indeed. "Though with our customary lack of luck, they will hear by tomorrow. But not tonight."

Carin grinned, gazing up at him happily. They did not really move. Nor did it matter Gerald had broken into another rousing ditty with no dignity. "No, not tonight."

"Am I forgiven for last night?" Adrian murmured.

Carin blinked. "I thought you said you couldn't apologize for it."

"I will," Adrian said with a sigh. "If that is what you wish. If that is how it must be."

Carin stared at him. "I—I . . ."

A shriek arose. Carin froze, as did everyone else. They looked quickly to the source. Teresa was doubled over, clutching her stomach. Her eyes were wide and frightened.

Dickey stared, his arms dropped at his side. "What? What did I do?"

"Nothing, you nincompoop," Lady Vincent said, stomping forward. "Someone already did it before you. Are you all right, child?"

"No?" Teresa whispered. She flushed a fiery red, looking down. "I think . . ."

"She's going ter have her baby. *Now!*" Bertha cracked.

"What?" Dickey shouted. He sprang four feet in the air.

"A baby!" Ferdie choked, toppling back. He would have fallen if Lizzy had not supported him.

"Gadzooks! What do we do?" Lord Trevor bounded toward Teresa, skidded to a halt, then bounded away. "What in blazes do we do?"

Carin blinked. If she thought the men had been active in dancing, they now hopped and leapt in a frenzy.

"We get her to her room," Bertha ordered.

"Good idea. Good idea." Dickey nodded. He swiftly bent and scooped Teresa up into his arms. She shrieked. "Zounds." Dickey's face turned purple and he swayed from fear and the unexpected weight. "Help!"

"God," Adrian murmured, stepping forward. He need not have. Five men had sprung to Dickey's—or Teresa's, according to how one considered the matter—aid. They crowded around, bolstering each other.

"Go! Go!" Lady Vincent barked, swinging her cane. She rapped Gerald in the stomach with it by mistake.

"We must have a doctor," Adrian ordered.

"I'll get him!" Gerald wheezed, his blue eyes bulging. He straightened up and sprinted toward the door.

"Me, too," a friend of his exclaimed, pursuing him.

"Me three," another lord called and barreled after them.

Bertha smirked. "That'll keep at least some of them busy. Come on girls. We have a baby ter deliver." She nodded to Lady Vincent. "Mildred, after you."

Carin sat on a chair in the foyer. Adrian, his chair pulled close, sat beside her. Her hand was nestled within his. She drew comfort and strength from that firm clasp as she watched in a daze as seven men paced up and down the foyer. They had removed to there from the parlor a while ago, Dickey having demanded it. There wasn't enough "track to run" in the parlor.

A few of the maids had joined them, while others were like Carin. They sat, waiting nervously. Sally sniffed from her corner of the room. Like almost all of the women, she had been denied entry into the room of delivery. Bertha and Lady Vincent had been sharp and very autocratic about whom they permitted to assist them. Meg and Sarah were the only two women honored. Nelson was the only man approved. Though not inside the sanctuary itself, he was in charge of gathering hot water and towels.

"Where is Gerald?" Adrian muttered. "Why hasn't he come with the confounded doctor?"

Carin squeezed his hand. "I am sure they will be here soon. It *is* two days before Christmas Eve. And Lady Vincent and Bertha are in there."

"Yes." Adrian nodded.

"I can't stand this here waiting," Hez said. "Did ye hear her shout like she did?" He grabbed on to Marie's broad neck, for she sat sentry beside him. The pups were nipping at the pacing lords' heels.

"I did," Adrian said curtly. "Do not expound upon it."

"No, guv," Hez said. "Do you think she's still shouting?"

"It is painful to have a baby," Carin admitted, unable to lie.

"You can say that again," Adrian said, his voice tense. "And there are five more in this house."

"Blimey," Hez gasped, his eyes horrified. He looked at Marie. "Did you have ter do that, Marie?" Marie gazed at him adoringly and barked. Hez swallowed, his voice gruff. "Yer a Trojan. And you had three of them at one time."

The front door burst open.

"Thank God," Adrian breathed, springing up.

An echo of male exclamations sounded as Gerald and his friends entered with a man carrying a black bag. They converged upon him in such force that Carin and the maids were pressed to even hear the conversation, no matter how close they surrounded the men.

"We searched all over for the doctor," Gerald said. "He wasn't at his residence. Couldn't find anyone."

"Then we had a notion," another said.

"Came out of the blue," Gerald said. "We were coming home and saw this house with all these carriages. Thought if there was a large party, they might have a doctor there. So we stopped. They had one."

The men shouted, "Huzzah." Carin bit her lip, though she did not murmur like the rest of the women. At this moment she feared accepting an unknown doctor. The men, however, were delighted, and they clapped each other upon the back proudly.

"Do hurry," Sally broke into the male celebration, her voice shrill. "My sister has been in labor for an hour!"

"Do not worry, miss," the recruited doctor said in a condescending tone. "If this is her first baby, it may very well take all night."

The exclamations of sheer horror rose to the vaulted ceiling. The doctor coolly ignored them and asked to be led to the lady. This time the women refused to be dismissed; they twittered around the doctor, leading him away with their own questions.

"All night?" Hez asked, dragging back to his chair.

"Gads," Dickey muttered, wiping sweat from his face. "Don't think I respected my mother enough."

Adrian growled and took Carin's hand, leading her

back to their chairs. When he sat, he put his arm about her. "It will be all right, I am sure."

Carin's eyes widened and she cast a covert glance about. No one appeared to notice his improper display, since everyone had resumed pacing. Sighing, she relaxed into the curve of Adrian's arm. If the others did not notice, what did it matter? But she enjoyed her position so much, guilt twinged her conscience. Poor Teresa was suffering the pains of child labor, and Carin was reveling in Adrian's arms.

After fifteen minutes passed, the doctor appeared from the back of the house with his black bag. He wore a dark, fierce expression. One so frightening, that Carin buried herself deeper in Adrian's arms.

"Doctor," Sally cried, springing up. She hurried over to him, wringing her hands. "How is she? How is my sister?"

"I am sorry," the doctor said. "There is nothing I can do."

The intake of frightened breath in the room must have surely devoured all the air allotted.

"Oh, God," Sally cried, falling to the ground. "Please, no. You must do something to help her. She cannot die."

The doctor sprung back, alarmed.

"Please," Sally sobbed, raising clasped hands toward the heavens. "Let her live. I promise I shall reform. I shall change my wicked ways."

"You do not understand," the doctor said once more. "There is nothing I can do."

"I will be a maid," Sally cried to the Almighty. "I will never be a prostitute again."

The doctor gurgled. "No. I cannot do anything because the old woman threw me out. She swore she smelt liquor on my breath and she'd not have it."

"What?" Sally asked from her knees.

"Lady Vincent," Adrian groaned. "Oh, Lord."

"I have never been so insulted," the doctor said, his forbidding expression erupting into open rage. He rattled his bag and delved into it. He drew out a pewter flask. "She threw this at me."

"No," Carin gasped in amazement. "It was Bertha!"

"She said she didn't need any bloody more," the doctor said. "She told me to take it, but if I had anything in my cock loft, I'd learn from her. Here, you may take it."

Sally flushed. Her gaze roved to the ceiling. She shook her head vehemently. "Er, no, thank you."

Adrian jumped up. He strode over to the doctor. "Please keep it, doctor. You do not know what a true gift you have received."

"Very well," the doctor said, though he still growled. "You will receive my bill on the morrow."

"Here now," Dickey objected. "You just can't leave us!"

"I will pay it." Adrian nodded quickly as the doctor pocketed the flask and steamed toward the door.

"Please, dear Lord," Sally cried again.

The men jumped back readily as the women all dashed over to her to murmur and reassure her.

Adrian, a musing look upon his face, walked back to Carin. He stood staring at her.

"Would you like to sit down?" Carin asked. She wanted to feel his arm about her once more. She wanted to lean into him and savor the moment, while she prayed for the next.

He gazed at her with an unreadable expression. "I said last night you could not win them all. Perhaps you can."

"No," Carin said, flushing. "I have nothing to do with this night. It is Teresa who went into labor. It is she who is having the baby, and that comes from God." Her own eyes widened. Even she, as strongly as she believed, was still surprised. "It was—"

"No. Do not say it," Adrian said, sitting down swiftly,

staring off into space. "I am having enough trouble as it is."

Carin shivered. She didn't mind being silent. She was herself attempting to assimilate it. This time she leaned over, shoring her shoulder up against Adrian's. He immediately put his arm about her. She sighed in satisfaction.

They sat there and time passed without definition of seconds or minutes. Everyone appeared buried in his own contemplation. Carin's thoughts led her to finally shake her head in bemusement. "Will wonders never cease?"

At that moment Nelson appeared. He walked solemnly forward. Though his demeanor was dignified, tears streamed down his face.

Carin slowly stood, her heart ramming hard against her chest.

A wail rose from Sally. "Lord, I promise!"

Nelson mercly stood gazing at them. He swallowed and bowed. "I am proud to announce that it is a girl. A fine, healthy girl! With a blooming strong mother." He beamed finally. "Or so it was reported."

"Wonders apparently don't cease," Adrian murmured, standing with a wide smile. Carin, in sheer exuberance, flung herself into his arms. He caught her up, almost cracking her ribs as he lifted her and swung her around in wild circles.

The sound of jubilation arose. The men clapped each other on the back shouting, "Jolly good," and "We did it, old man!" The women sufficed with bursting into tears and hugging each other.

Nelson bowed. "I shall leave you. The ladies are still wrapping matters up, I am told. But soon we can present our new addition."

"Who has a cigar?" Dickey shouted. "We need cigars."

"I do!" Sally shouted back. For one moment the room fell silent. She smiled, tears streaming down her face.

"You all smoke them proper like. I won't be entertaining any gentlemen anymore. I'm a sister and an aunt. And I promised!"

She rushed away amongst shouts and applause.

"Oh, Adrian, isn't it marvelous?" Carin breathed, well wrapped in his arms.

"Yes," Adrian murmured. His head lowered toward hers. Carin, feeling all the best of life streaming through her, lifted her lips to his. They just barely touched.

A small body knocked against them, disturbing the budding kiss. Small arms wrapped around them.

"I am just so happy!" Hez said, sniffing.

"Yes, Hez," Adrian muttered.

"Yes, dear," Carin said, putting her arm about him too. "Isn't it wonderful?"

"I don't want ter go away," Hez sobbed. "I don't."

"You might not have to," Adrian gritted. "If you will just lay off."

"What?" Carin asked, wide-eyed.

"What?" Hez asked, his small face twisting. His eyes suddenly widened and he grinned. He released them, stepping back. A wink lowered his left lid. "Yes, guv. You two discuss it, why don't you? Discuss it well."

Carin swore Adrian returned that wink, but he presented a solemn face to her. "Yes?"

"You won't send him to boarding school?" Carin asked.

"I don't know," Adrian said, appearing confused. "But at this moment, I question the idea."

Carin laughed. She understood. At this moment the best of life was flowing around them. "I understand."

"No, Carin, you don't." Adrian smiled wryly. "You are supposed to convince me."

"I have thought," Carin said, blushing, "you might be right also."

"Do not confuse me. We can discuss it later," Adrian murmured. Once again he lowered his head. Once again

Carin lifted her lips in anticipation. Once again they just barely touched Adrian's.

"Do you want a cigar, my lord?" Sally's voice asked.

Carin blinked as Adrian lifted his head with a groan. He looked at the maid, who held up a quality cigar.

"No," Adrian gritted. "I don't need a cigar. Give mine to Gerald!"

"Yes, milord," Sally said. She dipped a proper curtsy and moved away.

"Confound it," Adrian muttered. He looked at Carin. "Just kiss me. And quickly."

Carin giggled. It did not seem an outrageous suggestion. It seemed so very right on this wondrous night. She leaned up, pursing her lips. Adrian lowered his head.

"Here they come," Gerald shouted.

"Blast!" Adrian exclaimed.

"What?" Carin gasped, looking over quickly.

"But . . . but . . ." Dickey gurgled. He dropped the cigar he was lighting.

Carin's eyes widened as she saw what confused him. Nelson escorted both Bertha, who held a bundle, and Lady Vincent, who held another bundle in one arm while she employed her cane with the other.

Nelson smiled and bowed to a gaping assembly. "My previous announcement was mistaken. Or doubled, might I say. May I present young Christian and young Noel."

Everyone merely stared the more.

"Marie Antoinette," Hez said into the silence, "she came close to you, but ye still topped her. She had two, but you had three."

"Not so," Gerald hooted. "These two are Christmas babies and that balances it out."

"They were off by only two days." Bertha grinned. She cast a clear, but teary gaze to Carin and Adrian. "Maybe next year, I can be delivering someone's baby on Christmas."

"Good God," Adrian muttered, springing back.

Carin froze.

"Blast, if this ain't the best party I've ever been to," Dickey cried. "We are uncles or something, ain't we?"

The men roared their approval and rushed up to Lady Vincent and Bertha, with the maids close behind.

"Keep your distance," Lady Vincent cried, holding Christian close.

"Yes, ye great loobies," Bertha said. "Ye can peek and nothing more. Ye won't be breathing any of those fumes on our little ones."

Carin remained standing, Bertha's comment burning in her heart. She didn't want a peek at the babies. She didn't want to see what she could never have. The best of life flowed around her. The very life she had vowed to her mother never to have. If there were Christmas babies, they would never be hers.

Chapter Eleven

Eleven Pipers

Adrian walked down Bond Street. He kept an eagle eye out in case any of his friends might be passing. Though he did not see anyone he knew, he still felt as if every pedestrian upon the street was looking at him. Looking at him and knowing.

He'd had very little sleep last night. Gerald and his friends had not left until the wee hours, all remaining to relive the stressful moments they had shared and to muse in the wonder of it all. That alone destroyed any sleeping hours remaining. For Adrian relived the moments before Bertha and Lady Vincent arrived with the Christmas babies and the moments after, when Bertha had looked at Adrian and Carin and openly demanded a baby from them. He assumed she had expected for marriage to be included.

Then those moments had grown worse. Adrian knew he had sprung back from Carin. Yet her frozen reaction was graver. She had not even looked at the babies. Neither had she said good-bye or good night to anyone. She had merely excused herself and retired.

Adrian stopped in front of a store window, not even seeing what was before him. The emotions welling within him were wild. Hurt, desire, fear. All linked with confusion. One more emotion whirled with the rest—one he refused to name. One he knew he didn't believe in.

"It's bad enough that I am doing this," Adrian murmured. Once again he looked hastily about. His gaze met that of a little girl passing by with her nanny. She knew! She knew he was buying Christmas gifts. Adrian Hazard, the marquise de Chambert, was out wandering the bedecked streets like those other pitiful fools he had scoffed at, out wandering and wondering over what gifts to buy. And what concerned him more was that, on this day before Christmas Eve, most of the other pitiful fools about were of his gender.

His jaw clenching, he focused upon the shopwindow. Then he cursed as the first thing to meet his gaze was a glittering array of rings. He redirected his gaze. Buying a ring was out of the question. However, this store offered more. He would enter and throw himself on the mercy of any clerk who could tell him what to buy a lady.

Carin strolled along the crowded street with Lizzy as her maid. It was the same street she had strolled along before. The street where they had found Marie and her court, the street where stood the infamous jewelry shop that had led Hez to his trespasses. Yet this day, the day before Christmas Eve, it positively bustled, and the feeling of Christmas permeated the air. It lifted Carin's spirits, and despite Lizzy's exasperated warnings, she nodded and offered Christmas greetings to the other pedestrians.

Their coachman, she knew, followed behind, searching, looking for another place to halt. Already the coach was filled with gifts and ornaments for the tree. They would decorate the tree tomorrow eve, then light the candles and sing carols. In truth, with everything that had happened, Carin had forgotten Adrian would not possess ornaments for a tree, let alone candles. When she returned home, they would apply themselves to stringing popcorn chains. Hez would enjoy that.

Now, however, she must find one last gift. Adrian's. For a moment, her spirit dimmed. She forced the dark pall away from her heart. It was Christmas. She was and would be like Meg. She would love and care for the things she did have. There was no use in wanting the things she couldn't have.

Her mother had begged Carin never to marry and Carin had promised not to. The memory flooded back. She remembered the love and fear in her mother's eyes. She remembered the peace that had entered those eyes when she had given her mother her word. It was a memory she had blocked all this time. Yet today it came back to her. Her heart tightened. In truth, it was a memory that had come back to her last night when she had gone to sleep, as if her mother had come to confront those longings that Bertha's pointed words had triggered. "I love you, Mother."

"What?" Lizzy asked, frowning.

Carin started. She had not realized she had spoken. "Nothing."

She drew in a deep breath. It was Christmas and she must not forget the blessings she had been given. She saw a door. She did not even look at the shop itself. "Let us go in here."

"Yes, miss," Lizzy said with a shrug.

It appeared the store they entered sold antiques. A wild assortment of items hung from the walls, rested upon scarred furniture, and stood alone in corners. The sheer quantity of items crowded into the space was overpowering. What little space was left at the moment was taken up by one small clerk and eleven large, burly men.

"We'll find nothing good here," Lizzy whispered. Her gaze was scandalized.

"Why?" Carin asked, though she could not help but study the eleven men herself. They wore bright plaid skirts, so their broad legs were bare from the knees down. Carin flushed. No, they had another name now that she considered it. Kilts were what they were—Scottish kilts. Carin bit her lip as she noticed the men also shouldered bagpipes.

"Here, lass. It would be a sure fine bargain you'd be making. Shawn McKenzie does nay offer up his pipes lightly." The intensity of his brilliant blue eyes and the shake of his grayish red mane of hair caused one to readily agree.

"I am sorry, sir," the little clerk said, her cheeks blanching. "This is an antique store, not a pawn shop."

"Is it now? You fooled me there, lass." Shawn McKenzie frowned. He and his men peered about with due seriousness. He winked. "Then I'll be offering you an antique, I will. These braw pipes have been in my family for generations." He rolled his eyes. "Ah, me, the great battles they have seen, wailing as my ancestors went to fight. We are great fighters don't you know, lass?"

"Were you?" the little clerk asked. She cringed back.

"Don't frighten her, Shawn," the man beside him whispered.

"Me? I'm the first peace-loving McKenzie," Shawn said quickly. "Fergus here will tell you."

"He is, lass." Fergus nodded. The rest of the men added hearty ayes.

"We must leave," Lizzy hissed.

"No," Carin murmured. She noted that the men then looked to her with speculative gazes. She quickly moved toward a table, pretending interest in the array of items upon it.

"Peace loving I am," Shawn boomed. "But if you don't take these pipes, lass, my men won't be having gifts for their sweet lasses or their babes."

Carin's heart wrenched. She tried to focus. Then she did. Amongst the tarnished pewter candlesticks and cracked china, a large music box rested. A delicately carved Christmas tree rose from the center of the box. Three dancing couples surrounded the tree. Carin reached out and wound the key. The haunting melody of "Greensleeves" played forth. The dancers whirled, slowly revolving around the tree and twirling.

"How lovely." Carin smiled. Here was Adrian's gift.

"Begorra. Look at that, lads," a deep voice exclaimed from behind.

Carin spun. Shawn McKenzie towered over her. He grinned at her even as Lizzy waved frantically and shook her head. "That's a fine box, ain't it?"

"Yes," Carin breathed in excitement. "It is."

"Would you like it, miss?" the clerk called out eagerly. Then the clerk circled around Shawn. She clearly wished to ignore him. "It is a fine box. Very old."

"My pipes are old," Shawn offered up just as quickly. The men behind him laughed.

"You finally admit to it then, Shawn," one called.

Shawn frowned, waving a hand at them. The motion coincided with Lizzy's frantic signals. "Don't you be speaking like that in front of the wee colleen."

Carin looked down for a moment. She feared she must disappoint him. "I am sorry, but I wish to purchase the music box."

"Don't fash yourself," Shawn said. He grinned. "Not many a body can play the pipes right. You can't give them as a gift to just anyone."

"Right this way, miss," the clerk said, dashing to pick up the music box.

"Thank you," Carin said and followed the clerk to the counter. Feeling all eyes upon her, Carin paid for her purchase. Yet she found she could not close her reticule. She spun. Shawn and his men were standing about, pretending to look at the merchandise. Carin drew in her breath. "I would like to buy your bagpipes after all, sir."

"What?" Lizzy squeaked.

Shawn's bushy brows rose. "Would you? And who would you be buying them for, lass?"

"Yes, who?" Lizzy asked, eyes narrowed.

"I do not know yet," Carin confessed.

Shawn laughed. He shook his head. "Nay, my sweet darling. It is kind of you, but Shawn McKenzie and his band won't take charity."

"You are a band?" Carin asked with interest.

"Aye, the best pipers in the land," Shawn said. His eyes twinkled. "The mighty Duchess of Rutledge will be regretting it tomorrow when she doesn't hear our bagpipes a-calling."

"The Duchess of Rutledge?" Carin asked.

"Aye." Shawn nodded. "She commissioned us to play for her tomorrow night at her grand ball."

"Then she told us nay," Fergus growled.

Shawn's voice rose to a falsetto and came just shy of an English brogue. " 'I have been informed by Lady Winston—my bosom bow, don't you know—that Scottish pipers are no longer the fashion. They are outré. It is the Pandian pipes I must have. And harps during the dinner removes. I do not require your services.' "

"Oh, dear," Carin sighed. "How dreadful."

"Here you are, miss," the clerk said, shoving a music box wrapped in brown paper secured by twine toward her.

"Thank you." Lizzy nodded, grabbing the package. "Now, Miss Carin, we must go."

Carin suddenly had a vision. She had never heard Scottish bagpipes before. They would not be outré to her. It would be a special surprise for the household, too. "How would you like to play for us tomorrow?" she asked eagerly. The pieces all fell into place. "We will pay you what the duchess offered. Only it will not be as grand. It will be a private gathering."

"Ah, lass," Shawn said, shaking his head, "we need no charity."

"No," Carin said firmly. "You will play for the marquise de Chambert."

Shawn's eyes glowed. "If that be the truth, then my band and I would be pleased."

"Yes," Carin said eagerly, turning to walk out of the store. Lizzy, sighing, followed. So did the band of eleven Scottish pipers.

"There is our coach," Carin exclaimed, seeing it waiting across the street. Her mind churned as she walked toward it. "It will be famous. And I am sure we can pay you in advance."

"Can you, lass?" Shawn puffed, trailing behind.

"Oh, yes." Carin nodded. Shawn did not need to sell his pipes. Carin and the family would have a special Christmas celebration. It could not have been more perfect.

She stepped from the curb to cross the street.

"Lass!" Shawn McKenzie shouted.

"What?" Carin cried as the large man bolted directly at her.

Adrian entered the town house, exhausted. Shopping for Christmas gifts wrung a man out to his last drop of blood. He was still uncertain of his purchases. He swore a wartime decision to attack had come easier than this day's decisions of what to purchase. Carin's gift had been the most taxing. Had he been an idiot? What had possessed him to buy it for her? All things considered, he didn't know.

The sound of laughter drifted to him. It came from the parlor doors. Adrian frowned. He looked around and sighed. He had grown accustomed to Nelson's absence at his post and even that of Gaskins. Yet now there was no one at all present for him to interrogate.

Shaking his head he walked toward the parlor doors. He opened them and stepped into the room. He halted, frowning as he took in the scene. The Christmas tree, which had been lying outside, was now set upright in the corner, its limbs bare. The three pups gambled beneath it, gnawing on the lower branches. Marie Antoinette sat, watching with unmotherly concern.

Carin rested upon the settee, actually sitting with her legs outstretched upon it. Eleven men in kilts—their legs bare to the public, and the ladies present—populated the room. One large giant leaned over the back of the settee, grinning down at Carin. Lady Vincent, Meg, Bertha, and Hez sat around in chairs, smiling and approving the scene.

It took only a moment for Adrian to observe it all. Though for the notice he received, he could have whiled away an hour.

"A sweet darling lass," the behemoth leaning over the couch murmured. "You—"

Adrian did not wait a moment more. He strode directly into the conclave of bare-legged foreigners and traitorous family—family for whom he had exhausted himself in obtaining the perfect gifts. "Good afternoon."

"Adrian!" Carin exclaimed, looking up at him with a brilliant welcoming smile.

Adrian stiffened, his muscles coiling with a hair-trigger tension. A cut ran across her forehead, her hair unable to hide it.

"What happened? What happened this time?" he gritted out.

"Here, man," the Scottish behemoth boomed, straightening to a height that matched Adrian's. "Go softly with the wee colleen. The poor darling has had a day, she has."

"Poor darling?" Adrian growled and glared at the Scotsman. Adrian had just now begun to openly call her Carin and the Scotsman was calling her darling already. "She is no poor darling. She brings it on herself."

"I said, here now," the Scotsman roared and strode around the settee, standing between Adrian and Carin. A low rumble came from the other men. "Don't you be barking at her."

"Shawn." Bertha rose to walk over to him. She placed a hand upon his arm. Her eyes were bright and she winked, "This here is m'lord. We've talked of him."

The man looked at Adrian and guffawed. His large hand shot out and rubbed Adrian upon the arm. Adrian's fists clenched. "Would you look at me, lad? I'm old enough to be her Da. Sweet Mary, I might be old enough to be yours."

Adrian flushed. The man's blue eyes were brilliant upon his, but now up close, he saw the lines splaying from his eyes. He saw the gray in the man's red hair was from age. Contrarily, it angered Adrian the more. "Just how did she save you?"

"What?" Shawn asked, his tufted brows snapping down.

"No, Adrian," Carin's voice drifted from the couch. "He saved me!"

"How did she save you?" Adrian repeated, eyes narrowed. "Are you homeless? Did you steal something? Was someone going to kill you?"

Shawn's eyes narrowed. "Ye are a banty rooster, aren't you, lad?"

"He called his nibs a banty rooster," Hez exclaimed with awe.

"Shawn," Bertha persisted. "I think we ought ter clear out now."

Shawn tore his eyes from Adrian and looked at Bertha.

He clapped his large hand over hers. "You're right, darling. I'm a peace-loving man."

Carin swallowed hard, watching Adrian pace back and forth in front of her like a caged tiger. If her foot were not hurt, she might stand up and dash after everyone else. Not even the dogs had remained to comfort her.

"I am sorry, Adrian," Carin said. "But Shawn is here because he brought me home. I wasn't looking where I was going and I stepped in front of a carriage. He pushed me aside before—" The way Adrian stopped and glared at her caused her to choose her words more cautiously. "Nobody was hurt. I twisted my ankle very slightly and received this cut on the forehead. That is all."

"That is all?" Adrian's body seemed to shake. He spun away and resumed his pacing. "You need a keeper."

"I beg your pardon?" Carin whispered.

He halted and turned back. Fear traced through his eyes. Then they hardened and his lips tightened into an uncompromising line. "That is it. You need a keeper."

"I do not think—"

"Marry me," Adrian said.

Carin halted. Her eyes widened. "What?"

"We need to marry," Adrian said, his tone brisk. "That is the only answer."

Carin stared at him. He spoke in the cold, reasonable manner she remembered well. It was the way he spoke about Christmas and love being drivel. She shivered. His tone was so reasonable that it unreasonably sliced like a knife through her. "No, that is not the answer."

His eyes darkened, but he did not move. "It is, Carin. You try and save everyone, but who will save you?"

"I do not need saving," Carin murmured.

"Don't you?" Adrian asked lowly. It seemed a taunt to Carin. "You collect people as others do wine or snuffboxes or those ugly Sevres shepherdesses. You cannot resist. It hurts you not to care. Not to help. If we do not marry, what will you do?"

"What do you mean?" Carin asked. She lifted her chin. "Father will return, I am sure."

"Your father!" Adrian's voice rose in wild anger. "Do not be an innocent. He left you here with me because he was all to pieces."

"What?" Carin gasped.

A pulse leapt along Adrian's jaw. He looked away. "Your father is not the type to look after anyone. He did not look after your mother. He did not look after you. He cannot even look after himself."

Carin attempted to keep her chin up, but it sank. "I will not marry you."

Adrian's eyes flared. "Listen to reason, for God's sake. You must have someone to take care of you. And"—he sighed—"we cannot continue like this."

"I see," Carin murmured. Fear rose within her. She felt cornered. Lost.

"Marry me, Carin," Adrian said again. Carin could only stare at him, knowing emotions of vulnerability must show in her eyes. Adrian turned his gaze from her. "It is the only answer. I will take care of you. I will take care of Bertha and Hez and baby Joy. And everyone else." Finally his gaze turned back. It burned with pride and determination. "I am the only man who will offer you that, Carin."

"The only man," Carin murmured. His confidence showed in his eyes.

Carin's rebellion flared. *Man!* Her mother had warned her. Her dying eyes with their fear and desperation supplanted Adrian's gaze even as Carin heard his voice. "Carin, please."

She shook her head blindly. "No. Never! I will never marry."

"Will you listen to me?" Adrian cried.

For a moment Carin's sight cleared. The look in Adrian's eye held its own desperation, and something more: a fire in their black depths. She choked, "No." She swung her legs from the settee to the floor. She attempted to rise. Pain shot through her leg. Pride demanded that she sit back down. She had nothing else left, but she would not fall to the ground in front of Adrian. Not now. "Please leave."

"Are you all right?" Adrian asked, rushing toward her.

Carin looked up, the anger of a wounded animal glittering in her gaze. Adrian halted in his tracks. "Do not come near me. I understand this is your house. I understand everything. But please leave. Leave me."

The color drained from Adrian's face. His gray eyes were as dark as coal. "Very well."

He strode from the room. Carin blinked. She would not cry. She would not cry.

Carin sat upon her bed. She hung her head. Now, late at night, with only the moon shining in to watch, she cried. She cried because she knew the answer. It was not marriage. Her mother had warned her men would cause misery. The pain she had felt bespoke the truth. At least it had finally subsided. Only because the sheer power of it had numbed and cauterized its own wound.

She rose and looked at her bed. On it were the gifts she had bought that morning. The ornaments for the tree were there. An envelope lay amongst it all. The answer.

She turned. Picking up a satchel she tread silently toward the door. The gentlest smile touched her lips. There was a kindness, a memory to take with her. Hez surely must have slipped from the house many evenings before.

He had slipped out because of five golden rings. He had slipped out because he loved.

The smile slipped. She would slip out as well, because she loved.

Chapter Twelve

Twelve Drummers Drumming

Adrian sat, watching from his chair. With all the many hands assisting, he never doubted the Christmas tree would be decorated within minutes. Eleven Scottish pipers, Hez, Meg, and Nelson were certainly enough of a crew. At least the maids were not present. They had chosen to have their own Christmas celebration in the servants' hall. At least, Adrian chose to believe that, since none of the maids would either speak or attend him this Christmas Eve day.

"No, no," Lady Vincent said from her vantage of a cozy chair. "Fergus, that is your name, is it not?"

"Jamie, milady," Jamie said, a glass ball dangling between his large fingers.

"Do not place that ornament there," Lady Vincent ordered. "It cannot be seen. Move it to the right five inches."

"Shawn," Bertha said as she too rested in a chair, rocking baby Joy. "Are ye tall enough ter put another candle on that branch there? It's bare as a . . . er . . . it's bare."

Then again it might take all night. Adrian clenched his teeth. He wasn't sure he could tolerate it. The day had been interminable as it was.

Hez sighed loudly, putting his nimble fingers to work stringing a popcorn chain. Richelieu was devouring the other end, which lay behind Hez on the floor. Yes, it might take all night if the two kept pace with each other as they were. Adrian refrained from comment.

"I wish you'd let me go to Miss Carin, yer nibs."

"No," Adrian barked.

"But she is all alone and on Christmas." Hez swallowed hard.

"She has her relatives," Adrian said tightly. He envisioned again the words in the note she had left.

I am returning to my relatives. Please do not anyone follow. Meg, take care of Hez, Bertha, and baby Joy. I know you will.

Adrian's fingers clenched. It was obvious that she didn't think he would take care of them.

I hope to be able to send for you all soon.

Adrian grinned evilly. That was a slim chance, better known as when hell froze over. "It was her decision."

"Was it, now?" Bertha asked.

"Yes," Adrian said, glaring at Bertha. He cringed to his very soul. It was embarrassing enough to have proposed, but to have everyone know he had been rejected was excruciating.

Of course, Carin had merely written:

My lord, I thank you for what you have done for me. Forgive me, but you were right. Things cannot continue like this.

It was the older women in the household who had immediately accused him of proposing and muffing it. He had unwisely attempted to defend himself as he did now. "I offered to take care of her."

"Just what a young girl afraid of marriage wants ter hear," Bertha snorted.

"If you did not say you loved her," Lady Vincent said sternly, "it was not a proposal."

"Sure, you darling ladies might give the lad a rest," Shawn said. For a man whom Adrian had at first detested, Shawn was becoming a strong support. "He knows the lass will be coming back to him. Don't you, lad? And she'll be as grateful as a lassie ought to be." He wagged a finger to Bertha. "And so should you be, my darling. It's out of his kindness that you are here."

"His kindness, my bloody—" Bertha began. Shawn offered her a broad wink. Bertha, the intrepid, subsided. She cracked an even broader smile.

Adrian blinked. Before he could say a word, however, Shawn clapped his hands together. "Now, boys, we were hired to play for this private party. Let's show them a fine time."

That was all he needed to say. Eleven Scotsmen dropped their decorations and their bare legs flashed as they found their bagpipes and lined up before the company. "It'll be 'Greensleeves,' my boys"—Shawn grinned and nodded to Adrian—"on the sad chance you don't open the wee colleen's gift to you." Adrian frowned as Shawn and his band actually struck up "Greensleeves," a rather odd choice for the bagpipes.

Hez scurried to under the tree and pulled out a box. He presented it to Adrian. "Open it, guv. *They* know what's in it and we don't. That ain't right, nohow."

Adrian, despite attempting to appear indifferent, agreed with Hez. He tore open the wrapping paper. He lifted a music box up. He wound the key. Though he could not hear the box play itself, he heard the bagpipes moaning "Greensleeves" as tiny dancers on the box twirled around a Christmas tree. *At last my love you do me wrong . . .*

Adrian looked up. All eyes were upon him. Just what the purpose of giving a music box to a man was eluded him. However, the ladies appeared to be nodding and weeping. Shawn's eyes twinkled as he blew into his bagpipes.

Then Adrian shook his head as something even stranger occurred. He thought he heard drums. It was quite impossible, but he heard them as a low rumble beneath the bagpipes. It must have been a lingering memory of the war coming forth to haunt him.

Shawn's face twisted. He drew back from his bagpipes, lifting a staying hand to his men. They ceased playing.

"Damn!" Adrian shot from his chair. The drums still drummed, playing the processional employed for royal occasions.

"It canna' be," Shawn murmured, his blue eyes wide. "I hear drums."

Hez dashed to the window. His jaw dropped. "Gore, you have ter see this."

Everyone rushed to crowd around the window.

Adrian did not waste his time. He strode from the parlor through the foyer and opened the front door. He halted immediately, his own jaw dropping.

Two carriages stood upon the street. Outriders and footmen accompanied each. More astounding was the parade of drummers behind the coaches. They stood two by two, marching in place and drumming. Even through the falling snow, Adrian counted twelve in all. They wore the bright red and black of Buckingham Palace's formal guards. They should have been in front of Buckingham, not here on the streets in front of his house.

"Is it the queen, guv?" Hez murmured. He had slipped up on Adrian. Indeed, the entire party had. Doors from across the square were opening as well and people were peering out.

"I don't know," Adrian said.

One carriage door opened and a man stepped out. He too wore brilliant red. He waved. "Adrian, my boy! How are you? Merry Christmas!"

"Blimey," Hez gasped as the man bolted toward them. "Is that St. Nicholas?"

"How is my little Carinna?" The man grinned as he came to a panting halt before them. "I have someone for her to meet."

"Bejesus," Hez squeaked. "St. Nicholas is here and he wants Carin to meet the queen. Yer in Dutch now, guv."

"It's a shame. I wanted to surprise my little puss," Lord Worthington said, shaking his head as he sat upon the settee. Hez and the dogs sat at his feet. The ladies had commandeered all of the other available chairs. Adrian, Shawn, and the band were forced to stand. The drum corps was not present, having been sent to enjoy Christmas Eve with the maids, although there had been one fractious moment when the English drummers and the Scottish pipers had mingled.

"Don't worry, Muffin," the new Lady Worthington said beside him. She was a buxom woman, nearly bursting from the red satin dress she wore—a red satin that matched Lord Worthington's stunning jacket. She possessed a harsh American accent, one Adrian found difficult to understand. His eyes widened as she reached over and squeezed her husband's knee. "We'll just keep those drummers until she can see them herself."

"Blimey," Hez breathed.

Lord Worthington shook his head once more. "I don't know. We can only borrow them so long, Molly."

"Pooh. I have the green." Molly waved. "They'll stay.

My money's just as good as your royalty's. Besides, I know how much you wanted to surprise your little girl. So did I."

"It was Molly's idea, you know?" Lord Worthington said, his tone proud.

"I was trying to think what kind of show we could give little Carinna for Christmas." Molly nodded to the group. "I figure, if you can't put on a show for the ones you love, what is life for?" She grinned wide. "Then I saw those guards outside that great palace. I knew then and there I wanted them." She grinned even more. "I like red, you know? When I heard they could play the drums, that was a fine and firm handshake to the deal for me."

"Indeed," Adrian murmured.

"You must be rich," Hez said in awe.

"I am." Molly grinned. "Filthy rich."

"Molly is an actress," Lord Worthington said, coughing.

"I would never have guessed," Adrian said.

"I also had two rich husbands," Molly said with a deep laugh. "That didn't hurt. Buried both, sad to say. But I've got Muffin here now." She beamed. "And he's made me a lady."

"Impossible," Lady Vincent muttered from her chair.

"Ain't marriage grand?" Molly asked.

"Miss Carin doesn't think so," Hez said, throwing an accusing look at Adrian.

"So where is my little puss?" Lord Worthington asked, frowning.

"Why don't you go get those gifts we brought from the carriage?" Molly said. She leaned her full chest into him and kissed him.

"Yes, sweetheart." Lord Worthington nodded. He sprang up and hastened to do her bidding.

"He still doesn't know he loves me. He thinks he married me for my money," Molly said, gazing after him with a fond eye. Only then she turned a sharp look upon them all. "Now tell me, before Muffin comes back, where is Carinna?"

"She went back to her relatives," Hez sighed.

"Adrian proposed to Carin and muffed it," Bertha said, nodding. "He told her he'd take care of her 'cause nobody else would."

Molly looked at Adrian. Her eyes brightened in challenge. "Then I reckon I'm here to upstage you, my lord. Little Carinna doesn't have to have anybody take care of her. Not with me around. I've always wanted a daughter. And Muffin is looking forward to finally having her too."

"Her name is Carin," Adrian bit out. "And she is no longer little."

"She's seventeen." Molly nodded. "Poor Muffin forgets. He has to for his own sake. If he keeps thinking she's a child, he doesn't have to admit he never was there when she grew up."

"Ye've got a head on you, don't you?" Bertha asked.

Molly winked. "We've got to think for them. That's not their strong point."

"I beg your pardon?" Adrian exclaimed, even as Shawn guffawed and his men muttered.

"Don't bust your stays," Molly laughed. "You men have plenty of other strong points to suit me right well. And if little Carinna ran off from you, you must have your strong points to her, too."

"She left me," Adrian said, anger and hurt welling up within him.

"Do you love her?" Molly asked baldly.

"I . . . I . . ."

"If you can't say it," Molly snorted and waved a dismissing hand, "then I've got a daughter for me to raise. It'll tickle me pink, it will."

"I . . . I . . ." Adrian tried again.

"I never met the other Lady Worthington," Molly said

to Bertha in a confidential tone. "But if she wasn't already dead, I'd kill her. What she's done to poor Muffin will take me an entire year to change. He's got a good heart, but he's afraid to love."

"Is he now?" Bertha chuckled. "I know some that are like that."

"I'm sure poor Carinna is the same." Molly nodded. "With a coldhearted bitch for a mother you can't expect much."

"I . . ." Adrian choked out.

"No, no," Bertha said. "Some may complain, but Carin's got the kindest, biggest heart a girl could have. She took us all in—me, Hez, baby Joy here, the dogs. What will ye do about that?"

"God love you," Molly hooted. "I plan to build a mansion as large as Buckingham Palace. You don't think I want to rattle around in it with just me and Muffin, do you? I like company. It's the only thing I miss from treading the boards. There was always plenty of company."

"I love her," Adrian finally shouted.

"What?" Lord Worthington asked, entering with his shoulders shrouded in snow. He carried a stack of gifts. Footmen trailed behind him with more.

"I said I love her," Adrian repeated. He glared at Lord Worthington. "I love your little Carinna and I am going to marry her."

"Here now," Lord Worthington said, his face darkening. "I won't have it."

"I love her," Adrian said again. It felt wonderful. A shocking release of the spirit that suddenly filled him with strength. "I love her and she's going to marry me." He glared at Bertha and Hez. "And none of you are leaving for some bloody mansion. Family is family."

"You are not going to marry Carinna," Lord Worthington objected.

"We will see," Adrian said, walking toward the door.

"Where are you going?" Worthington asked.

"To tell Carin I love her," Adrian retorted. "And to bring her back. Don't light those blasted candles on the tree until we return."

"No, you won't," Lord Worthington cried. He then smiled. "It's starting to snow heavily out there. You can't travel because it's so heavy."

"It doesn't matter," Adrian said. "I am going."

"Sit down, Muffin," Molly said in a soothing tone.

Adrian reached the parlor door when Hez called out, "Do ye have a ring fer her, guv?"

"No, blast it," Adrian murmured, halting in his tracks. "I don't."

Hez jumped up and ran to the tree. He snatched up a brightly wrapped package and dashed over to him. "Give her this one."

"Thank you," Adrian said. He thought a moment. Striding over, he picked up his own gift to Carin. "And she can open mine as well."

"What is it?" Bertha called as he strode back to the door.

Adrian grinned. "It is a fur muff."

"A fur muff?" Bertha's face fell. "Queer gift to give her. What does Carin want with a fur muff?"

Adrian began to retort. Then a worse thought struck him. "What are the directions to your country estate, Worthington?"

"You ask me that?" Lord Worthington howled. "Is that where she is?"

"His coachman ought to know." Molly grinned. "First coach in front, my lord. Now sit down, Muffin."

Carin sat quietly in front of the dying fire in the parlor. She stared into the fading flames. The only recognition and celebration of Christmas her relatives had eked out of themselves was to attend a Christmas service at church. They had then retired at their usual time of nine o'clock. Even that had not been permitted to be changed in honor of Christmas.

Carin rose and ambled listlessly around the parlor. The house no longer felt like her home. It was barren of any decorations. It was barren of the spirit of Christmas. Carin halted. It was barren of any spirit.

Carin picked up the lone candle and slowly, as if searching, walked through the darkened house. Memories came to her. Good times and bad times—times of laughter and times of tears. They seemed so very distant however. As if they had already gone cold.

She stopped. They indeed had gone cold compared to the life she had experienced this past month. Cold compared to the new memories of Hez and Bertha . . . and Adrian.

She shivered, for she finally felt a spirit in the house. Her mother's. Carin could see her mother now in her mind's eye. See as her mother went about her daily life. A good woman, but a woman who had given up on warmth and laughter. A woman who had given up on love.

Tears slipped down Carin's face. She didn't want to be the next woman to live her life out in this house without warmth or laughter.

"I am sorry, Mother," Carin whispered. "I cannot keep my promise. I love Adrian."

Carin waited. For what, she wasn't certain. Perhaps for some whirling wind or for things to start flying—some sign of anger and outrage from her departed mother.

Silence reigned. The wind that came was within Carin's soul. It was the whirling joy of knowing she loved a man— loved him so much that she would gladly live her days out with him. There surely would be heartache, but there would be love.

Carin laughed through her tears. Indeed, she had made a promise to her mother. Made a promise that had been unworthy, for it had denied the possibility of life and love.

She peeked up into the dark rafters. She made a new promise—the one she should have before—and to the right person this time. "Lord, I promise to love . . . and never to give up on it, no matter what happens."

She drew up her skirts and ran toward the stairs. She didn't belong here in this house. She knew where and with whom she belonged. She had missed Christmas Eve with him, but she would not miss Christmas Day.

Adrian burrowed beneath the coach blankets. The bricks at his feet were already cold. He ignored the cold. He was going to tell Carin he loved her and he would do so this Christmas Eve, the night she so dearly loved. It might be unworthy, but he knew Carin's fears and what he must overcome to coax her into marriage. If he could ride on the coattails of the special quality of the night, he would.

"Sorry about that," Adrian murmured. Then he shook his head, wincing. He didn't even care to think why he had said that.

Suddenly the coach jerked to a halt. Adrian sat a moment, hearing the coachman shout and crack the whip. When the coach still did not start up, he stifled his curses and opened the door. As he stepped from the coach, snow blasted him. He peered through the snow. He saw the coachman climbing down from the box. "What is the matter?"

"I don't know," the coachman said, his voice confused. "The horses just stopped."

"What?" Adrian asked. "What do you mean?"

"I only slowed to turn off this road," the coachman said. "And the horses stopped. They won't go."

Adrian strode up to the lead horse. "What's the matter, old fellow?" He bent down, checking the horse's hooves for stones. He found none. He ran his hand over its tendons and could discover no damage.

"You are all right," Adrian said, frowning. The horse neighed and shook his head. Adrian laughed despite himself. "Don't be a contrary beast. I have a lady I must see." He grabbed up the harness and pulled. "Now come."

The horse neighed again and stepped back rather than forward. The rest of the horses stepped back as well.

"Confound it," Adrian growled, no longer amused. "What the devil is wrong with you?"

"I've never seen the likes," the coachman said. He sighed and rolled out his whip.

"No, hold," Adrian said. He jerked on the horse's harness once more. Once more the horse dug in its hooves and refused to budge. "Faith. Are you a horse or a mule?"

The horse snorted and neighed, shaking his head.

"Help me," Adrian ordered the coachman. The coachman went to the other side.

They both jerked and pulled.

"You *are* a damn mule," Adrian panted close to the horse's head.

The horse bared its teeth. "Lay off, guv. I've got my orders."

Adrian jumped and stepped back. Reason asserted itself. He looked to the coachman. "What did you just say?"

The coachman frowned. "I didn't say anything."

Adrian stared at the horse. The horse stared back.

"Hello!" a voice hollered from the distance. Adrian tensed. He was almost too frightened to turn his head to discover if the voice was real and, if so, just who might be calling. Nevertheless, he turned his head just as the creature—for Adrian wasn't about to call it a horse now—leapt forward with a whinny. Adrian and the coachman were pressed to leap back as the coach took off.

Cursing, Adrian and the coachman ran after the coach. Fortunately, it stopped again fifty yards ahead. Adrian swiped the snow from his eyes. Another team of horses was stomping and snorting close to his team and coach.

"Adrian?" A well-loved voice called.

"Carin?" Adrian breathed.

Horses and teams were forgotten as Carin ran toward him from out of the blinding snow.

"Carin," Adrian cried, opening his arms wide as she flung herself at him. He held her tight to him.

"I can't believe it is you," Carin breathed.

"Nor I you," Adrian laughed. "But what are you doing here?"

"I was . . ." Carin drew in a breath and smiled. "I was coming home."

"Were you? And I was coming to bring you home," Adrian said, his voice choking. "I love you, Carin. Please marry me."

"I will." Carin nodded, her eyes brilliant.

"You will?" Adrian asked, stunned.

"Yes, I will," Carin whispered, holding him close. "I don't want to live without you."

Adrian drew back. He didn't want to say it, but he knew he must. "You do not have to marry me, Carin. Your father has returned."

"He has?" Carin asked. She smiled. "I thought I recognized his team and coachman."

"And they clearly recognized you," Adrian murmured. He shivered. "Even beforehand."

"What?" Carin asked.

Adrian shook his head. He couldn't speak of it yet. "Never mind. Your father has returned with a rich new wife. They can take care of you . . . if you wish."

"No," Carin shook her head. "I do not want anyone but you to take care of me. I love you, Adrian."

"Thank God," Adrian murmured. He lowered his lips to hers. The cold and the snow melted away with the warmth and tenderness of her lips beneath his. Awe filled Adrian and with it a devout intent. He would cherish this woman who had brought him, and taught him about, love.

"Excuse me, my lord."

Adrian lifted his head. The coachman stood watching. The man nodded, grinning. "We've got the other team of horses hitched to ours. That coachman said they lost a wheel on the carriage a ways back."

"Yes." Carin nodded. Her eyes grew solemn. "We decided to take the horses and walk. We didn't know the area, but we were afraid if we remained waiting, we'd freeze."

"Let us go," Adrian said, the chill passing through his soul. He clasped Carin's small hand in his and led her toward their coach. But he stopped before the lead horse. The horse whickered. Adrian, grinning, leaned over. "Sorry, old man. You had your orders." He gazed at Carin with open love. She frowned at him in confusion. Adrian laughed and looked at the horse once more. "And I've got my orders too, I believe. Please take me and my future wife home. Our family is waiting and we still have the candles to light on the tree."

Carin gasped. She looked at Adrian with stunned eyes. Adrian grinned and breathed in what he knew was the finest breath in his life. "Adrian, did that horse just wink at you?"

"Would ye look at them," Bertha whispered, peering into the coach as it stood before the town house. "Both sleeping like babies."

"Yeah." Hez grinned. "His nibs has his arm around Miss Carin."

"And look at that," Bertha pointed, smirking.

"Either tell us what is going on," Lady Vincent said from behind, "or step aside."

"Nothing but a blooming miracle is what's happening," Bertha said. She turned. "He didn't muff it this time. She's wearing his ring."

"She is." Hez beamed. "And I got the right size for her, I did!"

"Strike it up, lads!" Bertha nodded to those who waited behind her.

Twelve drummers began drumming. Eleven Scottish bagpipes blared louder. Eight maids applauded and laughed and cried with emotion. Marie barked. The puppies yapped. Baby Joy Partridge merely cooed from Meg's arms. Molly bussed a crying Lord Worthington on the cheek.

Carin opened her eyes. Bertha and Hez grinned at her from the coach's open door. She smiled mistily. "We are home, Adrian."

She heard a snort. Twisting her head, she looked at Adrian. A smile touched his lips though he didn't open his eyes. "I know, darling. I can hear it, as no doubt the entire neighborhood can."

Carin chuckled and snuggled back against him. She closed her eyes for one more blissful moment.

"Come on," Hez objected. "You two can't just sleep. It's Christmas!"

Carin smiled her own small smile as she fingered the ring on her hand. No, it was more than Christmas. Much more.

More Zebra Regency Romances

Put a Little Romance in Your Life With
Hannah Howell

__**My Valiant Knight**   **$5.50**US/**$7.00**CAN
    0-8217-5186-7

__**Only For You**   **$5.99**US/**$7.50**CAN
    0-8217-5943-4

__**Unconquered**   **$5.99**US/**$7.50**CAN
    0-8217-5417-3

__**Wild Roses**   **$5.99**US/**$7.50**CAN
    0-8217-5677-X

__**Highland Destiny**   **$5.99**US/**$7.50**CAN
    0-8217-5921-3

__**Highland Honor**   **$5.99**US/**$7.50**CAN
    0-8217-6095-5

__**A Taste of Fire**   **$5.99**US/**$7.50**CAN
    0-8217-5804-7

Call toll free **1-888-345-BOOK** to order by phone or use this coupon to order by mail.

Name _____

Address _____

City _____ State _____ Zip _____

Please send me the books I have checked above.

I am enclosing $_____

Plus postage and handling* $_____

Sales tax (in New York and Tennessee) $_____

Total amount enclosed $_____

*Add $2.50 for the first book and $.50 for each additional book.

Send check or money order (no cash or CODs) to:

Kensington Publishing Corp., 850 Third Avenue, New York, NY 10022

Prices and Numbers subject to change without notice.

All orders subject to availability.

Check out our website at **www.kensingtonbooks.com**